"What were you doin' in me room?"

Colm toyed with a tendril of her hair. Cool and damp between his fingers, it lit another spark of need within him. "I told you."

"Oh, aye. You came to see me," Maginn mimicked. Her face grew serious. "Why?"

Thunder rolled in the distance, prodding Colm to give in to his baser instincts.

He stole a glance at her lips, full, tempting. Compelled, he leaned down. His mouth touched hers.

Battle-lit eyes flew open. She thrashed wildly.

Without thought, he imprisoned her body against his.

He secured her tighter.

For one brief second, their gazes locked, warring. Her eyes darkened.

Testing her indifference, he tasted the slight part between her lips. Near madness, he groaned, bruising her mouth. Snaring her hair with his fingers, he pulled her closer still . . .

GOLDEN FURY

DEBORAH JAMES

DIAMOND BOOKS, NEW YORK

This book is a Diamond original edition, and has never been previously published.

GOLDEN FURY

A Diamond Book / published by arrangement with the author

PRINTING HISTORY
Diamond edition / November 1992

ISBN: 1-55773-811-4

Diamond Books are published by The Berkley Publishing Group, 200 Madison Avenue, New York, New York 10016.
The name "DIAMOND" and its logo are trademarks belonging to Charter Communications, Inc.

PRINTED IN THE UNITED STATES OF AMERICA

10 9 8 7 6 5 4 3 2 1

To my *girlfriends* Jeannie and Meg, who during the love and labor of this book, gently though firmly applied their fingerprints to my back.

To my other three mentors, Dianna, Sally, and Sue, who have taught me much more about life than mere writing.

And to my loving husband, Jim, who constantly reminds me that height puts no limits on how high one may reach if only she has the nerve to try, the stamina to endure, and a new pair of L.A. Gears.

I love you all

1

California, Winter 1875

No one spoke, no eye remained dry, no heart untouched, as the entire dispirited population of Marysville bowed their heads beneath the diminishing drizzle of a two-week-old flood.

Heated teardrops instantly cooled by the late January air tumbled silently down Maginn O'Shaunasey's cheeks, adding to the saturated ground beneath her feet. Were she to have raised her eyes to the doleful faces surrounding her, she might have seen the like of her own despondent tears, and not felt that she was so alone in her grief. But as it was, she remained motionless, head downcast, watching the rivulets of muddy water trickle into the as yet uncovered grave.

Against the echoic patter of rainfall, the

preacher ended the requiem, and as did the others, Maginn responded. "Amen." After making the sign of the cross, she reached down and dug her gloved fingers into the soggy earth. She stepped nearer the open burial pit and tossed the mud atop the small wooden box. "'Tis not a Catholic mass, me darlin' Tommy, but 'twill see your feet set upon the path of heaven even so," she whispered softly, the steady stream of scalding tears blinding her vision.

She allowed Reverend Jacobs to guide her to the head of the grave, though she could not respond to his consoling touch.

"We're so sorry, Maginn." Another hand grasped hers. Vaguely, she heard a woman's voice. "If there's anything you need, you just ask us, dear."

"If only that blasted pneumonia hadn't taken your pa like it did—" Rage inflected a man's tone.

Maginn peered up but remained oblivious to the man speaking to her.

"He'd have been here for Tommy. He'd have led us in the fight against those rich mine owners and their monitors." His voice stopped coming at her for a moment. He patted Maginn's hand and glowered toward the imposing mountain range of the Sierra Nevadas. "Should you need them"— he hesitated, then bent nearer her ear—"the resistance is always close by."

She forced an appreciative smile and nodded. And though she heard the sorrowers, she could not take their condolences to heart. The pain cut too deep, the anguish weighted her spirit, and the loss . . . Now she was left with no one and with nothing.

As the procession of blurred faces continued by, Maginn relived the last days with her father. She saw him again, lying so pale and weak in his bed, his breathing nothing but a labored wheeze. In one month's time he had withered from a strong and virile hulk of an Irishman to a worn-and-weary victim of chills and fever. Briefly, she squeezed her eyes closed. He hadn't even made it to last Christmas.

And now . . . Tommy . . . and the farm too, lost beneath a sea of mud . . .

Her chest felt as if it would burst with sadness. What will come of such misery as this? As if punctuating her pain-filled question, a sodden wisp of blond hair fell from beneath her plain black bonnet.

Another distorted face moved into view. Another meaningless utterance parroted the ones before it. She looked past the death masks looming in front of her, to the hills beyond. Lord, intervene! she railed inwardly. Stop those hellish monitors from gouging out the gold from the mountainsides with their jet streams of water and sending their waste down to bury us all in silt. Her gaze lowered to the ground ladened thick with mud. They're destroyin' our valley—killin' our children, and leavin' us all paupers here below 'em. Even more anger filled her body as she glanced down at the unadorned little casket.

Lips quivering, partly from the cold, partly from bitterness, Maginn drew in a deep breath. Don't sink into wrack and ruin, Maginn. Keep strong now. Think of Tommy and Patter. You're an Irishwoman, by God. Hold your head up and keep your heart still. You've a stout spirit. Show these people what an O'Shaunasey is made of. She shook her head mentally, gathered a purging gulp of air, and lifted her face to meet the challenge.

The rain had stopped, replaced now by a pale, thin fog that swathed the hills in a blanket of gray. "'Tis no soft Irish mist, but 'twill do," she whispered. Her gaze moved across the river basin. A crescent of muted colors arced down from the heavens. "What's this? A rainbow, now?"

"It's a sign of love from God, my child." Reverend Jacobs startled Maginn.

She had not realized she had spoken out loud.

4

"It's a remembrance gift of Tommy," he offered further.

Tracing the course of the vivid curve, Maginn lifted a questioning brow. The ribbon appeared to point straight to the mountains . . . and the gold mines burrowed so deeply within them. At once she understood the sign all too clearly. Blood for blood, blow for blow.

At last the remaining townspeople took their leave from the churchyard, leaving her alone with Reverend Jacobs beside Tommy's grave.

The minister clasped his hands fervently around his Bible. "I'm sorry we didn't have a clergy of your own faith to perform the last rites and a proper mass for the boy, Maginn. I know you'd have liked it better that way."

"'Tis nothin' to be frettin' over, Reverend. You did a foin job of it. Father Fagan, back home in me own Templemore Parish, would've been pleased with the grand words you spoke over me Tommy."

"Thank you, Maginn. I'm happy you were satisfied with the services."

Silence lengthened the moment, and as if cued, both Maginn and the clergyman trained their eyes on the mist-shrouded mountains.

"You know," Reverend Jacobs began in a soothing tone. "You must be willing to forgive the wrongdoings that have been done to your family. You must get on with your life.''

''I intend on doin' just that.'' Maginn turned to meet his compassionate gaze. ''But I'm curious, Reverend. Just who is it that you think I should be forgivin'?''

Peering at her as if she were some crystal ball he could use to see into the future, his weathered face remained expressionless, though his unwavering gaze seemed to move into her own, seeking out the truth of her heart. He grasped her hand gently and smiled. ''There are others who feel as you, Maginn. You're not alone in your pain. Many have lost much to this onslaught of mud from the mines, the same as you.''

Pretending ignorance, Maginn merely fixed a blank stare on him. ''I'm not certain I understand your meanin'.'' She fought the overwhelming urge to yank her hand free from the clergyman's grasp. How could he know how she felt? His warmth and understanding reached out to her through his touch, but she did not—could not—allow it to subdue the cry for justice shrieking in her soul.

''I think you do, child.'' He squeezed her hand. ''Only the Lord may seek vengeance, Maginn. No one else.''

Her eyes grew wide. Her inner torment pressed hard against her throat, nearly choking her with the realization that the man *had* read and understood her thoughts. "They can't be gettin' away with this, Reverend. Me mother's dead, as you well know. An' after battlin' the silt for two long years and finally makin' somethin' of our farm, Father too is gone." She fought back the tears, but they bested her efforts. She clamped her teeth together, tried to calm the quiver in her voice, but all for naught. "An' now our wee Tommy's drowned 'cause of them murderin' scoundrels— 'Tis too much! So great does this hammer-an'-tongs pound within me that even I fear its beatin'."

Setting her jaw hard, she narrowed her eyes defiantly, and with her lower lip trembling from the effort, she yanked her hand away. "I keep wonderin'. What can *I* do to stop those fiendish monitors? I keep hopin' the mine owners will see the anguish they're causin', but they never do—an' if they do, they don't care. Sweet Jesus—" She sobbed with all the pain of a possessed woman. "I cry for Him to help us. An' do you want to know the Almighty's answer? No, of course you don't. You'd rather sit round an' wait for some miracle." The words tumbled out in a rush. Her heart thudded against her breast. "Well, *I* won't, I'll tell you that for nothin'. *I'm* not one to sit and snivel an' wait for things to get better—to change. The Irish in me runs too deep."

"Maginn, please, you're overwrought with grief." The minister moved to console her, but she pulled away from his grasp.

"Overwrought, you say? Mark me words, Reverend." Fists clenched, she glared up at the distant mountains. "If it's to be the last thing I do, I'll see to the death of those damned water cannons—an' if need be, their pitiless owners as well!"

"Be sensible, child. You're not thinking clearly." His voice rang with full ministerial authority. "How can you know who's at fault here? There are at least fifty companies up there and they're all using monitors."

She pointed toward the Yuba River, still lapping small amounts of water over its levee. "Look there. They've filled the bottom of the river with so much mud that it can't even contain itself. They're *all* to blame!" She scowled viciously, blindly gesturing to the open grave as she spoke. "'Tis *my* little brother that lies so small an' cold in the ground there. 'Tis *me* that wears the sackcloth an' ashes. So 'tis my right to avenge his death. An' as to how? I'm not as yet certain. But as to who?" One company stood out in her mind. "Why not start at the top of the heap? That money-grubbin' Thimblerigger Minin' Consortium will be forever regrettin' their part in causin' the despair and ruination of the O'Shaunasey family."

Nevada, Spring 1875

Silence split the interior of the Little Gold Dollar Saloon. Though it was only early March, the air felt suffocatingly hot as a horde of onlookers watched the richest poker game to hit Virginia City. After five hours and an amount of twenty-two thousand dollars being won thus far, only three players were left—two partners of a mining consortium in California and a Wells Fargo agent.

"What'cha gonna do, boys? You're both cleaned out, far's I can see."

"We've got our mining interests."

"We can't do that!"

"You willing to just let him walk away with all our money?"

"No, but—"

"Well, me neither."

"Hold on now. I don't know nothin' 'bout no minin' interests. They worth any hard cash?"

"We both own one quarter of a gold consortium valued at ten thousand apiece. That good enough for you?"

9

"Ten thousand? Each?"

"Damnation. We came here to hire him to protect the mines—I know he's good, but nobody's worth forty-two thousand dollars!"

"He's up against both of us. One of us is bound to win."

"But August—"

"Stop whining, Hannibal. We've got no choice."

"So what's it gonna be, gents?"

"Will you accept our interests?"

A moment of deafening silence echoed through the room.

"Plunk 'em out there, boys. It's a bet."

A drone of whispers filled the sweltering air as the two partners scratched out their signatures and share holdings on scraps of paper, then tossed them out on the table with the twenty-two-thousand-dollar ante already lying in the middle.

The first, a little man with an overabundant, sandy mustache, placed three aces down.

With a satisfied smirk, the second peered across the table at his opponent, a small scar cupping his left eye like a tiny horseshoe. He set his cards down, one at a time. "Two. And a three of diamonds. A four of hearts. Another diamond. A five. And the last?" he said pointedly. "A six of hearts." Leaning back in his seat, he displayed a wide scramble of teeth, jumbled in his mouth like the beads of a faro dealer's cue box.

"Well, now. All I got is two pair."

"Two pair? You bet all this on two pair? That *is* a shame, isn't it?" The toothy man winked at his partner and reached for the pot.

"Well— Maybe not. How's 'bout one pair of kings and . . . another pair of kings? You think they'll beat that straight flush?"

"Eureka!" A chorus of yells surged through the saloon.

Beaming a playful, one-sided smile, Colm Wesley McQuaid looked up at the jovial faces crowding around the poker table. He glanced back at the two men seated across from him, their identical expressions appearing forlornly petrified as they stared down at all they had just lost.

Pulling the money toward him, Colm shuffled the bills into stacks. Motioning for a barroom girl to hand him his saddlebags draped across a nearby chair, he quickly stuffed his winnings inside without counting them. Carefully, he picked up the small pieces of paper and examined the writing. "Thimblerigger Mining Consortium. Hmm. Guess I don't have much choice but to take that gun job now that I own part of the mine, do I?"

Both men eyed him waspishly, but remained silent.

"No hard feelin's, now. It's just my day, I guess." Colm shrugged. "Bound to happen to all of us sooner or later. Your day'll come." Standing, he dipped his head to the jubilant bystanders as they slapped the agent on the back, congratulating him, and moved away from the table. He jammed the papers into his shirt pocket, then took them out again. "You boys do have the stock certificates on hand to back these up, don't you?"

"You think we're crazy?"

Colm chuckled. "Well, I don't know. Puttin' up everythin' you own, and losin' it in a poker game, sounds pretty crazy to me."

Walrus-lip flinched, making the ends of his mustache bristle like the hackles of a dog. "What about you? You did the same thing."

"No—not quite. I only brought fifty dollars into the game. I've been playin' with your money since the third hand."

The little man opened his mouth as if to retort but instead slammed it shut. Only the way his face turned poker-chip red made Colm think he might explode. Lips quivering, pressed tighter with each passing second, the man eyed Colm heatedly. Then without a word he jumped up, toppling his chair with the effort, and stalked out the swinging doors.

"Guess your friend's a mite upset, hmm?" Colm asked. He did not mean to be quite so full of himself, but at this particular moment, he felt as puffed up as a grouse looking for a mate. "Now, 'bout those stock certificates. You do have them?"

The larger man's scar deepened to a purple-red. "You don't think we'd carry something like that around with us, do you? Those things are as good as gold."

Colm waved the two folded pieces of paper. "These don't do me much good without the certificates."

"Look, Mr. McQuaid. We're businessmen. We're not ones for shirking on a deal. You come to Cavenaugh's Dig in California. We'll see you get your damn certificates!"

A gun exploded. A rush of surprised murmurs blustered through the room.

Following the remaining consortium partner, Colm made his way to the exit and pushed past the crowd. His expression was grim as his gaze swung to the ghastly sight outside the Little Gold Dollar.

Pitched over the side of the saloon's hitching rail, a smoking Knuckle-duster .32 still clenched in his hand, dangled the little sandy-mustached man, his face smeared with blood.

California, Spring 1875

Alert to the townspeople's movements, Colm kept a sharp eye out for a sign announcing the Thimblerigger Mining Consortium as he rode through the dusty main street of Cavenaugh's Dig.

He dipped his head occasionally and offered smiles to well-dressed ladies strolling along the planked walks. Like roving musicians, ever failing to keep an even tempo, they continually stopped to ogle some fancy piece of flounce or fluff in the windows of the various businesses.

In contrast, the men took as careful watch of Colm as he of them. The intensity of their blatant stares left Colm with an uneasy feeling. Did they know who he was? Or of the suicide of the consortium partner? Either way, the looks were becoming mighty uncomfortable. Holding his reins loosely in his right hand, he kept his left resting casually, yet prepared, at the juncture of his hip and thigh, just in front of his Colt.

"Hey, cowboy," a woman's syrupy voice cajoled from the balcony of a boisterous saloon. Wearing only the barest of essentials, a buxom redhead suggestively twisted the satin ties of her flimsy skivvy shirt.

"Ma'am." Colm touched the brim of his hat in greeting.

Lifting her brows, she glanced down at the horse's sweat-covered neck and flashed an evocative smile. "You always ride your mounts so hard?" Lounging a forearm on the railing, she leaned over, obviously to allow Colm a better view of her wares.

And naturally, Colm's gaze riveted on the tantalizing mounds of ivory flesh. A surge of adrenaline stirred his groin. He patted the animal's neck affectionately, then responded with a lopsided grin. "Ain't had no complaints yet."

"My, but aren't you the sure one?" She dropped the ribbons and lazily traced the upper edge of her partially unlaced bodice, proposing more with her movements than with the casual conversation. "You know. I'm pretty good myself—at taking a hard ride, I mean."

"Really?" Colm pulled his horse up alongside the saloon walk just below the woman.

She nodded. "And I do so admire a man who can endure as much and still sit a good saddle." She raked him with the heat of her scintillating brown eyes. "Care to join me in a ride?"

Stealing a second look at the ample exposure of her pale jutting breasts, Colm felt his groin tighten painfully. Her lusty gaze, bold and burning, gripped him with more than a twinge of interest. God, curse a beautiful redhead—even a not-so-pretty one. They had always been his weakness, and likely always would. But not now. He sighed heavily. Much as he would like to take the woman up on her savory invitation, he had business that needed handling. But after that—

Regretfully, he shook his head. "Can't right now. Maybe later."

With all the skills of an experienced actress, she pursed her lips in a forlorn pout. "Oh, that's too bad. Well. You come back and see me when your business is done." She curled a lock of that fiery red hair of hers around a finger, then wet her lips with a slow trace of her tongue. "Just ask for Blaze."

The woman was wreaking havoc with Colm's need. A trickle of sweat teased his ear, causing him to concentrate harder against his arousal. Forcing himself to remain settled, he gripped the reins tighter, resting his hand in his lap. Damn, but she was making it hard for him to decline her advances. He dipped his head and gifted her with a "you better believe I will" look. Directing his horse away, he called back. "Can you tell me where I can find the Thimblerigger Mining Consortium?" When she did not answer immediately, he shot a look over his shoulder.

She appeared dumbstruck, but quickly sobered as her gaze dropped to where his duster draped around his holster. "Uh—yea." She pointed directly behind him, then hurried into the bordello without so much as a "see ya later."

Odd. Why had her expression changed? She seemed shocked. Maybe even a bit afraid.

After crossing the street, Colm stepped down from his horse and looped the lead over the hitching post. The uneasiness had returned. He felt the stab of curious stares and the prick of wary whispers droning around him. The townsfolk had all stopped to gawk at him as if he were some strange animal on exhibit in a sideshow. So they *had* heard that he was coming. And they *did* blame him for Cross's suicide.

Cautiously, Colm pulled off his weighty overgarment. With the unusual early spring heat, the coat had become unbearable. And the way everybody was eyeing him, he felt a little more at ease with his Colt at an easy grasp. Experience had taught him to remain relaxed, go slow in his movements. So as not to alert anyone to his actions, he peeled out of his rawhide gloves and, free and easy like, slapped at the day and a half's worth of dirt covering his clothing, secretly unfastening his gun as he did so. Just in case he needed it real quick. Leisurely, he took the steps in front of the building marked Thimblerigger Mining Consortium. Too late, halfway up, he saw the woman.

Colliding, Colm reached out and caught her from falling backward. Their stares locked. Startled, he gazed down into large jade-green eyes flashing in the sunlight like wildfire in full flame.

Strangely compelled by their sudden closeness, Colm let his gaze wander over the woman's features. Tiny spirals of golden sundrenched hair had escaped the loose braid plaited down the full length of her back, provoking his already spurred senses with her soft fragrance like a beckoning finger. Instead of releasing her, he could not resist the urge to fan his fingers intimately against the small of her back and explore the soft, pliable curve of her body within his grasp. His mouth went as dry as the air around him. And after being tempted by Blaze so lustfully, Colm felt his palms itch painfully with the almost unbearable yearning to touch this woman in a more familiar manner. Inwardly he groaned. And her lips: full, tempting, soft as petals, only marred by a tiny scar on the bottom left corner, yet still perfectly formed for any man to savor their full pleasure.

Suddenly her gaze darted from him to the townspeople, whom their collision had obviously halted in motion. Her face turned crimson. She squirmed against the restriction of his arms.

Loosening his hold ever so slightly, he leaned back and smiled. "Your pardon, ma'am. I guess I wasn't payin' attention t' where I was goin'."

Chest heaving, back arched in his embrace, she glared up at him as if he spoke in some foreign tongue.

Too quick, Colm realized he had surmised wrong. She had understood him only too well.

"'Tis for certain you weren't, or you'd have steered yourself clear of the likes of this dev'l-infested lair." Jerking her chin high, she shoved her palms against his chest. "You'll be unhandin' me now—or shall I be callin' for the sheriff's assistance?"

Only slightly annoyed by her attitude, Colm stiffened. The little ungrateful— So swiftly did he release her, that he was almost forced to grab her again to steady her balance. "Your pardon again, ma'am," he said with forced courtesy and a touch of sarcasm. "But it wasn't all my fault."

Brushing primly at her sleeves and skirt as if

he had somehow soiled her, the woman hoisted one slender, uppity brow, her gaze cast downward in obviously snooty fashion. "Just you be watchin' your own plowin' row next time."

"Plowin' row?" Colm almost laughed out loud. His tension eased. The heavy brogue brought back memories of his childhood years at Fort Kearny when he and his mother had been taken from their Arapaho village. At least half of the soldiers had spoken with a similar Irish accent. He quirked a lopsided grin, tipped his hat gallantly, then mimicked her dialect almost perfectly. "'Tis for certain you may count on just that, but with none of the pleasure, I'll grant you."

Again their gazes fastened. Hers furious and hot, his daring and humorous. But something was wrong. Colm could see now that she was deeply troubled. But by what? Surely not by such a minor little mishap as this? The moment grew long, stretching between them.

Abruptly, her expression softened, ending the seriousness with an unexpected, but welcome gentle laugh. "I suppose I did come off a wee bit testy. An' you're right of course. 'Twas me fault as well. Do forgive me boorish disposition, sir, but—" She cast a hateful glare back toward the consortium building. "It seems to be all that's left to me of late."

Apparently suddenly embarrassed by the townsfolk's watchfulness, her gaze darted toward the passersby, and she began straightening her shirtwaist suit with a proper measure of composure. "I thank you for your help. An' now, if you'll be for excusin' me."

Curiosity piqued, Colm allowed her only one step down the stairs before he touched her elbow. "Pardon my noticin', ma'am, but do you have a complaint with the consortium?"

She turned back to him, her face darkened to blood-red. "'Complaint'? Lord, but I hate that word." Wheeling around, she lifted her skirts with more than ample force.

"Wait a minute. Maybe I can help—"

"Help?" She spun back, halting Colm with the strength of her angry tone. "An' why would you be wantin' to do such a thing for a woman you don't even know? Besides, what can *you* be thinkin' to do for me?"

"Well, for one thing, I can start off by introducin' myself. The name's Colm Mc-Quaid."

She stared at him as if his name meant nothing. Plainly, not everyone knew of his identity, or of his new partnership with the consortium.

He glanced around at the onlookers still watching the proceedings between him and the young woman. The tension returned to his body. He should just drop this and let the woman go on her way, but something urged him on. He had to know what had infuriated her so. He gestured toward the building behind them. "I guess the consortium hasn't announced it yet, but—"

"Sweet Jesus!" she all but shrieked. Glancing down at his gun, her eyes grew wide. She peered past him, gesturing to the building with a nod, then back at him. Rage and loathing marked her tone. "You bastard! You're him!"

Crack!

Colm's head snapped back. The flat of the woman's palm sent the full potency of her anger into his unprotected jaw.

❧ 2 ❧

Heat flamed the spot where the woman had struck Colm. "What the hell was that for?" he muttered. As he stared after her, his irritation shifted to amusement. The hard line of his mouth eased. His gaze remained fixed, heedless of the passersby still observing the scene on the consortium steps.

He watched as the pretty blonde hiked her skirts scandalously above her ankles. Her hips swished back and forth beneath a small but generous flounce of dainty blue checks.

She quick-marched across the street, straight for the Rowdy Rose Saloon.

Shaking his head, Colm grinned, then wiped the beads of sweat from his upper lip. "Shoulda known she was one of them." Turning up the stairs, he flashed a wide, triumphant grin at three older women huddled in front of the mining office's multipaned window. "Afternoon, ladies." He rubbed his stinging cheek. "Mite warm, though."

"If you ask me," he heard one call loud enough for him to hear, "she should have hit him harder."

Another insisted, "Well, if she hadn't been at the consortium, trying to cause trouble again for all our menfolk—or didn't spend all her time drawing those alarming pictures for that rabble-rousing paper, it wouldn't have happened." She held her hand up to her mouth and leaned over to her friend. "You know, they say she's one of *them*—you know, that resistance rabble."

Ignoring her friends, the third stretched her wrinkled face into a demure smile, and secretly waved at Colm when the other two were not looking.

As he reached for the doorknob of the building, he winked at her.

"Oh my." She flushed and tittered, drawing the attention of her companions.

"Really, Agatha! Act your age."

Chuckling at the old ladies, Colm started to turn the knob but hesitated. He had the strangest feeling he was being watched—*again*. But even before he looked over his shoulder, the right corner of his mouth lifted into a bold smirk. This time he did not feel uneasy. He knew who it was. He glanced across the street to the opposite walkway. And there she stood.

Back to him, her stance defiant, chin turned toward him, she resembled a newly erected statue of stately womanhood.

Their eyes clashed and held, but for just a second.

Colm spoke his interest in one look—one quick tip of his head. He squinted at the sign beside the barroom doors.

Beer—25¢
Whiskey—50¢
Repartee—Free
Other Diversions—Inquire Within

Looking back at her, he grinned lustfully.

Obviously bewildered by his expression, the young lady eyed the advertisement. Her mouth flew open and she whirled around.

Colm could almost hear the gasp. The outrage in her expression nearly caused him to laugh aloud. An indignant whore? Blaze's image goaded his memory. *Too bad she ain't a redhead. But I'm still goin' t' have t' sample that one.*

Darting him an angry glare, the woman puffed out her chest. Then with deliberateness, she tugged down her waist-shirt more securely and stalked down the walk.

He chuckled to himself. Proud and defiant—
just the way I like 'em.

Still gripping the handle, Colm opened the
door and went inside. In the paler light, it took
a moment for his eyes to adjust from the
outside to the dark-paneled interior.

The room reeked of quiet. So much so,
Colm could just about hear the scratching
from a pen across the office.

A bald pate bobbed above a large desk.
"May I help you?"

Colm moved to stand before the secretary.
When he did not answer, the man looked up
and squinted through the thick lenses of wire-
rimmed eyeglasses. "May I help you, sir?"

Reaching inside his vest pocket, Colm retrieved two folded pieces of paper. He held
them out. "The man that gave me these mark-
ers said t' come here. Said t' ask for him by
name."

The beetle-browed man accepted the notes,
then glared upward. "What man? Who are
you?"

"Read 'em," he answered, indifferent to the
perturbed fellow. Tucking his gloves up under
his gun belt, Colm took in the coldness of the
sparse room. Except for the desk and chair in
front of him, a woodstove standing against
one side, and a filing cabinet opposing it on

the other, Colm could have been waiting in some lonely prison cell.

This place feels like a tomb. He strode toward the sole means of light, a highly polished window overlooking the busy main street of town. He peered out. Tailor shops, a millinery, mercantiles . . . His gaze gravitated toward the Rowdy Rose Saloon, and again he read the meaningful sign displayed beside its swinging doors. *Yep. I'm definitely goin' t' have t' try that little blonde,* he finished in a whisper. "Rowdy Rose."

"'Scuse me. But this says that you're Colm McQuaid." The man's voice seemed deeper now—a bit nervous.

"Sure does."

"But I was under the impression that Mr. Willard had hired you to protect the mines."

Colm shot the man a piercing look. "You thought wrong."

"Look, just who are you, really?" The little man jumped up from his desk, shaking the papers. "And how did you acquire these promissories?"

Every muscle in Colm's body tightened. "Stop right there, mister. I don't know what's goin' on here, but I'm not in the habit of bein' called a liar. And I'm gettin' damned tired of bein' attacked every time somebody hears my name."

"I—I'm sorry, Mr. McQuaid." The secretary instantly lost his courage. "I didn't mean to attack you."

He gave the scrawny little guy the once-over. Attack me? Him? He fought the grin pulling at his mouth. "No harm done," he said with controlled effort. "Now, I'd like t' see Mr. Willard. There's still the matter of signin' over the stock certificates."

"Sorry, Mr. McQuaid. But he's out at the number two."

"Where?"

The man jerked his thick brows upward, his glasses sliding to the tip of his nose. "There was an explosion out at the number two mine a couple of days ago. Our company president, Mr. Jameson, was badly hurt. So Mr. Willard's trying to sort out the mess and figure out who did it."

"Explosion! Damn it t' hell. Are the mines still intact?" Colm ground the words between his teeth as if he were chewing rawhide. "I figured this would all get shot out from under me. I knew it was too good to be true."

Retreating a pace, the secretary crinkled the papers tighter. "There's nothing really to worry about. Everybody already knows who's responsible."

"Who?" Colm nearly leapt at the man. His fists bunched. He had waited too long for this chance to see his mother set up with money and respectability. And by God, she'll damn well have it! No more dirty laundry and sneers from the officers' wives for her.

"Why, the farmers from down Sacramento Valley way, of course."

"What do you mean, of course? And how do you know it was them for sure? Didn't you say Willard was *tryin' t'* figure out who did it?"

"Well, yeah. But that's just for proof. Everybody knows who did it." The little man flicked his head in the direction of the street outside. "Did you notice the woman leaving just before you came in?"

Notice her? Mister, it was a sight more than just *notice*. Colm nodded.

"Well, that's Maginn O'Shaunasey. She's an artist for a small paper here in town, *The Badger's Winze Gazette*. She drew up a picture of the whole thing."

"You mean she's not a—"

"A what?"

"Nothin'. Go on."

The secretary leaned forward and glared through his thick lenses. "She hates the mines. Has a personal grudge against all of 'em. So she makes sure anything the farmers' resistance movement does gets sketched and put in that blasted newspaper. She and her boss,

29

Lance Taggert, really like stirring up trouble for us. You know the type.''

"No. Tell me. Why would a woman want t' get herself involved in somethin' as dangerous as all this?''

"Oh, she's got some fool notion that the mines are responsible for her pa's and little brother's deaths. They died a couple of months back.''

"And are they?'' Colm frowned. Maybe there was a reason for the woman's ill-temper and her attack on Colm after all.

"Nah.'' The secretary waved his hand as if he were swatting at a fly. "Her pa died of the chills. They got themselves a levee built on the Yuba River down there, and the dang fool stayed out in a bad rain one night trying to keep it braced so's it wouldn't spill over and flood his land.'' He shook his head. "He caught pneumonia and died a couple of days before Christmas.''

"And the woman's brother?'' Visualizing his mother and the pain he had felt for her all these past years, Colm felt his emotions stir. He peered back out at the walk across the street, imagining the pretty blonde as he had seen her moments before, devil-eyed, flustered, and angry. "What happened t' him?''

"He drowned in that flash flood they had down there last month.'' Joining Colm at the window, the secretary removed his glasses, wiped them off with a handkerchief, then held them up for inspection before setting them back on his round pink face. "Now, I ask you. Just how is any of that the fault of the mines?"

Colm shrugged. Something about all of this just did not add up. The O'Shaunasey woman had been too upset. He felt certain there was more to this than just what the secretary was telling him.

"Now back to these," the bald man said, returning Colm's attention to the matter at hand. "How did you say you acquired them?"

"In a poker—"

"Mr. McQuaid!"

Colm wheeled around to see August Willard standing in the doorway of one of the offices behind the desk.

"I see you were able to terminate your employment with Wells Fargo sooner than I anticipated."

"Mr. Willard. I thought you were still out at the number two." The clerk appeared surprised.

"Just got back." A broad smile plastered on his face, the stocky man hurried into the room. Shoving a hand out, he shook Colm's vigorously, as if they were old friends. "I'll take care of Mr. McQuaid, Covington. Go on home now."

"But Mr. Willard." The secretary took out his pocket watch and stared at his boss with wide, uncertain eyes. "It's only ten past three."

"Surprise your wife. Besides, it's just too damn hot to be cooped up in this building."

"But—"

Snatching the papers from his employee's grasp, Willard gestured for Colm to go into his office, then glowered over his shoulder. "Just go home, Covington," he said forcibly. "Be here early tomorrow morning to make up for the lost time."

Willard waited in the doorway until Covington had left the building. He turned to Colm, and his jovial expression of a moment earlier vanished. "I thought you weren't going to be here for a couple of weeks."

Colm moved to the man's desk and sat down. Casually, he lounged back and propped his feet up on one corner of the oak top. "Like you said. I was able t' quit my job sooner than I thought."

Willard suddenly appeared nervous. He took a step farther into the room. "But I thought—"

Leaning an elbow on the edge of the desk, Colm rested his jaw against the back of his fist and stared at the agitated man. "What did you think?"

His face a blotched red, Willard took off his Stetson and hung it on the hat tree in the corner. "I thought I'd have a little more time."

"Time?"

Taking a chair against the front wall, Willard nodded. "You probably heard about Mr. Jameson?"

"Yep."

"And, of course, you know about Mr. Cross as well—"

Colm felt a twinge of guilt at the sound of the dead man's name. Tensing, he nodded. "Go on."

"Well, since I'm the only able partner at the moment, and with the valley people lashing out at us like they are and causing us trouble . . . well I, uh, haven't had a chance to transfer the stocks to you."

Suspicious of Willard's intentions, Colm studied the stout man for a long moment before he spoke. What's he up to? "Why not? Those notes you have there make *me* the only able partner, not you."

"Well, yes. You're right. But I—I just haven't been able to break the news to Mr. Jameson yet."

"Who's this Jameson you keep talkin' about? And if he's so all-fired important, why *haven't* you told him yet?"

"Roark T. Jameson. He's the largest stock-holder in the Thimblerigger Mining . . ."

Roark T. Jameson. Colm did not listen to the rest. His mother's white husband— Here. How could this be? Colm felt his stomach clench. After the raid, and freeing of all the white slaves from the Arapaho Village, he and his mother had been brought to Fort Kearny. Jameson had sent a single wire in response to the commanding officer's inquiry. He would never forget his mother's tear-filled expression as she read:

> MY WIFE, JENNIFER JAMESON, IS DEAD.
>   ROARK T. JAMESON

Hatred for the man suddenly filled his be-ing. Eighteen years of watching his mother slave over a washtub as fort laundress, scrub-bing the soldiers' clothes, her hands cracked and bleeding—the painful memories crowded his mind. The hushed whispers of the officers' wives echoed through his thoughts. He could almost hear them speaking.

"Even her own husband doesn't want her."

"No wonder, flaunting that half-breed boy of hers in his face."

"Any decent white woman would've killed herself rather than let some savage touch her."

"She got what she deserves—"

Got what she deserves? Colm's inner voice railed at the venomous phantoms that haunted him still. What did she do to deserve their hatred? Survive? How many times had he lashed out at the fort's so-called ladies? Or fought the children over their cruel remarks? And always with no true triumph. It never ended. He could not remember a moment when his mother was ever afforded any real leisure. Always cooking, cleaning, more dirty laundry, yet still she would take a little while to sit with Colm before bed and talk of dreams—dreams that would someday see them with a fine house, living in comfort.

And now, when it was within a hand's reach, Jameson—again—blocked the way.

"Mr. McQuaid?" Willard leaned into Colm's line of vision. "Are you okay?"

Glaring at the fat man, Colm nodded. "Get on with it."

"Well, as I was saying. I was hoping we could—that is, I could persuade you to work with us before I told Mr. Jameson of my and Mr. Cross's misfortune."

"You mean he doesn't know about any of it yet? The poker game? My partnership? Anythin'?"

Willard shook his head. He seemed to be assessing Colm. "No, nothing." He barely spoke aloud.

Colm remained motionless, staring at the obviously distressed man across the desk from him. He had thought everything would be settled by now. Willard had told him in Virginia City that there would be no problems. He had assured Colm it was all a matter of procedure. The new partnership would be explained, the transaction and introduction made, and everything would be finalized very easily. Now, nothing about it appeared easy. "I'm not sure I follow your reasonin' behind all of this. Just exactly what do you want from me?"

"I want you to keep up the pretense of being the consortium's hired gun."

"What?" Colm sat up straight. He thought maybe he had not heard the man clearly. "You want me t' do what?"

"Please, Mr. McQuaid. Just relax. I can assure you nothing's changed," Willard insisted. He lifted the papers. "I'll still honor these."

Colm felt his irritation pulse through his body. It swept into his fists, stinging his palms. Unconsciously, he flexed his hands. He reached for the notes, but Willard jerked them away from his grasp.

"Try to understand." Though visibly tense, the pig-faced man straightened his spine. "Look, we need you. With your reputation you can threaten them—find things out. Once news gets around that you're here, the farmers would be crazy to cause any more trouble at the mines."

Colm stared at the man with amazement. Willard was obviously scared. So, why was he risking getting him riled? "Hand over the papers, Willard."

"Won't you at least consider posing as our security?" Willard leaned back in the chair, clutching the papers even tighter. "You can get more answers as a gunman than a share-holder."

Colm fixed his eyes on the man with a heated glare. "I don't seem t' be botherin' you any."

"I—I know if you wanted to you could kill me and take these—" A gleam of hope edged Willard's gaze.

Colm dashed it with an artful nod. Maybe he could intimidate him into returning the papers.

"—but I'm betting you won't."

"Willard." Colm lowered his voice in an effort to incite fear. "Somebody ought t' teach you how to t' gamble better. You're not very good. You've already lost everythin' you own t' me—" Lifting a crafty brow, he raked the man with a deadly scowl. Still and all, Colm thought, the man's got backbone. "If I did decide t' go along with this hoax, what do *you* hope t' gain?"

Red-faced, neck bulging over the edge of his collar, Willard stumbled over his words. "I— I'm a company man. I started out as an assayer with the first gold strike, and saved everything I earned until I could finally buy stock in the consortium. Mr. Jameson took a liking to me right off. He helped me to become a major stockholder. He's been good to me, and it's my hope that when all this trouble at the mines is over and done with, he'll remember my loyalty and keep me on."

Folding his hands beneath his chin, Colm rested his elbows on the arms of the chair. He eyed Willard pensively.

Nervously, Willard watched Colm. He took out a handkerchief and patted his forehead then, with apparent reluctance, held the notes out to Colm.

"You're givin' 'em back?"

Willard nodded. "I can see I'm not goin' to make you understand, so . . . This isn't your problem. We can go over to the bank right now. Soon as I sign the stock certificates we can start looking for a buyer for you."

"A buyer?"

"Of course." Willard looked up, his hopeful expression turned to one of defeat. "You're not a businessman, so I assume you'd like to sell your stocks to the highest bidder as soon as possible.''

Taking the papers, Colm began to understand the man's very real devotion to the company. He admired the man's loyalty. His rigidness began to waver. It can't hurt to find out who's causin' the company's trouble. After all, I'll only be helpin' myself too. Maybe the man's right—I *can* find out more as the consortium's gunman. He glanced away, then back at Willard.

He had to put a stop to the trouble, for himself, for Willard—and even for the O'Shaunasey woman. What if the next one hurt, or maybe killed, is one of them? I'll be damned if I'll have anyone's death on my conscience. He thought of his mother's white husband again and the years of misery the man had caused her. A thought spun in his mind. Unless, of course, it's you, Jameson.

Disgruntled, Colm could clearly see his mother's deliverance. He nodded. "Okay, Willard. It's a deal. I'll be your hired gun.''

❧ 3 ❧

Sitting behind her desk, Maginn smiled down at her latest collaboration with Lance Taggert for *The Badger's Winze Gazette*. Only hours after her arrival in town a month ago, she had heard about the proprietor's need for an artist through her landlady, Mrs. Penhaligon, and had rushed down to his office to show him her drawings.

Her mother always told her she had an eye for detail and could put anything she saw to paper. An' right she was. A grand day it was when I landed this job. An' me afraid I'd have to work in another tearoom, an' have to listen to all those rich, uppity crones, an' their pompous blather about this one or that. Hmph! It fairly drove me crazy havin' to be so polite all the time. An' them never really carin' for anyone but themselves. Always makin' fun of me determination.

Proudly, she scanned each and every detail of her sketch. She had well enough captured the catapulting of splintered wood and frightened men racing away from the previous day's explosion at the Thimblerigger's number three. People had been lined up outside the office this morning even before the papers were finished printing. Everyone hated the *Badger's Winze*, but everybody scooped them up right off the press.

Lance had told her what a scandal her work would cause when he had hired her, and he had been right. She had already learned to ignore the more belligerent townspeople who made crude remarks about her. With the pictures to illustrate the paper's stand against the monitors and their destruction of the mountainsides, a couple of government officials had finally taken notice and had begun to support the Sacramento Valley farmers in their fight for survival.

Pity you're not here to see all the commotion, Father. 'Tis a good feelin', it is, to be doin' somethin' at last about you an' the farm . . . an' Tommy. At the recollection of her loss, an involuntary shudder quivered through her heart. One day I'll not be feelin' the pain quite so sharp. An' soon it is I'm hopin', I'll only remember the glad an' happy times we all had together.

A drone of voices just outside the office drew her attention and she smiled anew. Even now, hours later, the town buzzed with talk about the Grain versus Gold resistance group and the trouble they had caused the mines again.

"Aye, me sketches sure have an effect on the 'good townsfolk' here," she said to herself.

"They do indeed, Miss O'Shaunasey!"

Startled, Maginn stared up at the intruder. Wide-eyed, she held her breath. Eyes the color of hammered copper—and every bit as cold—stared back at her; it was the consortium's hired gunman.

"Damn it, woman!" he bellowed before she could catch her breath. "If you're so all-fired determined to print the *truth*, as you people call it, why don't you name names?" He slammed down a half-folded copy of the newspaper atop her desk.

She looked up, feigning shyness to conceal her wicked pleasure. "An' let you be knowin' who they are?" She had expected Colm McQuaid would be one of the first to come and try to get more information about the explosion. But what she had not expected was the delicious feeling of self-gratification at having something he wanted. It felt good to be the one in control. Her first triumph in her fight. To think, the great and infamous Colm McQuaid callin' on meself for answers. She knew who the vigilantes were rightly enough, but she was not about to tell *him*.

"Look!" He ground out his words between clenched teeth. "Whatever your beef is with the mines, you can't justify this kind of lawlessness," McQuaid railed savagely.

Maginn paid no mind to his booming voice. Unable to stop herself, she stared at his tanned, chiseled face. When he spoke, the sharp set of the jaw of the ruggedly handsome man gnashed at her. Satiny-black curls caressed his dark skin, which glistened with beads of sweat from the heat of the day—or was it from his temper? Either way, her emotions shot through her, charging, crashing, exploding like fireworks on the Fourth of July.

"Are you so filled with hate that you can't see what's happenin'?" He slapped at the picture with the back of his hand, then seared her with a blazing glare.

Instantly her own body warmed and a single drop of perspiration tickled down her spine. Her stomach tightened.

"Don't you see what you're doin'? People are gettin' hurt. This ain't some sideshow. Seein' this kind of thing for themselves only gets folks riled up worse. Don't that matter to you?"

"Aye. It matters," she answered, her defensive tone edged with bitterness. Suddenly she realized what she had done. She had actually baited him into coming and seeking her out. She had chosen this sketch on purpose and had wanted him to be angry about it. But why? To get back at him for their first meeting?

He leaned nearer. "Wasn't it enough that this group of hell-raisers almost killed Roark Jameson?"

Maginn stared at him in disbelief. Jumping to her feet, she slapped her open palms atop the papers. "Jameson be damned! *I've* done nothin' to the money-hungry bugger. 'Twas not my fault he was hurt in the pure accident of it all. I simply draw what I see."

McQuaid's face darkened. His hard-bitten eyes blazed into her. "Oh, you beat all, lady. You might not have caused that first blast, but you sure as hell are enjoyin' its outcome, ain't you?"

Managing to keep her rage in check, she shrugged indifferently. "An' just what would you be knowin' of me joy? You know nothin' of me except me drawin's."

The corners of his mouth turned upward, but not with amusement. It was a smile of ruthlessness. He glanced down at the newspaper, then back at her, and his eyes took on a savage, untamed glint. "Oh, but what they tell of you, *me sweet Miss O'Shaunasey*. Too bad your heart doesn't match that beautiful face of yours . . ." He leaned forward, countering her defiance with his. "A man might find himself . . ."

"What?" she murmured more softly than she had intended. Her nerves jittered just under her skin.

"Eaten up by that same snarlin' hatred that's gnawin' at you." He leaned back from her.

Dazed, Maginn could not speak. Colm McQuaid had struck a raw nerve. How clearly the gunman had seen into her emptiness. In desperation, she tapped deeper into her anger. "So be it!" Of its own volition, her hand lashed out.

He seized her wrist and jerked her to within inches of his face. For one split second, his angry glare held her more a prisoner than his grasp.

Their eyes clashed.

His mouth tightened into a thin line.

Chest heaving, Maginn could smell the scent of heated leather, sagebrush, and wood smoke combined with his own male fragrance. So close now, she thought he might dare to kiss her. For one hopeful moment, she almost wished he would. Make her forget for just a little while. Let her feel something. Anything pleasant again.

Then, strangely, he grinned, flashing white, even teeth, his features luring her with bedevilry.

He released her so suddenly she stumbled back into her chair.

"Another time, Miss O'Shaunasey—" He moved to leave, but turned back at the threshold. "We'll finish this another time."

Slamming the door closed behind him, Colm sucked in a restless breath. Another minute and he might not have been able to stop. Hell, another minute and— He glanced back at the wood surface of the door and imagined the O'Shaunasey woman spilled back atop the desk, her pale hair fanning across the dark surface below her head, her mist-green eyes begging him to free her from— Shaking his head, he looked up at the awning and groaned. "There's one helluva lot of dynamite to that little package."

His mind stirred, voicing the inner whisperings of his body. *That's* one helluva woman! Period.

"True enough," he answered his thoughts. "But she's one helluva a lot of trouble, too."

Still, he had to admire her determination and spunk. She believed in what she was doing, even if it meant putting herself in danger.

Turning away from the door, Colm peered around as if he thought someone might have heard him talking to himself. No one seemed to have noticed. Good. He settled his Stetson lower on his brow, then glanced down the street in the direction of his next destination. "'Cause I got more than enough worries without addin' *her* t' my list."

Shoving open the gate to a large, immaculately kept yard leading to a white manor house, Colm took the steps up to the lattice-shaded porch encompassing Roark Jameson's house with easy strides. The man had sent word by way of Willard that he wanted to meet his newly hired man.

Standing in front of the house, he pulled off one leather glove and reached up to knock on the door. Red fire sparkled from the two rubies gracing the delicate ring his mother had given him when he had left her so long ago.

"Think about me from time to time," she had said just before he had mounted and ridden away.

He smiled to himself. How could he not? She was his reason for doing all of this. Taking a breath, he pulled the glove back on. He did not want to reveal too much too quickly. And he knew Jameson would recognize the ring. It had been a wedding present from Jennifer's mother and father.

He rapped on the heavy wood. No reply. He hammered again. Nothing. Looking around, he followed the portico to the side of the house. For years he had dreamed of this. He would finally confront the man for leaving his mother to waste away as a laundress. Someday, Mother, you'll have money. He looked through a pair of French doors and noted the dainty white furniture seemingly made of woven twigs. "And all that goes with it, as well."

A sudden pounding from inside caught his attention. He listened. Another repetition of thumps. He tested the door latch. It opened. He leaned inside.

The sound repeated. "Damn it, Mrs. Beeton. Someone's at the door."

Hesitantly, Colm entered. The downstairs appeared empty. He crossed through the small, glassed-in dining room to an elaborate parlor. The house was filled with exotic things from all over the world.

Hanging above the fireplace was an overly large fan with sketchings of a little blond girl at a strange tea party with animals dressed like people. And in almost every fold was a different signature. A beautiful stained-glass picture brightened the center of the three large front windows which formed a bayed sitting area. On a marble-topped cabinet the statue of a nude couple embracing seemed to leap out between two vases filled with white roses.

Colm's eyes narrowed. "All this splendor—and Mother with nothin'."

Angrily, he scanned the finely crafted furnishings of rich woods adorning the memorabilia-crammed house. Showcases of books of every imagining, portraits, more sketches, fringes of colored beads decorating silk shades atop heavily ornate lamps, oriental rugs—the list was endless.

"Is there nowhere the man hasn't been?" Colm said between clenched teeth.

"Mrs. Beeton?" a man's gravelly voice boomed from above. Another series of rapid thuds. "By damn, woman. Where are you?"

Turning toward the staircase, Colm slid a hand over the smooth texture of the baluster. "He can't come t' me, so I'll go t' him." When he reached the upper landing, he heard a softer likeness of the voice that had boomed only moments ago. He stopped to listen.

The man seemed to be mumbling to himself. "Blasted woman. How long does it take to have a steer trotted in and butchered?" Papers rustled from beyond the only open door out of three adjacent to the long hall. "That fool doctor must think starving's a cure for a broken leg."

Colm sneered at the man's belligerent tone. He took a couple of steps toward the open room. A floorboard creaked beneath his weight.

"Who's there? Mrs. Beeton—that you?"

Colm halted his step. His muscles corded. He suddenly felt strange. It was not fear. He was afraid of no man. Yet something inside caused him to hesitate.

"Damn it, woman. Answer me."

From the corner of his eye, he saw someone and jumped. Realizing it was his own image in the large mirror hanging between the two closed doors opposite him, he relaxed. But something else startled him. He could see the reflection of his own apprehension at finally confronting his mother's husband. His determination wavered. Maybe now was not the right time to demand answers about his mother.

Straightening, he shook off the thought. Hell! He was a notorious gunman. He had faced down many men. What was so different about this one? He wiped away the sweat from his upper lip.

He took a breath, then reached up and rapped on the doorjamb. "Jameson?" He did not wait for an answer. Stepping inside, he cocked his head to a slight tilt to conceal his eyes beneath the brim of his hat. "You wanted to meet me."

Slate-blue eyes darted a startled gaze at Colm. One bushy salt-and-pepper brow quirked upward. "Who the hell are *you*?"

Stunned, Colm stared at Jameson. Throughout the years, he had imagined that he looked like some evil spirit—a devil masked in all the horrors of a child's nightmares. But now to see him like this—confined to bed, and helpless . . . He was not sure how to react, and in that instant, his hatred was reigned up short.

Beneath a mussed crop of brimstone-colored hair fading into silver, the man's luminous eyes traveled Colm's length. His voice cracked and he cleared his throat. "I said, who *are* you?"

Instinctively cautious, Colm glanced around the interior. As downstairs, the room was filled with costly furnishings. Silently, he moved as if he owned the house, striding easily across the bright Persian carpet. Coming to stand at the foot of the large mahogany four-poster, he smiled without mirth. "I'm Colm McQuaid."

Jameson's stubbled cheeks puffed out and his full mustache of sorrel-grey bristles flurried beneath his still-necked gaze. He squinted through one eye, his gaze darting to Colm's gunhand. "Mrs. Beeton let you in?"

Colm shook his head.

Caution registered in the older man's eyes. He shifted his posture and squared his shoulders. "It's customary to wait to receive an answer to the door before barging into someone else's home. But since you're here—" He pointed at a chair. "Willard warned me you were an arrogant bastard."

Though the hairs on his neck stiffened, and he gritted his teeth, Colm remained stoic. *Don't push me, old man. I'm not in the mood.* His muscles tensed, but Jameson ignored it if he noticed.

"However, I'm sure that'll work in our favor." Setting aside a wooden cow-horned crutch, he picked up one of the many papers scattered across his quilt. "I don't usually tend to business from my bed, but as you can see, I'm in no condition to take care of it elsewhere." He flipped his hand up, pointing to a splinted leg protruding from his nightshirt. "Now then, let's get to the point of your visit, eh?"

Colm barely paid Jameson's babbling any attention. *Who the hell does this pompous ass think he's dealin' with?* He glared hard at the man, but remained motionless at the end of the bed.

Jameson's ramblings finally stopped and he looked up. "What is it, McQuaid?"

"Look, Jameson." Colm continued to glare at the man. "I came here at your request. Your housewoman wasn't here, so I let myself in." Spreading his feet apart, he shifted his weight. "I don't have time for any 'you better know I'm in charge' bullshit. I was hired t' find out who's behind all the trouble at the mines. I can do my job. I don't need you t' tell me how t' do it."

Jameson met the challenge of Colm's glare with equal fervor, then chuckled. "No bullshit, eh? I like that—I like you." One thick brow jutted upward again, and he glanced at the overstuffed chair to his right. "Take a seat, McQuaid. I assure you, I have no intentions of telling you what to do."

Though only slightly relieved by the man's words, Colm could not help but admire Jameson's straightforward attitude. And though still leery of his intentions, Colm's curiosity got the better of him. Keeping his focus securely on the dour-faced man, he crossed the room and took the seat.

Jameson fastened his eyes to the document in his hand. "Fix us a drink there, will you, McQuaid?"

Colm glanced at the decanter of whiskey on the small table to his left. Might as well.

Unplugging the stopper, he filled two glasses beside the container.

Without so much as a glance up, Jameson took his drink.

Sipping the amber liquid, Colm allowed his gaze to roam. His eyes came to rest on the side table nearest Jameson's bed. There a small daguerreotype caught his eye.

Fragile as a flower petal, a blush of joy on her cheeks, the dignified image of a woman with dark, fashionably upswept hair peered out from the picture. Colm swallowed. He leaned nearer in his chair. Never had he seen his mother look so radiant.

"Beautiful, isn't she?"

Startled, Colm suddenly felt embarrassed at being caught staring at the portrait. Hoping to appear indifferent, he only nodded. "Who is she?"

"My wife, Jennifer." Jameson picked up the gilt-edged frame, fingering the ornamental filigree with a loving touch.

Colm studied his white stepfather. He knew the man to be cold and unfeeling. Memories of watching his mother grow old before her time stirred his senses. His recollection of her pain and torment severed his reasoning.

He hated him. Despised his nearness. Glaring around at the luxury of the house, he envisioned the one-room shack the fort provided for his mother. His jaws clenched. He gripped the glass tighter. His eyes narrowed as he returned his gaze to Jameson. The little boy inside of Colm wanted to snatch the picture away. But the man within saw that the ruthlessness he had attributed to Jameson had all but disappeared, bringing a vulnerable light to his pale blue eyes.

When the older man set the portrait back in its original position, Colm thought he saw true pain in his face—or was it just regret?

"McQuaid." Jameson looked back at the papers lying in his lap. "I've been given some startling information that may or may not help you to discover who's behind the chaos at the mines. But actually, I hope it doesn't help you at all."

"The hell you say." Colm reared back. He hated delaying the matter of his mother and Jameson, but if he was to lift her from her impoverished state and set her up for life, he would have to get to the bottom of the trouble at the mines first. But after that—

He took another gulp of his drink and observed Jameson intently. After two days of watching and asking countless questions, he had not uncovered a single clue as to the identity of the vandals and thieves. If the truth be known, he could use all the help he could get. And now Jameson thought he had something but did not want it to be of use? Strange man. "You don't want the trouble stopped?"

"Of course I do," Jameson almost yelled. "But at what expense?"

"Expense?" Colm frowned. The man had him baffled. Focusing on his whiskey, he tapped the rim of his glass with his forefinger. "A man of your wealth shouldn't have a problem with money."

"I'm not speaking of money." Jameson lowered his voice. "It's my son, Andrew. I think he's in trouble."

"Your son?" Colm sat up. His mother had told him about his brother, but he had forgotten about him. With all the problems in the mines and that damn O'Shaunasey woman, now Colm was expected to deal with a brother—and one in trouble to boot!

"Damn you, Colm McQuaid." With the hem of her cotton nightdress hiked above her thighs, Maginn sat cross-legged atop the bedsheets, fuming in frustration. She stabbed mercilessly at the sketchpad in her lap. "Leave me be and let me finish me work."

Why so angry, Maginn? her inner voice chided. The gunman said nothin' today that wasn't the pure truth of it.

"Oh, shut up! What do you know?" She tossed the tablet to the floor and folded her arms over her chest. "The bugger's got a lot of nerve comin' an' tellin' *me* what's what. Just who does he think he is?" She cocked her head back and forth. "Pity your heart's not as bonny as your face, he says. Hmph! Snarlin' hatred, he says. I'll show him *snarlin' hate!*"

Forgetting her proximity to the headboard, she threw herself back.

Thud.

"Ouch!" She grabbed the back of her head, gingerly rubbing the spot that had just collided with the bedstead.

See now, her conscience scolded again. McQuaid's right. You *are* filled with hate, Maginn O'Shaunasey. Do you want the whole of the mountains infested with the same hatred as yours?

Shaking the thought, she picked up the sketchpad and flipped the page. She had to finish. Lance needed to approve the drawings for the paper in the morning. Taking her pen, she made a fresh start. "I'm not the one causin' the trouble," she said, continuing the argument with herself.

Aren't you?

Maginn shook her head as if someone else were truly in the room and speaking to her. "No. 'Tis those damnable water cannons, not me."

But without your drawin's to look at, folks might not get so angry.

"'Tis angry they should be. They must see the truth of things."

Facts are one thing, but you don't need to be cuffin' 'em in the face with it. There's no good to it.

"If people see it in front of their faces, it's harder to hide from doin' what's right. They'll have to get involved."

An' what about you?

"I *am* involved."

But is it for the good?

A twinge of doubt crept into Maginn's thoughts. She paused in mid-stroke as she worked. Could I be doin' wrong?

As if someone had suddenly gripped her shoulders, her conscience shook her from her thoughts.

Blindly she stared down at the drawing beneath her hand. They've got to see what's happenin' to them? She shook her head and clucked her tongue. "Here now, Maginn. You're all a-flutter." She dipped her pen in the inkwell on her bedstand. "An' you've let that man McQuaid get the better of you *again*. Painful or not, I only sketch the truth. Eventually folks'll see the right of me work an' come round."

So what truth is this now?

Focusing on the unfinished picture, her eyes suddenly widened, and she gasped. "Damn you, Colm McQuaid!" Rage, disbelief, and horror at her own creation clawed at her spine.

Like the kiss of an incubus, Colm McQuaid's soul-searching gaze leapt out at her from the paper.

"Damn you to hell!"

❧ 4 ❧

"Thank you, Lance." Maginn offered her employer a smile as she breezed past him and into the Sierra House. She waited nearby while he closed the door.

When he turned around, his gentle gray eyes scanned the available seating. He pointed to a table in front of the large window of the restaurant. "How about that one?"

Maginn acknowledged her approval with a dip of her head.

Doffing his tan cap, he smoothed back his thick mop of blackish-brown hair, then lifted his hand, motioning her to go ahead of him.

"Miss O'Shaunasey? Mr. Taggert?" Joelie Tollins bounded over to their table. She tossed her long carrot-colored braid over her shoulder, and though bubbly as usual, the young girl appeared a bit nervous. Her gaze darted around the room as she handed the menu boards to each of them. "Won't Mother be surprised to see you both here. Not that you're not welcome. I mean—you know? With all the fuss you people have been kicking up over there at your paper and all, well, it's got folks downright riled. I mean—well—them's awful nice drawings and all, Miss O'Shaunasey, but . . ."

Setting her sketch case and reticule in the extra chair, Maginn accepted the menu. "Aye, Joelie. I know," she answered, only half amused by the implications of the girl's words. The townspeople were becoming more and more agitated by the newspaper's stand against the monitors and in favor of the farmer's resistance. And her drawings only seemed to incite them more.

"I'll have the Sierra House special, Joelie." Lance smiled brightly, making the dark bruise around his eye appear even more pronounced.

"I think I'll just be havin' a cup of coffee with cream, a biscuit or two, an' maybe a wee bit of that wonderful orange marmalade your mother's so famous for."

"Would you like coffee, too, Mr. Taggert?"

"That'll be fine, Joelie."

"Good." Joelie's freckles seemed to leap out from her face as she beamed an overexuberant smile. "I know you're probably in a hurry to get back to the paper, so I'll tell Mother—"

"Oh, there's no rush," Lance said with an uplifted brow.

Joelie shifted uneasily. "But Mr. Taggert—"

"Don't worry. There's hardly anyone here." He indicated the nearly empty room with a wave of his hand. "I promise, we'll just have a quiet breakfast. No trouble. And then we'll leave. Okay?"

"Really? No trouble?"

"Really." Lance winked with his uninjured eye, his boyish good looks shining through his battered face. He wriggled his thick handlebar mustache at her teasingly.

Joelie giggled, revealing the little girl still left in the young woman. "Thanks, Mr. Taggert. It's not that we don't want you here and all, but this place's all Mother and I got. If we was to lose our customers on account of people getting the wrong idea about us and you— not that we don't feel the same, you understand. Well, it's just that we can't afford to take sides. It's the miners that butter our bread—if you know what I mean?"

"I do indeed." Lance reached across the table and took Maginn's board, handing both his and hers back to the girl. "Don't worry."

Appearing satisfied, Joelie nodded, then

wheeled around and disappeared into the kitchen.

"If we could only be gettin' more people like Kate Tollins to see the importance of the resistance, maybe they'd back us up."

Lance snorted. "Ideally, that's a wonderful thought. Realistically, they can't—at least not right now. You heard her. The money brought in by the mines is bread and butter to her mother as well as the other local merchants."

"Then for heaven's sakes, Lance, what in God's thunderous voice are we doin' this for?" Folding her arms over her chest, Maginn glowered at her companion. "Just look at yourself there. 'Tis quite the sight you are with your face all battered an' bruised like that."

Lance shrugged. "Comes with the territory." He grinned. "It's not like it's the first time, you know."

Maginn shook her head. "I don't understand you. You won't back off from printin' the truth an' you won't go an' see the sheriff to put a stop to this. Or will you be for tryin' to convince me that you don't know who did this to you?"

Lounging against the chair back, Lance set one ankle atop his knee, then folded his hands in his lap. "Does it matter who it was?"

"Of course it does. Don't you care?"

He glanced outside. "One fist's the same as

another. And if it hadn't been the men last night, it'd be someone else later."

"But—"

"Look, Maginn." His warm gaze washed over her with a consoling smile. "It just means they're starting to see the truth around here. The meat isn't quite seasoned yet. You gotta give them time to chew. 'Specially something that's as gamy and tough to swallow as the destruction the monitors are causing."

"You mean you're just gonna let them continue to buffet you round like this?"

"No." He looked out again at the street.

"So you're gonna fight back." Maginn grinned. Finally Lance was going to get *really* involved. The paper was a good thing. No one could deny the very real destruction the hydraulic mining caused when it stared them in the face, but now he was actually going to roll up his sleeves and physically *do* something. Leaning an elbow on the table, she rested her chin in her palm. "What's it to be now?"

"Here you go," Joelie said, startling Maginn. She set two cups and saucers down, then poured coffee from a steaming pot. "And I didn't forget your cream either."

"Thank you." Maginn forced a smile. She waited for the girl to move to the table across the room before she spoke again. "So what's it to be, Lance? Are you goin' to join the resistance?"

"I already have."

Her eyes flew open wide. "Wonderful!" After pouring an ample amount of cream in her cup, she took a sip, then peered at him over the rim. "What're you an' Drew goin' to do?"

"Drew?" Lance's dark brows drew together in a vee. "I don't know any Drew."

Puzzled by his reluctance to admit meeting Drew Jordan, the resistance leader, she tilted her head and studied his expression. "It's quite all right, you know. I met him meself. Matter of fact, the same day I met you."

"I'm sorry, Maginn. I really don't know who you're talking about."

She smiled complacently. Maybe Drew wanted to keep his identity a secret from Lance. Maybe he wasn't sure he could trust him. Or maybe he was afraid if Lance knew who he was, an incident like last night's just might bring his name out. "No matter. What is it that you're up to?"

"Well. While I was in Sacramento last week, I got in contact with a Mr. George Ohleyer and Mr. James Keyes. They've been fighting the usage of the monitors since the beginning. We've put a proposal to Assemblyman Berry and have retained a lawyer to recommend that an engineering team be sent out to examine the situation at the mines and that they prevent the opening of any more hydraulic claims like Thimblerigger's." Picking up his cup, Lance took a sip. He grinned triumphantly. "That ought to get the ball rolling in our favor."

Stunned, Maginn could only stare at him. "That's it?"

Lance frowned. "What do you mean, that's it? That's a lot." He swallowed another gulp of coffee. "I thought you'd be happy."

"Lawyers and assemblymen! They don't give a two-penny damn about the mountains up here, or the farms below for that matter. Besides, while they're waitin' round for all that legal twaddle to take root in some fool court, the mountains an' the farmers are sufferin'." She challenged him with a glare. "I thought you were serious about the fight."

"And so I am." Lance's usual composure had been dispelled. "I put myself in jeopardy every time I run off a new copy of the paper. Hell, I can't even go out at night without putting my life in danger—" Planting both fists firmly atop the table, he shot her an accusatory glare. "Or hadn't you noticed?"

"A-hem." Joelie seemed to appear from nowhere with the couple's breakfast plates. Setting Maginn's down first, she cast a nervous glance toward one of the other tables. "You promised, Mr. Taggert, remember?'' she asked in a hushed voice as she placed his food in front of him. "No trouble."

Lowering his gaze to his plate, Lance held up his hands. "You're right. No trouble."

Uncertainty marking her expression, Joelie cast a brief look first at Lance, then at Maginn. "Well—all right. I'll be back with some fresh coffee in a few minutes." Before another word could be uttered, she spun around and vanished into the back of the restaurant.

"An' just what was that supposed to be meanin'?" Maginn asked when the girl had departed. Her heart pounded. Her temper soared, and with it, her bottom lip began trembling. She stiffened, but as she did so, a movement caught her attention. She cut a glance to the back table. Her jaw slackened.

Chin resting atop his folded hands, Colm McQuaid sat silently watching her.

With the potent memory of the gunslinger's verbal attack clear in her mind, Maginn sucked in a deep breath and squared her shoulders. She glared at Lance. "I'm not some unfeelin' monster as you and others might be believin'. I've noticed all right. But you surely can't be for thinkin' that pitiful black eye of yours can compare to what meself and others have suffered?"

Colm McQuaid leaned both forearms on the

67

table and allowed his hands to droop below the edge.

A tiny feeling of victory sparked inside of Maginn. She had his full attention. She wanted him to know of her suffering and the reasons for her convictions. Wanted him to feel her pain. But why?

"Men! What an infuriatin' lot of gouty-limpers you are. You talk of the trouble, an' you even manage a good boast or two. But when push comes to shove, you sit 'round on your butts and do what? Why, talk some more." Shaking with the full fury of her ire, Maginn grasped at the single thread of composure she still retained. Then, with the deliberate intention of irritating Colm Mc-Quaid, she raised her voice. "Why, if *I* were a man, I'd *really* be doin' somethin' to stop those damned water cannons! But as 'tis, I'm only able to do this!" She grabbed her drawing pad and slapped it atop the table.

A chair scraped across the floor.

Beneath lowered lids, Maginn snatched a glimpse of the gunman.

With a cold, fixed stare, McQuaid reached into his pocket and pulled out a three-dollar gold eagle. He tossed it onto the table. Crossing the room with quick strides, he jerked his Stetson off the hat tree near the door.

A flood of gratification surged through the

full length of Maginn's body. Affecting an air of indifference, her eyes cast downward, she smiled to herself. With a haughty lift of her brows, she picked up her cup and brought it to her lips. But she could not help looking at McQuaid. She wanted to enjoy his retreat.

"There's that beautiful face again." It was the deeply resonant voice of the gunslinger.

Startled, she peered up. She almost dropped her coffee. So close that his holster touched the table, Colm McQuaid goaded her with a lop-sided grin.

"But still no heart." Apparently indifferent to Lance, the gunslinger's expression hardened. "You really don't give one damn that men are bein' seriously hurt, do you? Or that you're helpin' the ones that're causin' the trouble?"

Maginn felt the blood rush to her face. She ignored her first instinct. A slap. But she had to do something. She was not about to just sit there like some stupid lack-wit. "Helpin'?" she echoed. Restraining her temper, she lowered her voice. "Oh, 'tis hopin', I am, that 'tis much more than just *helpin'*, Mr. McQuaid." With great effort, she reached down and withdrew her reticule, then looked at Lance and stood. "Thank you for breakfast, Mr. Taggert, but I seem to have lost me appetite with the here an' now of it. So, if you'll be excusin' me."

Lance slid his chair back and rose. "Maginn, wait, we need to go over the sketches."

Abruptly withdrawing from the table, Maginn ignored both men and stalked outside.

Staring after her, Colm shook his head. "If I live t' be a hundred, I'll never meet a woman more fulla trouble."

"She's got her reasons," the O'Shaunasey woman's companion interjected.

Colm cut him a questioning glance. "Ain't we all?"

"I don't believe we've met. I'm Lance Taggert, owner and editor of *The Badger's Winze Gazette*." The dark-haired man offered Colm his hand.

Unimpressed, Colm accepted the greeting.

"You're that Wells Fargo agent the consortium hired."

Colm nodded. "You make it sound like I'm some kinda murderer or somethin'."

"I assure you that wasn't my intention." He gestured to the O'Shaunasey woman's unoccupied seat. "Would you keep me company while I finish my breakfast?"

Colm eyed the man suspiciously.

Though strikingly handsome, Lance Taggert looked every bit the dandy in his fancy gray pants and tall, highly polished boots.

Peering down at himself, Taggert grinned up at Colm. "English riding britches, and Prussian boots."

"That a fact?" Colm moved around to the chair and sat down.

Taking his own, Taggert scooted his seat closer to the table. "They're quite comfortable."

"Mmm-hmm." Colm pursed his lips to keep from smiling. Some kinda milksop.

Taggert lifted his fork and gestured toward the door. "I take it you've met our lovely Maginn?"

"Maginn?" Strange name for a woman. "Well, 'magine that." Colm chuckled at his own wit. Then remembering their first meeting, he rubbed his jaw. "Yep. We've struck blows a time or two."

Taggert's gaze met Colm's and a strange, knowing smile turned into a grin. "Yea, I bet you have."

"How long have you known her?"

"Oh, couple of months now. Since the day she arrived." Taggert forked his beefsteak, then cut off a chunk. After only a couple of chews, he swallowed. "Why?"

"I'm just curious as t' what's got her petticoats in a snag with the consortium."

Stopping mid-bite, Taggert hesitated. He set

his utensil on the edge of his plate. "Why do you want to know?"

"Curious."

"Curious?" Taggert rested his weight on his elbows. His eyes narrowed.

Colm nodded toward the exit. "That woman's madder than a badger in heat. And she's aimin' everthin' she's got straight at the consortium. It only seems natural t' find out why. Do you know?"

As if worried that the woman still stood in the doorway, Lance Taggert cut a troubled glance over his shoulder. He looked back at Colm, then filled his lungs with air. "You've got a reputation for being a hard man, courageous, ruthless, and at times even savage." He eyed Colm thoughtfully. "But I've been watching you around town. And I like to think I'm a pretty good judge of character. I think you want to do right by the townspeople here in Cavenaugh's Dig, as well as the consortium. So . . . I'll tell you, Mr. McQuaid. But if you're half the man I think you are, I guarantee you won't like what you hear. And once you've heard, you just might want to take another look at your own standing with the consortium."

Colm spent the rest of the morning and afternoon in Lance Taggert's room. They had gone over studies that were done by an eastern researcher Lance had hired to find out how much damage the hydraulic mining was really doing to the land.

"Thanks for the information, Taggert," Colm said from the doorway.

"My pleasure. I'm glad I was able to prove the truth about the monitors." He lifted a hand. "Maybe it'll help you take care of things from your side."

"Yea. Maybe." With that, Colm dipped his head and made as if to leave, but another door opening and closing down the hall drew his attention.

Maginn O'Shaunasey, slightly bent, stood locking her bedroom door at the back of the house. Outfitted in a worn pair of men's dungarees and a red cotton shirt, the pretty blonde tossed back her thick hair tied with a ribbon at the nape of her neck.

Where's she off t' now? he thought. Curious, Colm decided to follow her. After hearing her story from Taggert, he could understand why she was so up in arms over the hydraulic mining. But if she was not careful, she would probably wind up dead like the rest of her family.

He followed her downstairs at a discreet distance. Once she had left the house, Colm walked to the front window and watched. She pulled on a pair of gloves and crossed the yard, heading straight for the livery stable.

When he had made sure he had not been seen, he stepped out into the heat and soundlessly closed the door to Penhaligon's Boarding House behind him. Unconsciously, he tugged at his gunbelt, then pulled his hat down low against the bright ball of orange lingering above the rooftops.

Spurred by his new information, an urge to protect the woman waged another battle within him. He suddenly wanted to make things right for her. Wanted to correct the wrong done to her. But why? She was nothing to him.

A few minutes later, a sorrel mare was led out to her, whereupon she mounted and trotted out toward the west. This made the third time that week he had seen her leave town at sundown.

Mighty queer. Looking up and down the street, Colm watched to see if anyone else had noticed. Other than a few meaningful glares tossed her way, no one seemed to pay her any mind.

Crossing the yard, he looked next door at Jameson's house. The facts Taggert had given him flashed through his mind. He would definitely go out and see the mining operations for himself. He wanted to know firsthand what he was up against before confronting Jameson with this discovery. If all that Taggert says is true, maybe the farmers and these . . . What the hell did Taggert call them people? Ecologists? He rubbed the back of his neck. Yeah, ecologists. And the reports. He grimaced as he recalled what they had revealed.

The monitors were gouging out fifty thousand tons of earth a day, leaving stripped-out canyons of some five-hundred-and-fifty-feet-deep pits in their wake. Lance said the cliffs would probably be left barren for over a hundred years to come. And the silt and debris sent down in the drainage to the valley was filling up the riverbeds, waiting for another storm to come and flood the fertile farmland. And for what? To make the rich richer.

His glare deepened as he thought of Jameson. Not for long. *This* is just what I need to destroy the man.

Another thought struck him. If it was true, he would be ruined too. Damn. Now what?

Colm went to the livery and saddled up his paint, Scaramouch. Then, free and easy like so as not to draw attention, he followed the woman out into the first shadows of night.

Even with her head start, Colm caught up to the O'Shaunasey woman in a short period of time. He stayed back, just out of sight. She seemed to have a set direction, climbing steadily into the mountains.

This ain't just no carefree night ride. Wary of every sound and movement, Colm's senses were sharp. Less than an hour later, a strange owl's hoot caught his attention.

Too soft to be a real bird, the sound, he knew, had to have been made by the woman. A second later another, huskier call answered the first. Dismounting, he tied his horse's reins on a mountain scrub. Hunched down, he made his way to a rocky hill and peered into a small moonlit meadow. But he saw no one. No movement. Nothing.

"He's too close to findin' you out, Drew." The O'Shaunasey woman's voice touched Colm's ears.

Hugging the mountainside, he inched his way to an overhang and looked down. The darkness hindered his vision.

He was so close he could hear the woman breathing. She spoke again, her tone urgent, a hint of fear in it. "He's a ruthless bastard, he is. He'll kill you—kill you dead if he gets half a chance."

Silently, Colm pulled off his hat and crawled to the edge. A cloud passed beyond the moon and a movement caught his eye.

"Come here, you."

Someone was with her. A man. Heart racing, Colm held his breath. He peeked over the ledge.

Barely a good drop below, Maginn O'Shaunasey leaned into the embrace of a stranger, a man who—to Colm—appeared way too familiar with her . . .

❦ 5 ❧

Moon-mad, the silver shades of night did little to hide Colm's intrusion on the couple below. Pressing himself flat-bellied against the still-warm hillside, he continued to observe the two carefully. He squinted into the darkness.

Concealed beneath a dusty black hat, the stranger tipped his face down to the O'Shaunasey woman.

Thunderous silence rumbled in Colm's straining ears. Then a throaty, masculine groan echoed, answered by the distinct sound of a woman being thoroughly kissed.

Stroked by the soft, female noise, Colm felt the blood surge to his groin, stirring reactions that had never before remained so long unsatisfied. He clenched his jaw and glowered downward. So this is how the little upstart gets what she wants. Her earlier words rolled through his mind.

He narrowed his eyes. Some kinda helpin' you're doin', lady. Is this the way you *help* the resistance? Struggling with the urge to jump down and disrupt the woman's secret meeting with her lover, Colm chose instead to wait and see if he could learn anything that might help him. But he only found himself wishing *he* were the man holding the lovely blonde. He restrained a smile. His heart quickened its thick beating. His manhood stiffened to the point of pain. He grimaced.

Three times during the last week he had seen Blaze at the Rowdy Rose and had been invited to join her in her room, but Colm had always declined. Normally, he would have snatched her up without a thought, but with so much on his mind lately, he had not been interested. Tonight, however, he would make sure things worked out differently. Tonight he was definitely interested.

"Drew. Please," the O'Shaunasey woman whispered breathlessly. "We've no time for such things. This McQuaid is not such a blunderer as you might be supposin'. He's been askin' quite a lot of questions round town."

"So what?" the man replied arrogantly. "What's there to find out? Taggert's the only one who could possibly know anything and after our meeting with him last night—"

"So, you have met him? An' him pretendin' none the wiser about you."

"What're you talking about?"

The man's voice seemed to border on anger—or was it fear? Colm could not be sure. Turning his head, he tilted his ear toward their conversation.

"I took a late breakfast with Lance this mornin'. You know, I wondered why he was so deadset against knowin' who you were. Why, he even took a beatin' for us last night. An' since you say he met with you, it couldn't have been long afterward, I'm supposin'." She took a breath. "You're right to trust him. We'll never have to worry about the likes of him givin' away the show. Even without that scrap, he's shown the true color of his heart, an' 'tis clearly not cast in *gold*."

"What did Taggert say about the men who roughed him up?" he asked quickly.

Intrigued, Colm held his breath for a moment so as not to miss the woman's answer, or her lover's response. He stretched closer to the edge.

Distancing herself a space, Maginn O'Shaunasey leaned against a boulder and shrugged. "Very little. He won't even go to the sheriff about it. Odd, hmm?" She picked a sprig of sagebrush from a nearby clump and held it up to her nose. ''You'd think for certain he'd be wantin' to turn the minin' scurvy into the law, wouldn't you?''

''So, he said the miners roughed him up, hmm?''

Colm brushed the bead of sweat from his upper lip against his shoulder. Something about the way this guy acted made Colm even more suspicious. Strange, too, he had not asked if Taggert had been seriously hurt.

The woman shook her head. ''He didn't say who 'twas. Who other than the miners would've been so black-hearted, though? Everyone knows Lance is against the use of the monitors.''

''Of course. You're right.'' The man's overbearing manner returned almost immediately. Using two smaller stones for a foothold, he stepped up to the boulder where the O'Shaunasey woman rested and sat down beside her. He reached over and began massaging her back. ''Okay. I know you're worried—but why are you so flustered about this two-bit gunslinger? The consortium's just trying to scare us.''

''Scare, you say?'' She whirled around and faced the man.

Colm ducked.

''Listen, Drew Jordan. He's no one to be

triflin' with. I did some checkin' with the Wells Fargo Company an' it seems he's earned himself the reputation for doin' what he's hired to do."

Puzzled, Colm lifted his head and stole another look. He wanted to see if the woman truly appeared as anxious as she sounded.

The man below shrugged. "So?"

The O'Shaunasey woman leaned away from her lover and stared at him, moonlight distorting her face.

"Oh, come on, Maginn. I can't believe a hellcat like you is afraid of anyone—gunslinger or not."

"I'm not afraid," she snapped. Then, folding her arms across her middle, she clutched her elbows as if she were suddenly chilled. "But you better be, Drew Jordan. 'Tis you he's after."

"So's a lot of others, and they haven't caught me yet. What makes you think he can?"

She looked up into the restless sky. Her voice softened. "'Tis his eyes."

"His eyes? What's so strange about them?"

"Like agates thrust up from the burnin' pit of hell, they reach inside an' sear your soul. He's the dev'l's own beast, he is."

Jordan's body tensed. "For somebody you hate, you sure have noticed an awful lot about him. You know, with all the fuss you're making, I'd almost think you liked this gunman."

A weighty pause suspended Colm's curiosity like a puppet dangling powerless from its strings.

The woman's expression was contorted with rage. She drew a breath of air. "Like him? I hate the pure sight of him. He's 'bout as likable as a rattlesnake's kiss, that one!"

Colm frowned. Yes. She had *always* met him with a challenge, cursing and scorning his every word. But now it seemed as if she were just a bit too quick with her denial.

"Maginn, you're shivering," Jordan said, sounding almost as surprised as Colm felt. Briskly, he rubbed her upper arms. He pulled her closer. "You can't let this bastard get to you, Maginn. He doesn't know anything, or he'd have come after us by now." Cupping her chin, he tipped her face up to his. "And I wouldn't make too much of his reputation, if I were you. It's probably all talk anyhow."

Noting the look of anger still creasing her features, Colm could see the man had not changed her opinion.

Clutching her, Jordan leaned back, his head cocked to one side. "You hear me?"

"Mmm-hmm."

A cloud scudded angrily across the prying moon. And though the light dimmed her features, Colm envisioned the woman's forced smile.

Jordan tapped her nose. "He can't be that good. I've never heard of him." He chuckled. "Hell, given a slug at a dead run, I bet he couldn't even blast its butt."

If the night had not been so quiet around them, Colm might have missed the nervousness of her laughter. Her response grated on him sharply, causing a slow burn to ignite in the pit of his stomach. He glowered down at the couple below and watched as Maginn O'Shaunasey allowed the man to gather her into his arms.

Colm felt his muscles contract painfully against his bones. His insides twisted. The man had stomped a mudhole in his pride, poked fun at his well-deserved reputation, and worst of all, revealed the woman's fear of him. Colm had never felt such hate or contempt. He had seen enough—heard enough! Let her be afraid. He had a job to do. His plans depended on it.

He stabbed the man's back with a savage glare. As for you . . . walk soft, Drew Jordan. Colm backed away from the edge, then rose and made his way to where he had left his paint.

By the time he had reached the bottom of the mountainside and Cavenaugh's Dig, a light drizzle had begun. Midnight draped the town in a blanket of darkness. With the exception of a stray cat, or the whimper of some unseen dog, all remained quiet. After stalling Scaramouch at the livery, Colm trudged out into the rain, his mood as black and murky as the sky above. He wanted nothing more than to go to his room at the hotel and fall into bed, but that would have to wait. With quick strides, he ate up the distance between the stable and Penhaligon's Boarding House.

Careful to conceal his presence, he kept to the shadows and bushes surrounding the building until he had made his way around to the back. Checking one last time to assure himself that he had not been seen, he jumped up and grabbed the edge of the balcony. Though the rain did its best to hinder his movement, he managed to pull himself abreast of the railing and climb over.

Remembering the O'Shaunasey woman's room was at the back of the house, Colm halted at her window. He hesitated. Though he knew she was still with Jordan, he peeked inside. Dark and quiet. He raised the window-pane, threw his leg over the sill, and slipped inside.

Her petal-soft fragrance caught him off guard even before his eyes adjusted to the unlit bedroom. "Why does she have t' smell so damn good?'' Catching the glint of an oil lamp's glass chimney, he made his way to a small table beside the bed. He felt around until he found a tray of matchsticks. Taking one, he struck it to flame across a rivet on his pants.

After lighting the wick and replacing the dome, he turned the lamp down to the barest hint of a glow. There had to be something here that would help him discover just exactly what the O'Shaunasey woman's accomplice was up to. He had to be part of the resistance, that much Colm felt was certain. Maybe he was even the ringleader.

Colm glanced around the room. Exposed to his view, it revealed the delicate woman hiding within the brittle shell of Maginn O'Shaunasey. Primly neat, the room held nothing but the remnants of female vanity. Drawn to the articles atop the bureau, Colm moved across the floor, causing a board to creak beneath his weight. He froze and waited. Nothing stirred.

He looked down. A pair of tortoiseshell combs inset with a scroll design lay one on top of the other next to a mahogany hairbrush. Picking it up, Colm thumbed the soft, thick bristles. Strands of pale golden hair, as rare a color as the elusive palomino, glimmered in the light.

Ever since that first day, Colm had wondered how soft her hair would feel gliding between his fingers, or splayed across his skin. His gaze wandered to where a small clear bottle with a yellow bow sat filled with amber liquid. Colm picked it up.

A tiny bouquet of flowers and the words "Victorian Posy *Eau de Toilette*" decorated the gold-edged label. Opening the stopper, he took a sniff. The soft fragrance of wildflowers tweaked his sense of smell, leaving a dewy kiss where the bottle had touched his nose. He smiled. Almost, but not quite right. Without the added essence of Maginn O'Shaunasey, something was missing. He closed his eyes and inhaled again, teasing his manhood. His nostrils flared, recapturing her womanly scent. The moment lingered, nearly diverting his purpose.

He opened his eyes and gritted his teeth with a throaty groan. Damn that infernal woman! Plugging the container, he set it back in its original position. He suppressed the urgency of his need with another promise to visit Blaze before going back to his room. She might not smell as good, but she's willin'.

Sweeping the interior with another glance, he noticed a pad of paper hidden just beneath the edge of the bed. Maybe she had written something down. He crossed the room and lifted the scalloped border of the quilt, then retrieved the papers. He sat on the bed and smoothed the crumpled top page, then held it up to the light.

Astonished, he stared at the perfect likeness of his own image. What the hell? He flipped the sheets over one at a time. With every turn he discovered still another drawing of himself in various settings and situations around town. "Son of a bitch! She's been watchin' me!"

Muffled voices echoed up the staircase, followed by footsteps in the hallway.

Colm tensed. She was back. He looked at the window. Too late. He would never make it out before she came inside. He blew out the lamp.

A key clinked, the door opened, and Maginn O'Shaunasey's silhouette appeared in the doorway.

Motionless, Colm listened. Primed for any noise, he could almost hear the unfastening of each button down her front, the heavy swipe of wet fabric being tugged out from her dungarees, and above it all the chattering rasp of her chilled breathing. She took a step toward the foot of the bed.

Tossed over the nearest bedpost, her shirt slapped at the wood in a soggy heap. With an unladylike groan, she pulled off each boot in turn, sending them across the floor with a clunk.

Colm felt his stomach clench. Never before

had he paid attention to the sounds of a woman undressing. But now, without being able to see her, he found his other senses sharpening, stimulating him to a dangerous arousal. Another bout of silence, and he knew she was loosening the buttons on her pants. His pulse quickened. He had to stop her. He could not stand any more.

"You better hold it right there, lady."

Like a startled cat, the woman froze.

Colm struck another match. "I don't think you want t' take off much more." Remembering her fear of him, he decided to put it to good use. He lifted the flame closer to his face before lighting the lamp.

"You."

Glancing up at her, Colm sucked in a breath. Her wide eyes flashed green fire. Soaked to the skin, she looked more beautiful than he had ever seen her.

His blood heated. Held captive, he forgot his intent. His gaze swept her rain-misted face, the honey-sweet pout of her mouth, and the drenched tumble of her hair. Wet, wild, and wind-blown, it fell limp down her back, dangling just above her waist. He lifted his stare, letting it come to rest on the gentle swell of her breasts straining against the thin material of her flimsy undergarment. His pulse jumped. No woman had ever disarmed him as she did now. Unable to tear his eyes away from the dark thrust of the nipples pressing the wet fabric, he gawked openly like a puckish schoolboy.

She followed his gaze. Her eyes were riveted to his. Covering herself with her hands, she backed away. "Whatever are you doin' here?" she asked in a panicked whisper. Fear marked her expression.

Colm remained silent. What could he say? He did not want to admit that he knew about her lover, or about their secret meeting. He had no proof that either of them were involved in the troubles at the mines . . . yet.

"Are you daft?" she asked from the middle of the room. Her face flushed red. Her bottom lip trembled. "Answer me!"

Colm blinked. He looked her square in the eyes.

Full of terror, they searched his face, demanding a reply.

Outside, the steady drizzle grew louder, intruding on the quiet.

When he still did not speak, she lunged for her shirt. Snatching it up, she shoved her arms through the wet sleeves and pulled it together in the front. She yanked the weight of her hair from beneath the collar and glowered back at him. "I asked you a question."

Colm still did not know how he was going

to get out of this. If he told her the truth, she would probably yell for help. Hell, no matter what he told her, he was sure she would set to hollering. And if she screamed, the whole town would come running, ready to loop a rope around his neck. That much was certain. He decided to gamble on her temper. He knew that once riled she would not stoop to feminine weakness. She would try to fight him on equal terms. "I came t' see you."

Her jaw fell slack.

"We didn't finish our conversation at breakfast this mornin'."

One thin glistening brow rose. She folded her arms across her chest and squared her shoulders. "Really? I think we both had quite a say, don't you?"

"You didn't let me finish—"

"Let you finish?" She wiped the moisture from her face.

Colm watched while he formed his plan. Inwardly, he grinned.

Enraged, Maginn puffed up like a bloated calf. "You mean I didn't allow you the last word?" A hate-filled smile played across her mouth. "Did I wound you so?" She lifted her chin and set her hands atop her hips. "Aye, I'm supposin' I did. I can see where that wee bit of banterin' might've put a ruffle in the haughty plumes of such a notorious gun-slinger as yourself.''

Colm almost laughed aloud. And as long as he kept her hackles up, he would have time to make a plan to get himself out of her room unseen and with little to no trouble. He would come back later when she was gone again—when it was less risky. But how to do it? The sketches. That was it! She had to be attracted to him a little. Otherwise, she would not have filled the entire pad with his likeness.

He shook his head and flashed her a bold smirk. Rising to his full height, he peered down at her. ''You've got me dead t' rights, Miss O'Shaunasey. You did get me a bit riled.'' He lifted the sketchpad. ''So, here's where I get even.''

Her gaze shifted to the pad. Her face drained of color, then torched red-hot. She snaked out a hand, aiming for the sketches, but Colm yanked them from her grasp.

''Give those to me!'' Thunder punctuated her command.

He raised each sheet with slow deliberation, taunting her with his dramatic perusal of every drawing. ''You seem t' take great pride in your work, Miss O'Shaunasey. And what feelin'.''

''Damn you, Colm McQuaid. Give those back!'' she all but shrieked. ''Or are you thinkin' to become a thief as well as a hired killer?''

Colm could feel his own temper smolder. He could not afford to lose control. "Thinking? Tell me—" He lowered his voice suggestively, then turned the paper for her to view. "What were *you* thinkin' when you drew me?"

Glancing at the sketch, she balled her fists. She was shaking with fury when her eyes returned to his. She could not deny the evidence of her own handiwork. Nostrils flaring, she took a deep breath. "Why did you come here?"

"I told you."

Her posture suddenly relaxed and she appeared to gain fortitude. She smiled wickedly. "'Tis a fair bit of nettlin' I must've caused your pride to provoke your comin' here to do this." Moving to the bureau, she leaned against its edge, her hands braced behind her back.

Colm frowned. What's she up to? "Do what?"

"Why, to kill me of course."

"What?" Colm nearly choked. She really did believe him to be a mad killer.

"I can see the headlines in tomorrow's paper: 'CONSORTIUM'S HIRED GUN MURDERS HELPLESS NEWSPAPER ARTIST.'"

Was she crazy? Colm stared at the woman. If it had not been for the flicker of lightning through the window, Colm would have missed the slight upturn of her lips. *So, she thinks she can put one over on me.* Folding one arm across his middle, he rested the other elbow atop his fist, and rubbed his chin. Beneath furrowed brows, he looked up and taunted her, mirroring her own grin. He relaxed his posture and chuckled softly, his gaze clinging to hers. "Lady, you're about as helpless as a baby rattler. And if that's all I wanted, I could've killed you earlier in the woods."

Dark-gold lashes flew upward, exposing her shock. "You followed me?" She bolted toward him, fists pounding against his chest. "You bastard!" She whipped a hand upward, knocking the sketchpad from his grasp.

On his guard, Colm caught her wrist midswing. He grabbed a handful of hair and yanked her head back, forcing her face to meet his. "I'm on to that tactic."

Her teeth flashed white. "An' this?" She jerked her knee up.

Feeling her body tense, Colm pulled her tighter so that the strike met his thigh and not his groin.

She struggled harder, twisting and writhing until she threw both off balance. They plunged to the floor. Colm landed hard, Maginn to his side.

She squirmed, almost gaining her freedom.

In one quick movement, he secured her hands beneath her hips and rolled on top of her. Her heart pounded against his ear. He looked up. His chin brushed the wet fabric barely concealing her breasts.

Someone pounded on the door.

"Maginn? Dear? Are you all right?" Constance Penhaligon's sharp tone cracked at the door as if it were a bullwhip ripping through flesh.

Colm gave Maginn O'Shaunasey a mocking lopsided grin.

She opened her mouth. "H—"

"Careful. Or tomorrow's headlines might read: 'GAZETTE'S ARTIST DRAWS MORE THAN SKETCHES.'"

Agony registered in her expression. "You wouldn't—"

"I wouldn't have t'," he finished in a throaty suggestive whisper. He shot a glance down the length of their entwined bodies, only to return his eyes to hers with a teasing look. Even in the dim light, he could see her face flame red.

"'Tis all right I am, Mrs. Penhaligon. I simply lost me balance with me undressin'."

"Can I come in—I could help you."

Pale eyes grew paler still, widening to their fullest. "Oh, God. The door's not locked," she whispered.

Colm pretended a lack of concern. He lifted his brows helplessly.

Glaring at him, she shook her head and called to the proprietress. "I'm not decent."

Colm's grin deepened. He curbed a chuckle. He found himself rather enjoying her predicament.

"You're a love for worryin', but I can manage meself. Be off to bed with you now. I assure you, I'm quite unharmed."

"Well, all right . . . if you're certain?"

"Aye."

An audible sigh drifted through the door. "Night, dear."

"Good night," she called back almost too cheerfully.

Colm held his breath and waited. He did not want the elderly woman suspicious any more than did Maginn O'Shaunasey. He listened as the sound of receding footsteps traveled the length of the hall and down the staircase.

"Get off me, you great lummox, you." Her voice grated between clenched teeth. Wriggling, she managed to free one leg enough to plant her heel into his calf.

Colm threw a powerful limb over hers and repositioned her within his strength. He decided to take advantage of her distress and have some fun. "You didn't answer *my* question, Miss O'Shaunasey."

"What!" Obviously startling herself, she darted a look at the door, then lowered her voice. "What question?"

He nodded toward the sketchpad lying upside down on the floor next to them. "What were you thinkin' when you drew all those pictures of me?"

She thrashed her head back and forth, heaving her chest, her breasts shoving into Colm's face.

A shot of adrenaline stung his groin. "Miss O'Shaunasey," he scolded with a sneer. "Best you relax and hold still."

"Get off me!" she demanded, though panic had returned to her voice. "I can't breathe."

"You'll behave?"

She nodded.

Colm cocked his head to one side and squinted at her questioningly.

"Please. You're hurtin' me hands."

Colm relented. But just enough to give her a measure of comfort. Deliberately rubbing against her, he shifted to his side, keeping one leg draped casually over hers—just in case. "Now. Answer me."

"Why did you follow me?"

"I didn't follow you," he lied. "I saw you ride out."

"So, how did you know where I was goin'?"

He shrugged. "You did take the north road."

"Oh." She seemed to relax, then tensed again. "What were you doin' in me room?"

Lounging on one elbow, Colm unconsciously began to toy with a tendril of her hair. Cool and damp between his fingers, it lit another spark of need within him. "I told you."

"Oh, aye. You came to see me," she mimicked childishly. Her face grew serious. "Why?"

He grinned. "T' murder you of course."

For a moment, she appeared to believe him, but all too quickly met his threat with a challenge of her own. She tipped her nose up and closed her eyes. "If that be so, be done with it then."

Studying the length of her form, he noted how, even though he had long since released her wrists, her hands remained immobile, relaxed at her sides. He lifted the blond strand of hair to his nose. Her soft fragrance touched off his memory. Victorian Posy. He swept a gaze over her face.

Proud and defiant as a storybook queen, she lay against the lamp's golden hue. He followed the perfection of her profile. God, but she was beautiful. How many times in his dreams these last two weeks had he been tortured with this same vision? Too many. His heartbeat thickened, his blood heated.

With a low, almost seductive groan, thunder rolled in the distance, prodding Colm to give in to his baser instincts.

He stole a glance at her lips, full, tempting. More than that, inviting. Compelled, he leaned down. His mouth touched hers.

Battle-lit eyes flew open. She thrashed wildly.

Without thought, he imprisoned her body against his.

A tiny gasp escaped her.

He secured her tighter.

Her movements stilled.

For a brief second, their gazes locked, warring. Her eyes darkened. She looked up and stared at the ceiling.

Testing her indifference, he tasted the slight part between her lips.

She did not fight him.

Colm closed his eyes. He wanted to feel something more from her than hate.

Gently, he savored the sweetness of her mouth. But his lust rose too quickly, overwhelming him. He needed release. Moving a hand to her rib cage, he felt her shudder beneath his palm.

Near madness, he groaned, bruising her mouth. Snaring her hair with his fingers, he pulled her closer still.

Her tongue touched his, searing his flesh. Her arms encircled his neck and she arched against him. She moaned, deepening the kiss.

Colm froze. What the hell? *She* was kissing him. Baffled, chest heaving, he pulled away and stared.

Her lashes fluttered upward. Dark-fringed, her eyes revealed the passion-fed storm silently raging within her, demanding more.

Damn it! She continually played him for a fool. She wanted him to desire her, but he was on to her game. Once he gave in to his need and surrendered to her wiles, he would probably find her nails ripping out his eyes.

Tossing his head back, he exhaled a deep-pitted growl. The little she-cat was a dangerous fusion of bliss and brimstone.

Drenched with nectar, her voice stroked his ear. "Colm?"

His muscles went taut. She said his name—had succumbed to his touch. Why? She hated him—feared him. He searched the delicate contours of her face, looking for a sign of deception, but none surfaced. He wanted to trust her, bury himself within her—

But like a viper, suspicion reared its ugly head as he remembered her lover. Damn it t' hell! Wordlessly, he released her and pushed himself away. Rising, he stalked to the window.

Lightning flashed.

Rain splattered against the sill in a coaxing tattoo, urging her name to his lips. But he could not voice it. If he spoke, he might not leave. Colm shot her a sidelong glance.

Encompassed within the lamp's soft, amber light, she sat stock-still, green eyes emitting a look of quiet desperation. But why? Because of Colm? Or simply was she toying with him? Was this just another way of interfering with his investigation? He could not be sure. He had to find out. But not now. He could not trust her . . . or himself.

6

Tears burned Maginn's eyes as she watched Colm disappear into the downpour. What had she done? A slap would not have hurt so much as the abruptness of his silent departure. Standing, she made her way to the window and looked out through the doubled panes of glass. She squinted against a flash of lightning, barely catching a glimpse of his dark head as he leapt from the balcony to the ground. She wanted to call out to him, but something stopped her. Damn her Irish pride.

As if agreeing, a low roar of thunder rumbled around her.

Through the glistening shower, she saw him splash across the yard. He stopped and turned toward her, his silhouette barely visible against the backdrop of the alley. She could feel the weight of his stare on her. And as powerfully as when he had held and touched her moments ago, a shudder rippled through her body.

She wet her lips, tasting again the intoxicating sweetness of his kiss. Filled with frustration, she could not prevent a groan from slipping away from her. Why had she allowed him to do that? She remembered the solid warmth of his embrace, the excitement of his touch, and the sudden need to feel something—anything good after enduring such a long period of cold emptiness.

Maginn almost strangled on the realization. She was lonely. Eyes fixed on the man in the alley, she struggled to gain a fortifying breath.

In the distance, thunder rolled, a mere murmur of its earlier voice. Softer now, lukewarm rain splattered her as she stood in her stocking feet. And though still tethered to the dark figure across the street, Maginn's gaze blurred. She was tired of having to be brave, of having to seek retaliation for the injuries inflicted on her family, and most of all, the isolation her dutiful promise inflicted upon her. She sighed determinedly. All she wanted right now was to sleep, to forget this night had happened, to retreat back into the protection of her indifference, and away from Colm McQuaid. Reaching up, she grasped the frameworkand slowly, firmly pushed the window closed.

As she slept, Maginn was assaulted by a tumble of dreams. Misshapen images, familiar faces, tortured sobs, and taunting challenges crowded her rest. The quiet horror of her father's death, Tommy's lifeless form, her flooded home, long-nuzzled beasts roaring, spitting, cutting her flesh, and newspapers whirling around her like helpless birds caught in the wind. Her heart constricted, filled with vengeance. She was the heroine—alone, she would fight them. Fearlessly, she met the monsters, battling with all her might until all were silenced and dead.

A shape loomed in the shadows.

Chest heaving, she moved nearer, focusing on the phantom. Her breath lodged in her throat. The gunslinger. He was her only obstacle, and he was coming for her. She braced herself, but something was wrong. She did not know how to defeat him. Her strength nearly depleted, she lashed out, but caught no more than air. She darted from his path, only to find him looming closer. Afraid, Maginn froze. She had to get away. But she was tired—so very tired. Searching for an escape, her gaze came to rest on his face.

Like sunburst, he smiled at her, holding out his arms.

Her body swayed, his warmth drawing her ever nearer. She wanted to go to him, to feel the comfort of his gentle embrace and forget. Hesitantly, she moved toward him.

Drew appeared. "That's right, whore! Go to the murderer. Give yourself to him. Turn away from your family's cries."

Shame stung Maginn's cheeks. Her eyes flooded with hot tears. "Please, Drew. You can't be for understandin'. I don't want to hurt anymore."

Drew sneered hatefully. "You think he won't hurt you? Fool! He doesn't want you—he wants to *use* you—"

Heart pounding, Maginn woke with a start, her face wet with tears. The reality of the nightmare still upon her, she lay very still, allowing herself a few extra minutes for recovery. She shivered. Just a dream . . . rather, a nightmare. Plucking up her courage, she shook off her fear. None of that now, Maginn, me girl. 'Twas nothin' to be fearin'. Only children are frightened by nightmares.

She sat up resolutely, then stretched. Her muscles ached. She felt more exhausted now than when she went to sleep. Her mind stirred with thoughts of Colm McQuaid, and she turned her gaze toward the window.

The softly breaking pale light of dawn crawled in through the glass, dappling her room in muted shades of morning. Maginn sat for several moments staring out at the yellow-robed sky.

Was he still in bed? Aghast at her own folly, she looked away. How could she think such a thing? Her gaze fell on something dark on the floor. As she peered closer, Colm McQuaid's gray Stetson came into focus. Her eyes grew wide and she smiled. Tossing back the covers, she jumped up and grabbed it, disdain and scorn forgotten with the discovery. She fingered the felt curve of the brim. As real as if it had just happened, his kiss came back to her, and of their own volition, her fingers traced her lips. The single action did more to fracture her resolve than the disturbing dream.

Wheeling around, she pitched the hat atop her bed, bolted over to her bureau, and yanked open a drawer. She suddenly felt exhilarated. Come what may, she wanted to see him, and the hat was a perfect excuse.

"Good day to you, Wheet," Maginn called out with a wave to the smithy, Mr. Buffman, across the street.

Standing in front of his anvil, he strapped on his leather apron and smiled. "Mornin', Miss Maginn. Off to work, eh?"

With a flourish, she nodded and closed the gate between her and the boarding house. She gestured to the bright ball of orange just cresting the rooftops. Even at this early hour it had already heated the slight breeze. "Mind you, that's a peppery sun this morn, likely to bake your brain and scald your skin, an' with no charge atall. Keep you to the shade now, you hear?" Without waiting for a reply, she made her way across the street. She beamed a contagious smile to Kate Tollins as she all but skipped past the Sierra House. "Grand day, isn't it!"

"Isn't it?" Mrs. Tollins answered, a look of astonishment on her face.

Clasping her bundle closer to her chest, Maginn almost crashed into Doc Farnham on his way to breakfast. "Your pardon, good Doctor. Gorgeous mornin', now, isn't it?"

Dipping his head, his mouth fell agape beneath a silver handlebar mustache.

Maginn grinned. She knew she had shocked them all with her unusual good humor, but she could not seem to help herself. She lifted the object within the confines of her shawl and sniffed. Powerfully masculine, Colm McQuaid's scent fired her stride to a jaunty step.

She thought of his expression when he had left her so suddenly the night before. For all his faults, the man was shy. You were a lusty wench, Maginn, me girl. Poor man. What must he think of you? Hiding her amusement behind the bundle, she giggled softly.

Her footsteps slowed. Oh, me good Lord! What must he be thinkin' of me indeed! What'll I say to him? She looked down at the concealed hat. An' just how am I to be givin' this back? What if someone sees? What'll *they* think? It'll be all over. Merciful Jesus. I hadn't thought of that!

"Mornin', Miss O'Shaunasey."

Startled, Maginn blinked. The very fastidious Downie Williams, the hotel manager, stood smiling at her. A heavy odor of oil assailing her senses, she watched the thin wisps of black smoke curl upward as he blew out the wall sconces on either side of the entrance.

"Something I can do for you?"

"Hmm? What?" Gathering her wits, she peered around. Without realizing how she had come this far, she found herself standing in front of the building where Colm McQuaid roomed.

"I say, something I can do for you?"

"Umm—I—" Heat rushed to Maginn's cheeks. She could not think. What was she going to do about the hat?

"If you're looking for Mr. Taggert, he's already left."

"Left?"

"Yep. Came by about an hour ago to see Mr. McQuaid."

"Colm?"

"Mmm-hmm." Downie bobbed his cottony head. "You just missed 'em."

Her sterling mood suddenly dulled. What was Lance doing with the consortium's gunman? Wheeling around, Maginn stormed toward the newspaper office.

"Oh, they didn't go over there."

Maginn spun back on her toes. She cocked her head to one side and squinted at the rail-thin man.

He stood pursing his lips with a look of amusement. He seemed to be enjoying her confusion.

"Well?" Gripping the shawl-covered hat in the crook of one arm, she planted the other fist atop her hip.

He nodded toward the growing sound of hoofbeats behind her, then chuckled and turned back inside the hotel.

"Maginn." Lance Taggert's smooth and easy voice called out to her.

She whirled around, almost dropping her bundle. Securing it, she looked up to see Colm McQuaid riding up next to her friend.

"I didn't figure to see you until I got back."

"Got back?" she questioned when they had reined to a stop in front of her. "Where is it that you're goin'?'' She fought to keep her eyes trained on Taggert, but to no avail. Colm McQuaid's riveting stare drew her gaze. She held her breath. Her pulse quickened.

Astride his black-and-white Indian pony, he appeared almost savage. Gleaming blackish-brown hair feathered away from the strong lines of his face, tapering to the back of his neck just short of his shoulders. The solid square line of his clean-shaven jaw flexed as he continued his all-too-apparent appraisal of Maginn.

A tremor raked through her body, but she managed to hold strong. The moment lengthened between the two, gripping, pulling, straining like wet leather drying in the sun. Catching a movement from the corner of her eye, she saw Lance shift in his saddle. He was saying something. Conscience-stricken, she forced herself to look at him. ''What was it you said?''

He shook his head and smiled, his gaze darting between Maginn and McQuaid. He pointed down to her package. ''I asked what you had there.''

She stood firmly rooted to the ground as a flush of warmth muddled her thoughts. She glanced down at the bundle, then met Colm McQuaid's disturbing stare again. There was no way out now. She had to reveal her burden.

She bit her lower lip. Boldly, she met his unswerving scrutiny. She took a breath. Clutching the felt brim, she yanked the hat from beneath her shawl, and thrust it out at the gunslinger.

His brows drew together, and his horse flinched away from her quick movement.

Lance straightened in his seat and his forehead creased with his intent assessment of the pair.

"You forgot this."

The gunman frowned.

She was not yet certain of Colm McQuaid, nor the meaning of the previous night's ordeal, and so could not allow him advantage over her. No matter what the outcome now. "You remember," she offered loud enough to insure anyone watching that her lie must surely be the truth. She forced determination and strength into her tone, and though she almost weakened beneath the potency of his regard, she lifted her chin stubbornly and met his stare with unyielding defiance. "When you stormed into the newspaper office an' hurled that nasty bit of temper at me?"

His dark eyes glimmered and a slow smile lifted one corner of his mouth. He glanced at Taggert before raking Maginn with an amused look of tacit understanding.

Relief washed over her. But no matter how

grateful she was for his willing participation, she could not abandon her ruse. She gestured for him to take the hat with another flick of her wrist. But it did not end there. Her glib Irish tongue took over her common sense. "'Tweren't for the heart that you've plainly stated I've not got, your property might not've been returned atall, Mr. McQuaid." Instantly, she regretted her gibe.

His stare darkened. Bending down to retrieve his hat, he leaned near her ear. His rich voice caressed her while his fingers stroked the back of her hand. "I would've come back for it . . . Maginn."

Straightening in his saddle, Colm pulled his Stetson low, and secretly grinned at her stunned expression. Why had she gasped? Wasn't that what she wanted to hear? Maginn O'Shaunasey definitely fascinated him more than any woman he had ever known. But why? Was she more beautiful, or more arousing than any other? The question strongarmed his heart. He peered deeper.

Braided like a wreath crowning her head, sun-drenched hair sparkled around an angelic face. His gaze slipped to hers. Whether the flicker in the willow-green depths of the woman's eyes was cold or balmy, Colm could not be certain. But the dangerous undercurrent of passion swirling within their depths could most definitely penetrate the thickest wall of restraint. Damn her! Did she have to look at him like that?

Startled by his own thoughts, he glanced away, focusing on the road ahead. Anger raised havoc with his self-assurance. He did not have time for this. He had to put some distance between himself, the woman, and his lusty appetite. "You ready, Taggert?"

"Just waiting for you."

Ignoring the hint of amusement in his companion's voice, Colm spurred Scaramouch forward. Without so much as a backward glimpse, he urged his mount away from the dust-flying bustle of town, and toward the fortifying coolness of the forest.

Silence stretched the passing of minutes like hours before Taggert broke the quiet.

"Didn't you have your hat yesterday evening when you left my room?"

Colm cut Taggert a glare. The barb had found its mark, causing him to shift uncomfortably in his seat. He reined the paint to a stop. "You got somethin' to say, Taggert, you spit it out."

Chuckling, Lance lifted his hands and flashed an apologetic grin. "Just asking a question."

Colm pulled his gaze from Taggert's and pressed his horse onward with a light tap to its flanks. Damn newspapermen! They don't miss a thing.

Another stretch of time yawned between the riders.

"So?" Taggert finally forced the subject further. "What about it?"

Colm held his posture relaxed, his eyes looking forward, and his mouth shut. For once, he was not quite sure how to handle things. He would answer the man if he thought this question would be the only one. But Taggert was no fool. If Colm replied at all, there was sure to be more questions following this one.

What could he say? If he lied to protect the woman's virtue, Taggert would know. And if he told him the truth, Taggert, being her closest friend and all, would more than likely call him out for a showdown.

Beneath his brim, he studied Taggert. He did not display a gun, but Colm was pretty sure he had one on him somewhere. He was not certain why, but he could not shake the feeling that his companion could handle himself when it came to gunplay. Even though Colm felt sure his skill was superior, he liked the man and would not want to see them at odds with each other.

"You're not going to answer me, are you?" Lance asked seriously. Though his tone remained light, his mouth was set in a firm line.

"Look, Taggert." Colm could not stand the goading any longer. He jerked Scaramouch's lead so hard it clanked against the animal's teeth. One way or another he was going to put an end to this probing. "I don't know what you wanna hear. So, yeah, I had my hat when I left your room last night."

The man's dark brows flew up.

Colm did not give him time to respond. "And yeah, sometime between then and this morning, I saw Maginn O'Shaunasey. But what happened, and how she came to have my hat, is none of your damn business."

Taggert's expression flashed his surprise. His eyes flickered with anger.

Noting a slight flex of his companion's free hand, Colm readied himself for a fight. He sharpened his features and eyed the man beneath furrowed brows.

Taggert tensed, then after only a moment he relaxed, sitting more at ease.

Colm tested his control on the matter. His voice did not soften. "Okay?"

Taggert brought a gloved fist up to his mouth and cleared his throat, though the effort did not hide his mischievous smirk. Head lowered slightly, eyes laughing, he said, "Sure thing." Then, adding more surprise, he reached out to Colm, his white smile slashing his tanned skin. "Still friends?"

Colm hesitated, studying Taggert to determine his sincerity. When he saw no sign of deception, he eased up and took a deep breath. Catching the man's grip within his, Colm accepted the gesture willingly. "You sure you wanna be friends with me? It might prove to be more than a little interestin' at times."

Taggert shrugged. "Yes, well, as we both know, newspapermen like myself"—he motioned toward his black eye—"tend to lead rather boring lives. So if you can stand my humdrum existence, I can certainly stand the stimulation. And being friends with you, Mc-Quaid, is sure to stir up more than just *interest*."

Colm chuckled. "You got grit, Taggert, I'll give you that." Straightening in his saddle, Colm paused. In the distance, a whooshing sound suddenly grew into a loud roar.

Scaramouch tossed his head nervously.

Colm jabbed the paint in the sides and headed for the open sunlight gaping at the end of the tree line. As they broke through the timber, the rumble became deafening. The horse reared. Nearly thrown, Colm sucked in a startled breath. "What the hell!"

7

Colm regained control of Scaramouch, quieting him with soothing words and gentle pats. Riveted by the incredible sight below, he scarcely noticed the approach of his companion.

Nozzles in hand, garbed like firemen from top to toe, miners stood in a huge pit directing streams of water at the mountain face. "Son of a bitch!" he said aloud. But with the ferocious roar hurtling from the monitors, no one, not even Taggert sitting only a few feet from him, could have heard him speak.

Lance leaned over and pointed at one of the gushing cannons. "They say it can shoot a spray four hundred feet into the air," he shouted above the noise. "Aimed at a wooden building, the jet would turn it into splinters in a matter of minutes."

Staring down at the long-snouted beasts below, Colm could well believe the truth of their destructive powers. He scanned the collection of canvas-walled bunkhouses scattered along the gravel-covered roads that threaded the camp together. Dust and spray mingled in the air like a brown mist, saturating the whole of the area with its heavy vapor.

Soot-covered workmen used picks on the naked rock, dodging the congestion of hoses and ditches. Others labored with sledgehammers and hand drills, and all for the same purpose.

Taggert gestured for Colm to follow him down the narrow path into the bowels of the cacophony.

Eyes still glued to the throng of muddy workmen, Colm made a careful descent behind his friend. Nearing the bottom, he saw August Willard huddled with two of the laborers. As the man looked up, Colm saw that Willard's bushy mustache appeared to bristle above gaping lips. The man shifted his attention back to his workers, motioning them to be about their duties.

"McQuaid!" He hurried forward.

Even before Colm's feet hit the ground, he felt the solid whack of a personable slap on his back. Turning, he met Willard with a look of warning.

The man grew flustered. He rubbed the offending hand as if he had been scalded. His gaze shifted nervously between Colm and Lance. "So—ah—Mr. McQuaid, you've finally found time to come and see what we do out here?"

Colm dipped his head in response.

"I see you've brought our illustrious Mr. Taggert, as well."

"Yeah. He found time too." Colm did not like Willard's insinuation that Colm might not be doing his job properly.

"I hope you don't mind, Mr. Willard. I wanted to get a firsthand look at the situation for myself." Flashing Colm a wink, he grinned. "I wouldn't want to be accused of one-sided reporting in my paper."

"To be sure, Mr. Taggert." Willard cleared his throat. "But then everyone knows that you're strictly neutral and completely unbiased."

"Do they?" Lance smirked.

"Oh, yes, indeed." Willard looked as if he had just been thrust between a bobcat and a rattlesnake. "So, gentlemen. How about letting me take you both on a tour of the operations?" He motioned to a thin little China man to come and take the horses.

Colm gave over his paint's reins. One hand

resting on the butt of his gun, he smiled tolerantly. "It's your show, Willard."

"Wonderful." The bow-shaped scar under the man's eye deepened from red to purple. He seemed as delighted as if he were a little boy given a new pup.

"As you can see, gentlemen, this is the heart of our business. The number one was the first and richest discovery of the consortium." He pointed at one of the water cannons. "One man can now do in a day what dozens couldn't in a week."

Reaching inside his shirt pocket, Lance retrieved a small journal and pencil. "You don't mind if I take a few notes, do you?"

Willard flashed Colm a questioning look, then turned back to Taggert. "Well, I guess there can't be any harm in it."

"Good. Now, what kind of profit is the mine yielding—compared to before the monitors were brought in five years ago?"

"Well—ah—" Willard wrung his hands and swallowed, his gaze darting between Colm and Lance.

Knowing full well what Willard's hopeful look meant, Colm chose to disregard his plea. He wanted to hear about the profits too. Folding his arms, he waited.

After a couple of strained minutes, Willard cleared his throat with a cough. "Well, Mr.

Taggert. We've never publicly declared our earnings before. I don't see why—"

"I'm well aware of the consortium's declarations, Mr. Willard. But with all the trouble, don't you think it might be a good idea to let people know how much the company's clearing?"

Lowering his gaze, Willard shoved his hands in his pants pockets and kicked at a small rock. "Wouldn't that be like cutting off my own nose?" He glanced up. "I mean, once the farmers realize exactly what we're netting up here, they're sure to get pissed."

Lance cocked his head to one side. "That substantial, hmm?" When Willard did not reply, Taggert continued. He motioned out over the pit with a sweep of his pencil. "You know, it just might help."

A look of surprise marked old Walrus-lip's face. "How do you figure?"

"Think of the jobs and the capital you're bringing down into the valley."

Colm hid a smirk by brushing a bead of sweat from his upper lip. Slick, Taggert. He watched Willard's expression for a sign of comprehension. If he were smart, the man would realize that things like money and work would have already been taken into consideration by the farmers. Obviously, though, they were not enough. But how smart was Colm's thinking? Being a major stockholder in the consortium, he should have wanted to put an end to Taggert's interrogation. It could prove disastrous for the company. But he did not stop him. He found himself too curious— Just how rich was he?

Willard's demeanor brightened. "Yeah, I see your meaning." He rubbed his chin thoughtfully. "You really think it might help put an end to this mess with the resistance?"

Lance shrugged. "It might."

"Let me see here . . . ah, yes. As I recall, before we brought in hydraulic mining, our profits were about a piss-poor two thousand a year, give or take some. Since then, we've gradually brought it up, yielding some odd twenty-two thousand in seventy-one, to almost a hundred thousand or so this year. And it's only May."

Colm swallowed. He had not imagined such wealth. If these facts were true, he could bring his mother out from Nebraska before winter set in.

"Mmm. I hadn't realized just how prosperous the consortium was," Taggert said with raised brows. Squinting down at his booklet, he wrote his notes in a whirlwind of scratchings.

"Now, hold on there, Mr. Taggert." Willard's face flushed. "You can't hold our gain against us. We're creating quite a boom for the valley people as well.''

"Really?" Lance looked up from his writing.

Willard peeked at him out of one eye and jabbed a finger in the westerly direction. "You seen them wagons groaning up the roads from the Sacramento floor, ain't you? Well, what do you think they're doing with all that fruit, grain, and other goods? Why, selling them to the miners . . ."

Colm did not hear more, for in the next instant, a gut-wrenching tearing sound echoed down from the north rim of the pit. He cut a startled glance upward.

As if screaming in pain, a huge ponderosa pine fell down the earthen wall, its roots ripped out by the sheer pounding pressure of the water shooting from one of the cannons nearest the edge.

His gaze dropped.

Deep in the pit under the highest cliff, a multitude of men worked like a force of ants, half hidden in shadow. Spitting from the gigantic force of the monitors, water from some unseen reservoir surged and tumbled into foam, wickedly, viciously rushing from the huge black pipes snaking down over the wall of the hollow. Like retching beasts, the cannons washed huge boulders and clay down to the bedrock where blasters waited, dodging flying rocks some two feet around tossed up from the jets.

Although repulsed by what he saw, Colm could not look away from the huge area of devastation. His stomach churned violently. Only in battle had he seen such mutilation. But this was a fight. Men were at war with the mountain, and she was losing. Her beauty was being raped and plundered. And for what? Gold. As if bleeding, the cliff face oozed red foam that spilled onto the ground where the main destruction was taking place.

Colm felt sick. He remembered another such sight from his childhood—another pathetic, vile vision that had haunted his dreams for many nights to follow. A year before his mother and he had been taken away from the people of the Arapaho, he and two other boys from the village had taken their ponies for a ride, hoping to find the tracks of the great buffalo. Such a discovery for so young a brave would have gained them praise from their chief.

Early morning had seen young Colm and his friends lucky in their hunt. They had found the beasts' tracks. But at the end of the tracks there was a hideous scene. Everywhere, as far as they could see, the massive herd lay slaughtered, rotting in the sun, hides and tongues stripped from their decaying bulk. Only whites would allow so much to go unused.

Bile rose in Colm's throat as he recalled the moment he had thought long since forgotten. It choked him. Blinking, he glanced around the pit again. How could anyone do this? Like the buffalo, the land could not fight back. And like the white hunters, when these miners were through gutting out their precious gold, they would leave the land to lie in waste.

He glared at the two men who had turned to stare at him. Seeing the color of their skin caused Colm to grimace. He felt suddenly ashamed that he had turned his back on his Indian blood for the wealth his white half could help him gain. Chest heaving, he whirled around and strode toward his horse.

"Colm. What's wrong?" Taggert called after him.

Snatching Scaramouch's reins away from the little Chinese man in front of the foreman's shack, Colm stepped up in the stirrup.

Lance trotted over to his side and grabbed the jaw strap of the harness. "Hey, partner. You all right?"

Without acknowledgment, Colm looked past his friend to the frenzy of the pit. If the destruction up here was this bad, what could it be like down below? He thought of the O'Shaunasey woman, and what she had said of the valley's devastation. Was it truly as horrible down below as Lance had told him? Were the consortium and their mining operations really responsible for all her loss? No matter what the outcome, he had to find out the truth for himself.

"Hey!" Taggert yanked on the horse's bit.

Colm glowered down at Lance's troubled expression. "Let go!"

"What's wrong, Colm?"

At that moment, Willard huffed up beside them, cheeks puffing, exhaling in wheezes.

"I said, let go, Taggert," Colm ground out between clenched teeth. He could not remain in their proximity. He was confused, angered, and sickened. He had to think, to get away, to breathe fresh air. He jerked up hard on the reins, freeing Scaramouch from the reporter's hold, causing the horse to prance sideways away from the men.

"Where you going?" Taggert asked.

The question went unheard in the roar of the monitors as Colm urged his paint up the steep grade and out of the yawning mouth of violence. When he had crested the cliff, he peered down at the scrambling men, the cascading water, and the mayhem they caused.

Colm was reminded of the morning before, when she had challenged Taggert in the Sierra House, as he replayed in his mind Maginn

O'Shaunasey's sharp words. "If *I* were a man, I'd *really* be doin' somethin' about those damned water cannons!"

Colm sucked in a deep breath. He *was* a man and he *could* do something. Wheeling away from the pit, he rode toward the valley.

Maginn sat at her desk staring off into oblivion. She could not work. Her mind would not stay focused to it. No matter how hard she tried to concentrate on her sketches, her thoughts would constantly wander. And always in the direction of Colm McQuaid. Damn the arrogant bastard. Why did he constantly plague her mind?

She felt a sting of embarrassment as she remembered his parting words when she had returned his hat to him the day before. Had he meant what he said? Would he really have come for it himself? Just the thought of his seductive voice sent bolts of excitement racing through her body. Simperin' school girl. Oh, but the shades of red you must've turned. Jackdaws and dev'ls! Could you not've waited a bit, Maginn? Did you have to let the whole of the countryside see you make a fool of yourself with that man?

Another thought struck her. How much did Lance know about the hat and how she had come to have it? She squeezed her eyes shut.

Heaven help me. The braggart probably told him everythin'.

"These going to be finished by tonight?" Lance Taggert's voice sounded too close.

She gazed up into the warmth of his smoky eyes and flushed. "Hmm? What?"

Leaning half over her, the tall man looked past her at the drawings. "I asked if these would be ready by this evening. We start printing at six sharp."

With a great deal of effort, she pulled her thoughts together and turned back to her desk. Stacking the drawings, she shuffled them into a neat pile and handed them to him. "They're ready now." The light rustle of paper unaccompanied by the usual approving comments was enough to cause her to glance up.

Only the slightest tinges of blue and yellow still remained beneath the black lashes of her friend's abused eye. Pursing his lips, Lance frowned. "Is this it?" He flipped through the pages again.

Setting her mouth defiantly, Maginn searched his puzzled expression. "Whatever do you mean? Isn't it enough?"

Lance's forehead wrinkled. "One cartoon and a bunch of doodling?" He eyed her over the top of the papers. "It's hardly as much as I expected."

She grimaced as if she had bitten something

sour then rose to her feet and lifted her chin, though she kept her eyes turned downward. "If you're unhappy with me work, Mr. Taggert, I'll—"

"Mr. Taggert?" Lance took hold of her arm. He set the stack atop the desk. "What's eating you, Maginn? I didn't say anything about being unhappy with your work." He bent down, forcing her gaze to meet his. "Talk to me."

She tried to turn away, but he did not relinquish his hold.

Instead he gently pulled her face more toward his. He peered deeper. "What is it? You've never hesitated to confide in me before. You're not still mad at me from breakfast the other day?"

"No!" Her temper threatened her self-control.

"Then what?"

Maginn's stomach somersaulted. "Never mind! 'Tis nothin'." She was starting to get very angry, but not at Lance, at herself. How could she tell him of her overzealous daydreams about the gunslinger?

Concern crinkling the corners of his eyes, Lance let go of her arm, then pulled a chair up for himself. "Look. Ever since the other day with McQuaid in the street, you've been acting like a gut-shot grizzly, ready to bite my head off at every turn."

Fury and shame flooded her being. There it was. Like a knife in her belly, the words hit their mark. Lance knew that Colm had been with her in her room. Ordinarily, she would have lashed out, but this time shame held her tongue silent. Her cheeks burned. Lowering her gaze from his, her head slipped down. Tears mocked her Irish pride. The worst had happened. She was ruined.

Placing a finger under her chin, Lance lifted her face to look at him. Filled with worry, his pale eyes offered her understanding. He swept away an errant tear with his thumb. "What troubles you, Maginn?"

Unable to speak, she could only shake her head.

"Tell me," he insisted.

Of their own volition, words gushed from her mouth in her defense. "I'm not for knowin' what he was doin' there, and in truth, I guess 'tis not for matterin' now. But—" The tears came faster. Her lips trembled uncontrollably. "Oh, Lance. I didn't mean for it to happen—"

"He? Who? What are you talking about?"

Why was he playing with her like this? "You know very well that Colm—"

"McQuaid?" Lance sounded baffled.

Maginn nodded.

Black fury darkened her friend's face. His body tensed and he gripped her hands together in his, but his voice remained calm. "You didn't mean for what to happen?"

Maginn bit down on the soft flesh inside her cheek. She could not bring herself to tell him more.

"What did he do to you? Did he—did he hurt you?" Grasping her shoulders, Lance reassured her with a comforting squeeze.

She shook her head. "No."

"It's all right, Maginn. You can tell me."

But she could not. The truth would only condemn her further. Her heart pounded beneath his stare. Whatever Colm had told him was probably more than enough.

"Maginn?"

Reluctantly, she lifted her eyes to his.

"Is it so horrible that you can't even confide in your closest friend?"

Maginn could see that Lance would not be satisfied until he had heard every sordid detail from her. He was enjoying this. Some friend you are, Lance Taggert. She did not believe his concern for a minute. Men! You're all alike. Fine! You want to hear me confess? She took a deep breath and yelled, "He kissed me! There. I said it."

"What?" Lance leaned nearer. He appeared even more perplexed than before.

Closing her eyes, she struggled to gain a measure of control. "I said, he kissed me."

Lance's brows nearly shot up to his hairline. His face brightened. "He kissed you?"

Maginn bit her bottom lip and nodded. "An' I kissed him back."

A soft throaty rumble crept through Lance, drawing Maginn's attention to his irrepressible smile. Her cheeks instantly flamed. Her body nearly cramped with anger. Damn him! He knew all about that night, and he was laughing at her! Damn Colm McQuaid! Damn, damn, DAMN! Leaping to her feet, she almost toppled her chair. "Go ahead, laugh, you blitherin' idiot! Take your pleasure while you can." With that she reached down and snatched up her reticule from beneath her desk. Whirling away, she made to leave, but gentle hands stayed her movements.

"Wait, Maginn." Lance sobered. He turned her back around. "I'm sorry. I didn't mean to hurt your feelings."

It was not enough to see her humiliate herself, now he wanted to see her tears as well? She was not about to give him that satisfaction. She glared at him, her eyes filled with tears, before turning her face as far away from him as possible.

He leaned around and offered her a pathetic expression. "Really. I am sorry."

She ignored his apology with indignant aloofness, but only for a moment.

"You just caught me off guard, that's all."

"Off guard?" She glowered at him. "Don't be for givin' me that rubble, Lance Taggert. You know full well what happened. What glee it must've brought the pompous braggart to tell you. An' me the dolt for succumbin' to his charms so freely." With a huff, she thrust out her bottom lip and folded her arms across her chest.

One arm over his middle, Lance rested an elbow atop his fist and covered his mouth with the other hand.

But it did not hide his chuckle. Maginn well noted the half-concealed chortle and it pricked her sorely. Her temper flared. "An' you, Lance Taggert. 'Tis none the better you are. You claim to be me friend from one side of your mouth, while mockin' me from the other."

Obviously startled, yet apparently even more amused at her outburst, Lance sobered his features with a childish smirk.

She bristled. "Go ahead!" She threw her arms wide, gesturing toward the window in the front of the office. "Laugh your fool head off. Go an' tell the whole town how I let the consortium's gunman throw me down to the floor an'—"

"Stop!" Lance held up his hands. "Don't say any more."

Jolted to silence, Maginn could only stare at him. She had thrust herself so deeply into her tirade that her pulse skittered through her body like lightning, pricking her senses painfully. Glaring at him, her breathing came in leadened pants. "Why ever not? Don't I tell it as good as Colm McQuaid?"

Lance crossed the space between them with hesitant strides. "Look, Maginn. I don't know where you got all of this, but I didn't know anything before you told me."

Her eyes opened wide. More mockery. She threatened him with a ferocious glare. "Don't lie for him."

"I'm not lying. Look at me," he said seriously. "Do I look like I'm lying?"

Maginn frowned. She was not sure if she could believe him. But as far as she knew, Lance had indeed never lied to her. She searched out the honesty in his imploring eyes. Her heart fluttered. Suddenly, she knew. Her knees went weak. Sweet Jesus in heaven. She had told on herself.

৯ 8 ৯

Maginn sucked in a sharp breath. What a fool she was. Lance had not known anything about the night Colm McQuaid had intruded on her—until now.

"Hey?" His voice reached out to her in a half-whisper.

Maginn lifted an incredulous stare to her friend.

"You all right?"

Embarrassed beyond words, she could not look at him. Lowering her eyes, she concentrated on the one unfastened button of his ash-colored vest. How could she have been so lack-witted—and so mistrustful? Even if Colm McQuaid had told him, Lance would never have used it against her. He had proved himself a good and loyal friend so far. How could she doubt his loyalty now?

With fidgeting fingers, she gripped the sides of her skirt. Beneath her pleated shirtwaist, the torchon lace of her corset cover became suddenly uncomfortable, sticking and chafing her with the damp heat of her skin.

Lance reached out and gently took her hand, his reassuring silence drawing her attention. His ash-gray eyes spoke of his understanding even before he uttered a word. "I'm neither your judge nor your persecutor, Maginn."

Without warning, her vision blurred again. Her throat closed and her chest constricted.

Tilting his head to one side, he leaned closer and smiled. "What I am is your friend, no matter what."

"Oh, Lance. I'm such a—"

"Shh—none of that." He patted her hand.

"But—"

He shook his head. "Don't say any more. What did, or didn't, happen between you and Colm is none of my business. And though I don't know him very well, I believe him to be at least somewhat honorable. He doesn't appear to be the type that would take advantage of a woman. He didn't, did he?" The latter he asked with great concern.

"No." Her voice sounded small.

"Then I see no further need for this conversation. Matter of fact—" He pulled out his pocket watch and opened it. "Four-twenty." Replacing the timepiece, he tugged at his black oversleeves and pulled them off. "How about we take an early supper at the Sierra House?"

Lifting a hand to her nose, Maginn sniffled against the backs of her fingers. "But the paper? We have to set the type. You said we go to print at six."

Lance shrugged. "So we'll start a little later. We've got all night. But you . . ." He tapped the end of her nose.

Reaching inside her reticule, Maginn pulled out a handkerchief and dabbed at the corners of her eyes. "I'm quite all right now."

"No matter." Lance held up his hands in a gesture of silence. Walking to his office, he tossed the oversleeves inside and retrieved his jacket from the coat rack behind the door. "After supper, I want you to go home and relax. Read a book, visit with Mrs. Penhaligon, whatever you like, just take the evening for yourself."

"But—"

"No buts. You've let yourself get much too involved in all of this business with the mines. You're tired." Slipping on his suit coat, he came to stand in front of her. He gestured toward the discarded papers. "And it's starting to affect your work."

Maginn glanced down at her one and only

accomplishment for the paper. He was right. Still, she could not let him make up and press all five hundred sheets by himself. "An' just how do you think to do all of this without me?"

Lance straightened his collar beneath his worsted lapels. "You forget about Thadius."

Maginn frowned. No. She had not forgotten. At sixty-three and retired from *Harper's Monthly*, Thadius Bean enjoyed working on the *Badger's Winze* whenever he could. Still and all, locking up type and illustrations was a tedious and muscle-aching task, and without her assistance, the two men would be at it till the wee hours. "There's no help for it, Lance. Thadius is an old man. He can't work fast enough to see the papers finished by mornin'. You need me help."

"What I need . . ." Lance came to stand directly in front of her. He playfully though pointedly jabbed a finger in her face. "Is for you to take some time off. I need you well rested and sprightful as ever. Besides, I can always get the Mendell boys. With their huge family, they're usually looking for a way to earn some extra pay."

"They're just children."

"Twelve and fifteen are old enough. They'll do just fine."

"Lance, please. I'm quite all right now, I

assure you." As if a fresh breath of air was a medicament for her earlier thoughts of Colm McQuaid, she inhaled, deep and slow. "I just let me guard down, that's all. It won't happen again."

"No. Keep it down. A little impulsiveness is just what you need." His grin broadened. "Matter of fact, I not only want to take the night off, but tomorrow too."

Maginn's eyes widened. "What a lot of potty-twaddle." She threw up her hands, then plummeted dramatically to her chair. "First you tell me you're for wantin' me to take time off, then you're for tellin' me as much as me work stinks. An' now"—exasperated, she rolled her eyes toward the heavens—"after I've set meself to workin' even harder, you're tellin' me to take a full day off."

Shaking his head, Lance smiled. He gathered her hands, then hoisted her to her feet. "That, Miss O'Shaunasey, is exactly what I'm telling you."

She started to protest again, but he silenced her with a no-nonsense look.

"And that's exactly what you're going to do. Do I make myself clear?"

Floating on the warm current of the morning breeze, two bright orange and black striped butterflies flitted over the head of Maginn's rented sorrel. She smiled, watching their invigorated dance through the murmuring pines. Beneath her, the easy rocking motion of the mare's gait allowed her to relax and enjoy April's beauty coloring the land.

Tiny clusters of rose and cream myrtlewood blossoms had already popped through winter's remnants, dotting the snow patches. Ghostly white Indian pipes sprinkled with a colorful array of wildflowers dipped their petaled heads demurely, swaying to and fro as if directing Maginn to some hidden pleasure beyond the forest. Somewhere in the distance, a bluebird chirped, and everywhere, the air was perfumed with the spicy scent of arbutus.

Lance had been right. This was just what she needed. At that moment, two playful chipmunks began a game of hide-and-seek, scampering in and out of the underbrush and rocks. She laughed. Tommy would've gotten quite a lot of cakes an' ale out of them, he would. The thought struck a painful cord within her, but she allowed it only a mere moment's nesting. If he were only here, I'd— None of that. Forcing herself to smile, she peered up at the streams of light filtering through the woodland. Never hurrying, the sun climbed steadily higher.

Maginn's breath caught as she came out of the trees. Undulating with the gentle flurry of wind, a sea of tall grass adorned with welkin and sapphire lupine waved her nearer. She swept an admiring gaze across the meadow. On the farthest side of its pale green expanse, a crystalline pond shimmered like quicksilver in the morning sunlight.

The mare snorted. Patting the horse's neck, Maginn sighed wistfully. "So, 'tis the same as meself you're thinkin', eh, girl? But for me own sweet Ireland, we could not've found a more glorious spot to while the day away." She tapped the sorrel's flanks, coaxing the animal forward with little clicking sounds.

Edging around the small lake, she reined the animal to a halt beneath a willow tree. She rose up, standing in the stirrups. "Oh, aye. 'Tis quite glorious indeed." She swung her leg over the animal's rump and stepped down, allowing the mare a drink before tying her to a fallen tree trunk.

"Mmm." Lifting her face to the sun, she stretched lazily, then knelt by the lakeside to quench her own thirst. The cool liquid tasted clean and fresh, chilling her insides as it trickled down her throat.

When she had retrieved her saddlebags, she unwrapped her family's treasured stereoscope and an assortment of views from the blanket she had brought. Setting them carefully aside, she spread the coverlet beneath a large piñon pine, then placed the slides and her lunch in the middle.

A loud slap on the water startled her. Shading her eyes against the sun's glare, she peered out at the pond. Another splash and she saw the beaver. Her gaze moved ahead of the animal, locating a large mound of twigs and mud at the far end of the pool. Lost in the little beast's frolic, she remained immobile.

"Oh, but that does look to be fun," she murmured aloud. Her eyes widened with wicked delight. She looked about. All was natural, undisturbed. She grinned. "Why not? 'Tis just too temptin'." Tugging off her boots and stockings, she fumbled with the fasteners of her riding skirt, shucked it down and stepped out of it. Then, as quickly as her fingers would work, she unbuttoned her blouse and slipped free of its bindings. In nothing but drawers and camisole, Maginn ran headlong into the frigid pool.

Swallowed by the icy liquid, her body instantly rebelled. She surfaced with a throaty shriek, sending a small flock of waterfowl racing for the safety of the sky. Exhilarated, she laughed. It felt good to laugh. How long had it been? It seemed like forever since she had been with her parents and brother playing like this. She gave herself a mental shake. Lance had given this day to her and she would do well to take advantage of it. With no one about, she was free to split her sides with laughter if she wished. Who would see? After today, she could return to Cavenaugh's Dig and be the same straightforward, sharp-tongued woman set on vengeance's path . . . but not today.

She flipped over, allowing the water to pop her up like a discarded cork. Eyelids closed, heart still pounding from the shock of the cold, she rested peacefully, floating without thought or care as she listened to the gurgles of the tiny ripples all around her.

When finally she became a bit too chilled, she swam for shore. Teeth chattering, water sluicing over gooseflesh, she flung herself facedown atop the warm blanket, giggling all the while. She rolled onto her back and, with outspread arms, tipped her head back and offered herself up to the warmth of the sun's rays. "Mmm. Oh, Lance, thank you for this."

After indulging in a few more minutes of basking, Maginn turned onto her side and reached for the stereoscope. She picked through the views, then placed one inside the holder. Lounging on her back again, she held it up and looked through the lenses.

Before her eyes, Ireland unfolded its arms wide. Though void of color, to Maginn the pictures appeared as real and vibrant as if she were looking through some window enjoying the glorious green fields under gray scudding Atlantic clouds. She could almost taste the salt spray that weighted the crisp air, envision dark cliffs against the sea, meadows of yellow gorse, slate-blue rock, and brown boglands of her faraway home.

"Dear sweet Pater an' Mam, why did you ever make us leave there?" With the thought of her parents and of her homeland so far away, a weighty pang of sorrow crowded her heart. "What wouldn't I give to have the two of you with me this grand day." Her throat closed. "An' little Tommy too."

The realization of her own loneliness filled her mind, threatening to spoil her mood. "No!" she said firmly if not convincingly. "Only happy thoughts today." Blinking, she brushed a heartsick tear from the corner of her eye. She removed the slide and replaced it with another.

Ever awash with mist, the sky over County Tipperary suddenly splintered her recollection with bright-colored scenery. She found herself drifting through a space of timeless beauty, a whimsical fantasy beneath the shadow of some rain-worn castle of old. The smell of fresh-cut grass and lilacs teased her senses, drawing her deeper into her dream.

In a field of shamrock-green, shrouded in a

cool fog, she lay waiting for her lover. Leaping down from a painted steed of black and white, he came to her. She smiled and lifted her arms, receiving him with a rapturous embrace. Like a man starved, he twined the mass of her pale hair within his hands, and swept her into his arms, capturing her mouth with his.

His passion teased her, sending her soaring to dizzying heights, setting her body to flames of pure molten gold. When his mouth left hers, she gazed up into coppery eyes glimmering with need. Fiery shivers fevered her body. Wanting him to kiss her again, she pressed closer. A deep, throaty moan escaped her.

The audible sound of her own desire dispelled her daydream. As quickly as it had carried her off, it fell away. Heart pounding, she cautiously pulled her arm away from her eyes. Past its zenith, the sun still hung high overhead. She peered around and nearly fell limp. She was still by the lake. Rolling over, she set herself up on one elbow facing the water. Abashed, she glared at the light fretting across the surface. "'Tis a shameful thin' to allow your head to be filled with the likes of such flights of fancy." The latter she allowed to escape her in no more than a whisper, for even as she said the words, she saw him.

Rounding the opposite bank, a man reined his horse toward her. Her breath lodged in her throat. He rode the painted steed of black and white.

The sight of the animal made her suddenly aware that the lover in her dream and the man riding up on her was one and the same. "Blood and thunder—nooo—Please." Leaping up from the blanket, she snatched her clothes to her breast and dashed behind the tree. "Sweet Jesus in heaven—" she pleaded, her fingers moving frantically. She barely had time to step into her skirt, yank it to her waist, and tuck in her blouse, before the horse's muffled hoofbeats halted and a man's nearing footsteps replaced them. "Not him! Oh, please don't let it be him—"

Whirling around, she collided with a solid mass. Something clamped her arms. A scream stripped her throat.

"Ho there!" The man's rich voice rustled the air.

As if dumbstruck, Maginn stared up into the smiling face of Colm McQuaid.

"I'm not goin' t' hurt you," he murmured softly.

Unable to speak, she swallowed instead. Her gaze drifted to where her palm had parted his half-buttoned shirt. Warm and damp beneath her touch, his muscles rippled against her fingers. Was she still dreaming? She blinked hard, then looked up at him again.

"Miss O'Shaunasey?" His expression sobered. Gently, he squeezed her arms. "Maginn. It's Colm. Are you all right?"

Trapped by her own bewilderment and his sudden nearness, she strained for breath. Just managing to pull her wits about her, she gingerly moved from his grasp. "I'm quite well, Mr. McQuaid." She sought relief from the heat of his stare by wiping her cheeks with the coolness of her hand.

He grasped her elbow. "You sure?" Angling his head to one side, he studied her.

"Mmm-hmm." She did not trust her voice further. He was still too near, as was her dream. Unable to meet his gaze again, she walked back to the blanket. Brushing aside an errant strand of hair, she sucked in a breath, forcing herself to speak. "Whatever are you doin' out here, Mr. McQuaid?"

"I thought someone was hurt."

"Hurt? Whatever gave you that idea?"

He looked up, pointing a finger in the air. "Seems they thought so too."

Squinting against the sun's glare, Maginn watched as two buzzards circled above her, then disappeared over the treetops. When she returned her gaze to Colm McQuaid, he had moved to where her pallet lay atop the grass.

"Well, if you're sure you're okay—" He appeared to hesitate. "I'll be on my way."

Beneath his heated stare, she felt herself flush anew. She looked away. She could not hold his gaze. Did he know of her daydream? Could he read her thoughts? She could not bear to know. But when he turned toward his horse, she heard her own voice. "Will you stay?"

"Beg pardon?" he asked, looking back at her.

"I wondered if you wouldn't like to sit down for a moment or two?" She could not believe what she had asked. Why had she done that?

He cut her a strange glance, his dusky gaze growing even darker. As if giving her question a great deal of consideration, he regarded her for a lengthy moment. Something odd flickered in his eyes and he looked away. "You sure you want me to join you?"

When she followed to where his gaze had lingered, she saw that in her hasty dressing, she had not fastened her blouse. Maginn's face flamed. She was mortified by her carelessness. Nimble fingers could not button the fabric quickly enough.

He moved to his horse and retrieved the reins.

"Please." She scoured her mind, trying to think of a way to appear a little less frazzled. Catching sight of the saddlebags, she remembered her lunch. "''Tis past noon, 'tis true, but if you've not eaten just yet . . ." She suddenly felt tongue-tied and jittery inside. He did not turn around. Now you've done it. Why ever are you doin' this to yourself, Maginn? You know he'll say no.

Still, he did not answer.

Nervously, she studied the play of his taut back muscles beneath his shirt and waited. Of course he'll say no. You've shown him nothin' but the pure hate an' ruin of things since your first meetin'. What else can you expect? Knowing full well the truth of her thoughts, she nibbled at her lower lip. Then another chord of anxiety stirred her. What if he says aye? She had no time to ponder this question though, for at that moment he turned around.

"You sure you have enough?"

Deep and resonant, his voice disquieted her even more than the last of her queries. So much so, that she all but jumped when he spoke. Unsure quite how to handle his answer, she stared at him for what seemed like a full minute.

"Miss O'Shaunasey?"

"Hmm? Oh, aye." Pulling out the two sandwiches Mrs. Penhaligon had prepared for her lunch, Maginn lifted one up to him. "Have you a taste for roast beef?"

He looped his mount's reins over a tree

branch, then removed his hat and moved to the blanket. He dipped his head. "I like roast beef just fine."

When he remained standing, she presented him with a shy smile, then gestured, sandwich still in hand, for him to take a seat opposite her on the blanket. "Do sit down, Mr. McQuaid."

Kneeling, he quickly repositioned himself in front of her, sitting cross-legged, and accepted her offer. As if prompted by some unseen signal, both unwrapped the kitchen cloths from their meals and took a bite.

Neither spoke until Maginn, quite beside herself with jumbled thoughts on how to proceed, bit down on a large piece of meat, flopping it out on her chin. She tried to hide the unladylike action behind her napkin, but of course, Colm saw it.

Their eyes met, his crinkled with mirth, hers round with humiliation.

He chuckled, a slow, growing sound, glee-filled and devilish.

What was she to do? Pull it out, or chew it up? She suddenly giggled. How silly she must look.

"Hold still." His expression almost sobered, yet not quite. He set the rest of his sandwich down, then rubbed his hands together as if he were about to attempt a great feat. "If we do this just right—" He reached up and plucked the overhanging portion of beef from her bite. "There. Haven't lost my touch."

More than a little perplexed, Maginn drew in the remaining mouthful of meat and peered at him quizzically. "What?" The question sounded garbled.

"I can still tear it free without so much as a smear of dressing escaping." He took his napkin and dabbed at the corner of her mouth. "Well, maybe just a spot or two."

Searching his eyes for the meaning of his obvious joke, she frowned. She swallowed. "I'm not for understandin'."

"Really?" A twinkle of delight lit his eyes. "You mean you can't tell?"

She shook her head. "I'm afraid I haven't the foggiest notion as to what you're talkin' about."

"Well, I don't like t' brag, but I've rescued many a fair damsel from just such a horrible fate as yours." He grinned. His teeth gleamed white and even, one of them slanted ever so slightly over the other.

She cut him an amused glance, then smiled. "Aren't you the witty one."

"What? You don't believe me?" Opening his hands, he exposed his palms dejectedly. No small boy could have told a better fib, then looked as puckish as he.

She could not hide the smile tugging at her

mouth. She decided to play along. "So that's how you became the bold, notorious gun-fighter you are—by rescuin' women from the likes of such depraved cuts of meat as that?" She pointed at the offensive slab in his hand and giggled.

Tossing the slice of beef in the bushes near the edge of the lake, he peered up at her. "That sounds nice."

"What?"

"Your laugh. I don't think I've ever heard it before."

Feeling more than a little self-conscious, Maginn stilled beneath his watchfulness. Her body felt hot. She wet her lips. She had never known the full weight of a man's attention and what it did to her now left her more than a little uncomfortable. Feigning interest across the lake, she looked away.

Silence fell softly around them. Afraid and unsure of what to say or do, Maginn clung to the fragile cocoon of quiet for as long as she could. This is silly. Someone has to be for sayin' somethin'. "I've noticed you've not been around town for a day or so, Mr. Mc-Quaid."

"Colm," he corrected.

She glanced back at him.

He smiled. "My name's Colm. I'd like it if you'd call me that, Maginn."

The sound of him saying her name sent tremors through the very core of her being. Or was it just the familiar way in which he said it? She was not certain. Neither was she sure if she liked what it did to her. She lifted her brows indifferently. "So, *Colm*." She had to force herself to use the name as he had asked. It made her stomach flutter. "Where have you been?" This was a first. Never before had she used so few words or found herself unable to carry on a simple conversation.

He flaunted a lopsided grin. "Did you miss me?"

Her tongue stuck to the roof of her mouth. If he only knew half the truth.

Plucking a foxtail from a patch of grass near the blanket's edge, Colm twirled it between his fingers. Then, flipping it stem up, he bit down on the end. "I had to take care of some business."

"Oh. I see." She brushed absently at some bread crumbs on her skirt. "For the consortium." She really did not want to hear about his ill-doings for the Thimblerigger.

"No."

Maginn's interest was piqued. What other business could he mean? She studied the curves and planes of his features.

"I went down to the valley."

A quiver raced up her spine. "Really?" She

tried to keep the curiosity from creeping into her voice.

He nodded, his expression taking on a distant, unfocused look. He took a deep breath. "The other day when you saw me leavin' town with Taggert, well, we went up t' the mines."

Maginn shrugged. "So. 'Tis for certain you've seen a mine before." She was not sure why, but she did not like the direction of their conversation.

"Not these mines."

An unladylike snort escaped her. "You've hired yourself out to the consortium an' you've never been up there before?" She rolled her eyes. "What kind of man would sell his gun an' not know what it was he protected?"

He hesitated. "A desperate man."

"Desperate? You?" She squinted at him. "Is this another joke?" Half-hopeful, she grinned.

Pulling the grassy spike from his mouth, he tossed it to the ground. "I had t' see how things were down there for myself." He turned to stare out across the water, but his body remained visibly tense. "I had t' see, firsthand, why you hate the consortium badly enough t' risk your life."

"Had to?" Her breath quickened. Her heart pounded triple-time. "Why did you have to?" She wanted to know, yet did not. Was he toying with her? Did he want information? If so, about what? The resistance?

Sitting up, he looked her square in the eye. "Because I had t' know *you*, Maginn O'Shaunasey."

Shock flooded her body. Why would he want to know the likes of me? An excited tremor raced through her veins and she found herself daring to hope the most wanton of things. Could it truly be so? Could I excite him, like he excites me?

Maginn's only movement, a dazed blink, drew Colm to reach up and sweep aside an errant wisp of her sunlit blond hair. At that moment, nothing would have given him more pleasure than to set the heavy braid dangling at her back free of its bonds and run his hands through the silken strands. But the bold innocence staring out at him through those incredible pale green eyes held him more still than if he were looking down the barrel of a Colt .45.

Experience warned him to move away, examine the flame within her more clearly, see past it to the truth of her wiles. Yet even as the thoughts made themselves heard in his mind, Colm pushed them aside. It was too late. He wanted her. He framed her chin between his finger and thumb.

Smooth and warm, her skin felt downy

against his callused palm. His gaze slid to her mouth. He traced the tiny blemish creasing her lower lip. His breathing came faster, uneven. He bent his head. With a gentleness he had not known he possessed, Colm brushed her lips with his.

An almost imperceptible sigh feathered against his mouth as she lifted a dreamy gaze. She stared at him expectantly beneath a golden fringe of downcast lashes.

God, but she was beautiful, and innocent, and vulnerable. He leaned back and looked at her. He remembered the night in her room. He had kissed her then too. Was she truly as innocent as she appeared? Or was this simply a game to sway him to her side. He peered deeper.

Sunshine and shade dappled her eyes, revealing a strange flicker—a look of silent desperation, loneliness, and need. Colm had known many women in his life, but he had only seen that look in one other's gaze—his mother's. He pulled back. If only he had not seen that, he might have— But he had seen it, even more, recognized the pain of her emptiness. He wanted her, but he could not take her—not now, not like this—not when she was so exposed and defenseless. He cleared his throat. "I'd—uh—better be gettin' on int' town."

Head still tilted back, Maginn opened her eyes fully, her expression one of startlement. Tiny furrows appeared between her brows. "No, wait, please."

Without hesitation, Colm rose. He did not dare to look at her. But before he could take a step, she grabbed his hand. Like lightning charges, her touch shot through his body. He glanced down.

She must have felt it too, for in that same instant, she broke her hold. With one glance, she caught his attention then looked away.

Her nervousness showed in the way she chewed on her bottom lip, and the way she darted her eyes everywhere except at him.

He wanted to help her, reassure her somehow. But with his own emotions on the attack as they were, how could he?

"'Tis early yet," she finally said, so softly he almost did not hear her. "Could you not manage to stay a wee bit longer?"

He hesitated to answer. Yes, he could stay, but for what purpose—and at what risk?

Lifting her face, she peered first at the lake, then up at him. A shy smile pulled at her lips. "You've not told me why you're for wantin' to know meself so well. Do you not intend to?"

He watched her a moment longer. Should he tell her what he had discovered? Should he let her know that he had seen the desolation of

Marysville for himself, examined the remains of her ruined farm, and looked upon her father's and brother's graves—the two very visible, glaring scars of her agony? And if he did, how would she react? He remained silent another minute. Beneath that captivating surface of childlike candor beat the fierce heart of a wounded lioness ready to strike, or flee should he move too fast. *No more fence-sittin'*, McQuaid. *Make up your mind. Will you take the gold or . . .*

Standing, Maginn frowned. "What's wrong?"

He took a heavy breath and sighed. "I know now why you hate the consortium so much. I've seen your farm, or what's left of it."

Her smile faded. "What?"

Colm searched for just the right words to fill the awkward moment. "I had to." Not the best he had ever thought of.

She stiffened. The image of the lioness grew steadily clearer. "You've been to me home?" Her voice quivered.

"I told you, I had t' know why you hate the monitors enough t' risk your—"

"You've spied on me? Why do you think you've permission to poke your nose into the privacy of me life?" she asked accusingly, her tone even more agitated. Not waiting for a reply, she planted her hands atop her hips and scowled. "Just who in bloody blazes do you think you are, Colm McQuaid? You think either of those paltry kisses you've pasted on me lips entitles you to any part of meself? Be it personal or not, Colm McQuaid, I'll thank you to stay out of me affairs, I will."

Picking up a small black boot, she struggled to get a bare foot inside. After doing like to the other, she bent down and snatched up her stockings and saddlebag. Red coloring her cheeks, she grumbled unintelligibly in that Irish brogue Colm had become accustomed to hearing.

"Maginn, wait." He tried to sound apologetic, but it came out more as indulgent. He clasped her elbow. "You don't understand."

Glaring down at his hand, she jerked out of his grasp. "Don't I, now? Aye, I think I do. I'm not quite the lack-witted little Mick you might be believin' me to be. I'm onto your tricks, Colm McQuaid, an' you'll not be for fawnin' information about the resistance from the likes of meself, I'll tell you that for nothin'!" She started to gather her belongings.

"The resistance?" Colm's anger began to rise. The mouthy little hellcat. She thought he was trying to seduce information from her. He fought to keep his temper under control. "Look, Maginn—"

"Miss O'Shaunasey, if you please!"

Colm balled his fists. He took a slow, deep

breath, his eyes remaining fixed on her movements as she retrieved the remnants of their lunch. With controlled effort he finally harnessed his irritation. He had to make her understand the reason for his intrusion on her private pain. He had to tell her of his decision to take a stand with her. He blinked. Until this moment, he had not come to terms with all of the destruction brought on by the monitors, much less the effect the woman had on him. Nearly thrown off balance, he felt a tug beneath his feet.

"If you please!" Holding one corner of the blanket they had sat on against her puffed-up chest, Maginn glowered at him defiantly. She yanked again.

Colm stepped off. "Maginn, you're jumpin' t' the wrong conclusion."

"Really?" She marched toward her horse, then after slapping the saddlebags across its rump, stuffed the rumpled cover inside the leather pouch.

Coming to stand behind her, he whirled her around to face him. "Really."

"Take your hands off me!" She scrunched her face up like an angry little girl.

Colm could see the fright in her eyes and knew that she must be mustering every ounce of grit she had so as not to show her alarm. It made him feel all the worse. He did not want her afraid of him. "Look, I want you t' know that—"

"*You* want?" The force of her voice shook as did the entire length of her body. "I don't give a two-penny damn what *you* want, Colm McQuaid! I know what 'tis you're after, an' I'm here to tell you, you've come up against a stone wall. I'll not give over any information that might help the likes of you an' that damn Jameson's business!"

He flinched at the accusation. He had lost his trump card. Now how was he to play this out?

Wrenching free of his hold, she bumped against her sorrel. She cut a nervous glance toward the animal before sidestepping Colm and snatching the lead from around a dead tree trunk. Gathering the reins, she gripped both horn and seat, slammed her foot into the stirrup and hauled herself up.

"That's enough, Maginn!" Colm's temper got the better of him. He grabbed the bridle and held tight. "Damn it, woman. You're goin' t' hear me out if I have t' drag you down off that horse and sit on you." He glared hard but she met him with a scowl that mirrored his own.

Green eyes flashed like polished glass, cold and unyielding. "You think so?" Her expression impassive, she lashed the reins at his cheek, dug her heels into the animal's flanks, and sped off across the sea of grass.

Disgusted, Colm stared after her. He rubbed the back of his hand against his face. Enough was enough! It was time to end this little game of roulette.

Colm held Scaramouch to an easy walk as he approached the fence in front of Jameson's house. The nearer he drew to the yard, the more his purpose urged him to quicken his pace. But he would not. If he let his anger get the better of him, he might lose track of his goal. Stopping at the gate, his gaze shot over to Penhaligon's Boarding House. Was Maginn back yet? He glanced across the street at the livery. The sorrel she had ridden stood hitched to a corral post. He touched the cut slashing his jaw and sighed. *I'll deal with her after I'm done with Jameson.*

Swinging off his mount, he draped the lead over a picket rail. With an affectionate pat, he swept a hand across the curve of the animal's rump and rounded the horse's backside. Colm peeled off his gloves and pushed open the gate. Reaching the porch, he stopped. Apprehension tightened his stomach. His thoughts commanded his attention. *What the hell's the problem? You know what you've got t' say, so* get it said. Lifting a hand, he rapped on the door.

Within seconds an apron-draped elderly woman appeared, her cheeks flushing pink, her eyes all but popping out of her head.

Colm tapped his hat respectfully. "Mrs. Beeton?"

"Oh, my! Mr. McQuaid." The pitch of her voice leapt up and down like the chirp of a cricket. She lowered her head shyly while fussing with a wayward strand of gray hair. "I can't believe you remember me."

Colm frowned. Remember her? Just her name from Jameson. To his recollection, he had never seen her before, but from the nervousness of her actions, he had no doubt *she* thought he had.

"Oh, my!" she said again, looking past him out at the street, a secret smile smoothing away the wrinkles around her mouth. "Do come in, Mr. McQuaid. Is Mr. Jameson expecting you?" She took one last peek outside before turning and closing the door.

"No, ma'am." He removed his hat and returned her smile, though he still had no recollection of meeting the old girl. "I do need t' see him, though."

"Well, of course you do. I'll go tell him you're here." Wheeling around, she hurried for the stairs.

The way she trotted up the steps, a body would have thought she was as young and fresh as new paint. Colm shook his head and chuckled. He still could not place her.

Racing back downstairs, Mrs. Beeton slammed into him on the bottom landing.

"Ho, there." Colm caught her around her plump waist. He stared into wide, startled eyes and a crimson face. "You all right?" He braced her until she could stand on her own.

"Oh, I am sorry, Mr. McQuaid. Did I hurt you?" she asked breathlessly, a hand flying to his swelling cheek.

Colm grinned then stilled her movements. "No harm done."

She tittered bashfully, but allowed him to continue holding her hands.

The sound of her nervous laughter coaxed a flash of memory. He suddenly knew where he had seen her. The day he rode into Cavenaugh's Dig. The three old ladies in front of the consortium. He had winked at her.

Still unable to catch her breath, she swallowed great gulps of air. "Mr. Jameson says you should go right up."

Colm dipped his head. He took the steps two at a time but stopped midway and looked back. "By the way, Mrs. Beeton. How're your two friends?"

"Oh my, you do remember!" Her eyes became large saucers again and her hand flew to her mouth.

Colm winked. "Of course. I'd never forget a beautiful face."

"Oh my!" With this last chirrup, she hurried off in the direction of the kitchen.

Chuckling to himself, Colm mounted the remaining stairs to the upper floor. He glanced at his reflection in the hall mirror then, without knocking, entered Jameson's room.

"'Bout damn time you reported back to me." Roark Jameson sat in a fancy brocade-upholstered rocker beside the window with his splinted leg propped on a foot stool. Smoke filtered up over the top of the newspaper he was reading. "You been checking everything out real careful, have you?"

Colm moved farther inside. Jameson's superior tone was indicative of his disposition.

Paper rustled and Jameson's cigar-embellished face popped into view. Slanted upward above each eye, gray brows, thick and bushy, marked a stern expression. "Well? What do you have to report, McQuaid?"

Colm pinched the protruding corner of his hat's crown. He never had liked confrontations, but somehow, he always seemed to find himself smack-dab in the middle of one. And as always, he was not about to back down—especially from this one. But what to say? He still had not figured out how he was going to convince Jameson to do something about the monitors. But it had to be done.

"You gonna talk, boy?" Jameson pinned him with a pointed stare. He took the cigar from his mouth and flicked the length of ashes into a dish.

A muscle beneath Colm's eye twitched. "I'd like t' take this easy, Jameson—"

"Take what easy?" Slate-blue eyes looked worried, then relaxed. "Look, boy. I like you. Have right from the start. But I can't abide a foot-shuffler. Now, you got something to tell me, you spit it out."

Colm fired a glare at the older man. "The name's McQuaid—not boy." His free hand flexed at his side. "And I got plenty t' tell you."

Jameson bobbed his head and pointed to the overstuffed parlor chair opposite him. "Well, *McQuaid*, get it said." He wedged the butt of tobacco back into the corner of his mouth and folded his hands across his middle.

Hat still in hand, Colm sat down. "I rode out t' the mines the other day, t' take a look at things for myself."

"And?"

Cutting his gaze away, Colm experienced that same stab of pain he had felt when he witnessed the unnecessary destruction being caused by the water cannons. "And what I saw, I didn't like." He targeted Jameson with a penetrating gaze. He paused, waiting to see how the man would react before continuing.

Jameson's features remained stoic, unreadable.

"What you're doin' up there is wrong—the same as what you're causin' down in the valley is wrong."

"It is, huh?" Jameson's belly bounced with a snort. "Just what in hell am I supposed to be doing? And just how did you determine that *I'm* causing all of this—uh—wrongdoing?"

"It's not just you. The North Bloomfield, the Excelsior Water Company, the Birdseye Creek, the Bluetent, all of you. You're all responsible." Jutting out his jaw, Colm tilted his head. "Hell, there's so many minin' companies up here tearin' up the land, I'm surprised there's a mile of solid ground left on any of these mountains."

Straightening to an upright position, Jameson glowered at Colm. "What the hell are you talking about, McQuaid? Who's been filling your head with all this horseshit?" He cut a glare out the window then jabbed a thumb in the same direction. "That newspaperman, Taggert? Or maybe that little Irish tart he's got working for him?" Jameson squinted out of one eye. "Don't tell me you don't know what they're up to. Just look at this." He shoved the paper at Colm.

Puzzled, Colm looked at the latest edition of the *Badger's Winze*. Nothing seemed out of the ordinary. They were just as blatantly against the mines as ever. "What're you talkin' about?"

"Look at the drawing, man. Can't you see it?"

Colm studied the cartoon. Beastly looking machines shot a stream of water at helpless figures running away. No more sarcasm than usual.

Jameson leaned over and pounded a finger on the paper. "There—the woman's signature. Notice anything different about it? See how it slants up the side of the drawing?"

"So?"

Jameson grabbed a stack of newspaper from the floor. "Look at these. See how she writes her name straight on some and slanted on others?"

"Yeah, so?"

"Damn it, McQuaid. She's the key to finding out who's behind all the explosions and vandalism at the mines."

Colm pulled a frown.

Jameson snatched the papers back from him. He snorted again. "What in hell am I paying you for? Even laid up in this room with a broken leg, I can find out more than you."

Colm was beginning to think the man suffered from cabin fever. He shook his head.

"Don't you give me that poor-old-bastard look. I know what I'm talking about." He gestured out the window with a curt nod. "The day before every explosion or mishap of any kind at the mines, that O'Shaunasey woman takes herself a little ride just before sundown, and doesn't return until late in the night. And every time, she just happens to go after the paper's come out. And on every occasion, she's signed her name up the side of a sketch." Scrunching his face into a mocking glare, he puffed out his chest and huffed. "Now I call that quite a little co-inky-dink, don't you?"

With talk of Maginn, Colm felt the sting of her mark on his cheek again. Was Jameson right? She had met with that Drew fella a couple of days ago. He checked the date on the first paper. The same as her ride. Maybe it was true. He might have been angry before, but now this discovery only spurred his determination. He had to put a stop to the use of monitors before she, or somebody else, got hurt.

"Damn it, Jameson! All you can see is what everybody else is up t'. Don't you realize what you and the other mine owners are doin'?" He shook his head. "You're ruinin' everythin'. The mountains. The valley. Everythin'!"

Eyes probing Colm, Jameson shifted in his chair.

"Hell, the Yuba's so full of silt and debris now the farmers down in Marysville had t' build levees t' keep the water from floodin' their crops and orchards when it rains." Colm's voice rose with hostility. "And even that isn't workin'. You got the mountains so pocked with giant pits a man can barely travel a half day's ride without fallin' in one of the damn holes. You're fellin' timber and leavin' it t' rot, chokin' natural water systems, and leavin' the general lay of the land t' waste . . . and all for what? A shiny piece of yellow metal!"

By the time he stopped, Colm could feel the surge of blood shooting through his veins and pounding in his temples. He had never said so much all at once in his life and he was not finished yet. "And as for the O'Shaunasey woman— Hell, Jameson, did you ever ask yourself why she's ready t' stab you in the ass every time you bend over? Did you ever wonder?"

Jameson's face had shaded a deep purple-red long ago, but now the whites of his eyes seemed to be splintering with those same shades of violet. "I suppose you're going to try and make me believe that *I'm* the cause of some great catastrophe in *her* life too." As Jameson spoke, his upper lip lifted into a threatening snarl. His agitation was clearly visible in the way he worked his cigar back and forth with his teeth.

Colm nearly dropped his hat with the force of his temper. "Is that so hard t' believe? You've been the *catastrophe* in people's lives for years."

Jameson yanked his smoke out of his mouth and grunted. "That's your opinion. Yours and those blasted farmers down in the valley there."

Colm pierced Jameson with a hard stare. "And your wife? All you've given her was a life of scrubbin' soldiers' dirty underwear. What about her opinion?"

"What in hell are you talking about?" Pure rage burst across Jameson's face. "My wife died a long time ago. So you shut your foul mouth up about her."

Colm slammed his Stetson down on his head. He planted his feet apart and leaned toward the older man. "Fine, Jameson. I'll shut up." He turned on his heels and strode toward the door but stopped midway and looked back. "You know, I used t' hate you— But now—" His gaze raked over the pathetic man.

"I feel sorry for you. You're nothin' but a coldhearted, crippled ol' son of a bitch." He jabbed a finger at the footstool. "And I ain't talkin' about that leg neither!"

Plugging the cigar into the corner of his mouth, Jameson grabbed a crutch lying on the floor beside him. He leapt up and poked it under his armpit. "Who in hell do you think you are, *boy*?" he railed, spitting the words so hard he all but lost his tobacco.

Colm nearly cut the man in two with the strength of his glare. But something behind Jameson grabbed his attention. Reaching out to him from the gold-edged frame on the table near the bed was his mother's loving gaze. Eighteen years of rage stormed through his body. He turned his attention back to the hobbling man. "I'm Colm McQuaid, your new partner and co-owner of the Thimblerigger. And . . ." He held himself proud and tall, then pointed to the picture. "Your wife's Arapaho half-breed son."

❧ 10 ❧

Jameson wavered and sank down into the chair. "Son?" The old man's face drained of color. His gaze fell to the ring on Colm's little finger. Wide-eyed, he shook his head in denial. Then, just as suddenly, his expression changed and he looked miserable. His unshaven cheeks appeared to deflate, his mouth drooped, and his eyes brimmed with anguish.

Here was the moment Colm had waited a lifetime to see. Easing his stance, he studied the slumped figure of a once formidable man and felt a flood of pity. He had not meant to blurt out everything as he did—especially about himself and his mother. He blinked. What was this? Regret? Where was the victory? He should be happy. He had crushed Roark T. Jameson as he had always wanted to do. So where was the pleasure?

A spark of light suddenly glimmered within the tearful depths of Jameson's uncertain stare. "You son of a bitch." His voice remained low and even, although it regained its former strength. "You half-breed son of a bitch! Don't you defile my Jennifer's name! Get out!"

Startled, Colm felt a charge of bitterness bolt through his body. His face flamed hot. A turbulence of sympathy and anger quickened his blood. The room closed in on him, suffocating. He had to get out.

Jameson's voice rang through the house, chasing Colm's departure with a vile curse.

Colm's own rage bounced off the walls with the thud of his own heavy footsteps. Mrs. Beeton rushed forward, but he cut a brisk path around her. With a forceful yank, he opened the door then slammed it behind him with such velocity, the three front windows clattered against their frames. He stormed down the porch steps and walkway. He nearly jerked the gate off its hinges as he swung it wide. Colm snatched the lead from the fence rail, causing Scaramouch to sidestep nervously.

"Damn it!" He gripped the reins against the side of the saddle. He tossed back his head and closed his eyes, steadying his adrenaline. "Why did I let him get t' me like that?" He had let everything out. A heavy ache gnawed in his gut. But that was not his real torment. In the eyes of the white world, nothing would mar his mother's name more than revealing that she had borne the child of an Indian. "Damn it t' hell!" By his own admission, he had given Jameson the perfect ammunition to ruin any chance for Jennifer. He leaned his forehead atop his fist. He suddenly felt drained, defeated.

A door banged shut.

Colm cut a gaze over the horse's withers.

Freshly dressed in a ruby-red shirt and a black riding skirt, Maginn O'Shaunasey ran across the street to the livery. She was crying.

His body went rigid. What the hell? Something was wrong. He frowned. Surely she was not still upset from earlier. No, surely not.

After scrambling atop the rented sorrel, she wheeled the animal around. Her gaze shot back to the house. She did not notice Colm. Yet he was in the open. Without another moment's hesitation, she kicked the horse's flanks and charged out of town.

Where the hell's she off t'? Colm started to mount Scaramouch, but as he stepped up into the stirrup, his eyes caught sight of a surrey in front of Penhaligon's. Only one man in town had a rig like that—the doctor. "What the hell's goin' on?"

He glanced over his shoulder just quick

enough to see the last trace of Maginn's bar-
reling departure. He should follow her. He
looked back at the buggy. But first he wanted
to find out what had caused her to run away
like that. He strode determinedly to Penhaligon's front door.

Eyes round and red as October apples, a
handkerchief wadded tightly in her fleshy fist,
Mrs. Penhaligon opened the door to Colm's
persistent knocking.

He politely touched the brim of his hat.
"You remember me, ma'am? I'm a friend of
Mr. Taggert's."

Sniffling, she nodded.

"Look, I noticed the doc's rig." He pointed
to the surrey. "And—I just saw Miss O'Shaunasey light out of here like a whipped pup
so— I was wonderin' what was wrong?"

"It's Mr. Taggert," the elderly woman
croaked. "He's just an awful mess."

Colm did not wait for her to invite him
inside. Dashing through the entry, he bounded
up the stairs three at a time. They had only
known each other for a short while, but he had
come to think of Lance as a friend. He had to
see him—find out what had happened.

Entering the dimly lit room, Colm's gaze
flew to the figure hovering near the bed. He
froze. A chill snaked up his spine. He took

another step into the colorless chamber and a board squeaked.

The shape turned, revealing the doctor, a grim expression on his cast-iron face. Sighing heavily, he laid down the syringe he was holding and picked up a basin of water, crimson with blood. Withdrawing from the bed stand to a table across the room laden with towels and red-blotched rags, he remained silent.

"Doc?" Colm barely heard his own voice.

The man kept his back to him, but shook his head.

"God, no." Colm swallowed. His head drooped. Lance was dead.

Someone groaned.

Startled, Colm looked up. He peered at the doctor. Another moan. Colm's gaze returned to the figure lying so still beneath the quilts. Taggert—he was alive. Colm bolted to the bedside. He peered down. A lump lodged in his throat. Bandages were wound around his friend's head and half of his face, red seeping through the white cloth over the left eye.

Lance glanced up and pulled a weak smile. "You're back?" His voice rattled, barely above a murmur.

Colm sucked in a breath. His stomach lurched and his throat worked up and down so hard he could not seem to make himself speak. Taggert was hurt bad.

With obvious pain, Lance swept a look around the room. "Where's Maginn?"

Colm shrugged. "She went for a ride." He nearly choked on the words then cleared his throat for another stab at speech. He did not want to worry his friend so he tried to make his tone light. "She looked upset. Guess seein' you all trussed up like this musta scared the hell outa her."

Lance grimaced and shook his head wearily. "Nooo," he groaned in a hoarse whisper. "Go after her."

Colm watched his friend's distressed face. "Why?" He swallowed again, the question burning a path deep within him. Something else was wrong. "What the hell happened t' you? Who did this?"

Face twisted by an eruption of pain, Taggert shook his head again. "Doesn't matter."

Rolling down his sleeves, the doctor moved to the foot of the bed. "You better leave, Mr. McQuaid. He needs to rest."

But Lance did not give Colm the chance to comply. "Wait. I have to tell you—" He tried to raise himself up, but fell back.

"What?" Wariness rode a hellbent path through Colm. Whatever it is, it must mean bad trouble. But for whom?

"Mr. McQuaid! Unless you want him dead, you better go."

"No—not yet." Taggert peered up at the doctor through his one good eye. "Please, Doc. I have to talk to him. It won't take long."

The doctor stared hard at his patient before finally relenting. He glowered up at Colm. "Just don't aggravate him. I didn't fix him up just to see him buried."

Colm dipped his head. "Okay, Doc. Don't worry. I won't stay too long."

"I know." After gathering his coat, bag, and implements, the work-hardened physician slapped a black hat atop his head. He jabbed a finger at Lance. "That shot I just gave him'll see to that."

"Now," Colm said after the doctor had taken his leave. "What's so all-fired important that you got t' tell me?" He tried to smile reassuringly, but failed. Lance definitely had him curious—not to mention troubled.

"Maginn's going to see Drew Jordan."

Colm's brows shot up. "You know 'bout him?"

Taggert's lips formed a thin smile. "Of course I do."

"You mean, you're with that damn resistance group too?"

Lance blinked. "There's no resistance. Just Drew Jordan and his gang of marauders."

"What the hell do you mean?"

"All the trouble at the mines. It was Jordan. He's Jameson's son."

Colm frowned. He had been to the valley. He knew there was no resistance. In his quest for information, he had uncovered startling information about the high-living Andrew Jordan Jameson, known to his friends as "Drew." And he had suspected as much about the man himself. But, as of yet, he had not had the time to track the culprit. He squinted down at Taggert. "How do you know all this?"

"Listen, Colm. I'm—" Taggert pointed at the bureau. "Under my clothes."

Colm crossed the room and opened the top drawer. After rummaging around, he found a leather case. He lifted the flap, revealing a silver badge, and turned it toward the light filtering in through the curtains. Ornately etched in the shield's surface, five words jumped out at him: "U.S. SPECIAL AGENT, LANCE TAGGERT."

Colm's head snapped back at his friend. "You mean you're some kinda lawman?"

Lance motioned him to the side of the bed. Wetting his lips, he nodded. "Investigator with Governor Pacheco's office."

"What, or who, are you investigating? The mines, or Jordan?"

"Both. Jordan hates his father." Taggert's

voice faltered. His eyelids began to droop. "Must stop him . . . save Maginn."

"But she's on his side—he wouldn't hurt her."

"She doesn't know the truth about the resistance, or Jordan—" Taggert weakly gripped Colm's wrist. "I tried to stop him."

Colm clutched his friend's hand, a lump closing his throat. He shot Lance an enraged glare, his gaze lingering on the bloody stain. "*He* did this to you, didn't he?"

Taggert nodded. "Caught him setting dynamite at number one."

"You tell Maginn this?"

"'Fraid so." Lance sighed heavily. "He'll kill her."

Colm looked out the window toward the livery. He would have to hurry if he wanted to catch up to her. He tossed the badge onto the night table, then glanced back at Taggert. He quirked a brow. "Not if I kill him first."

He bore down on Maginn's trail, but it took close to two hours before he caught sight of her through his field glasses. A little less than a mile ahead of him, passing through a stand of trees, she pressed her mount at a fast pace. If the timber had not been so sparse on that low-rising peak, and if it had not been for that bright-red shirt she wore, he might not have seen her at all.

He raised his field glasses, leveling them on another rise of mountains. If she made that range, he might not be able to track her over the hard surface of the rock. He would have to do better than this.

Heart pounding with every beat of Scaramouch's hooves, Colm urged the animal into a lather before he was able to close the distance between himself and the woman. She had just descended into another little canyon when he clearly saw her for the first time without the aid of the glasses.

He sighed. Almost there. Something caught his eye. He peered harder. Another rider, from the opposite end of the ravine, overtook her. He looked at them through the binoculars. "Damn it t' hell!" Drew Jordan. He watched for a few minutes longer.

Face flaming, Maginn flailed her arms at the man.

He trained his vision on Jordan.

A murderous smile suddenly appeared on the blond man's mouth. With lightning speed, Jordan slapped her, almost knocking her from her seat, then snatched the reins away from Maginn.

Colm felt as if he had been wrapped in

barbed wire. Lowering the glasses, he glowered at them.

They were heading the same way Jordan
had come. The bastard was making off with
her!

Even with all that Irish courage, spunk, and
temper, Maginn was no match for a dangerous
man like Jordan. Lance had been right. He
would try and kill her.

Colm shoved his binoculars back into the
case and nudged Scaramouch with his heels.
Fear for Maginn prodded him on as he quickly
swooped down the slope. Blood-lust filling his
veins, he echoed his earlier vow. "Not if I kill
him first."

Near the edge of a clearing, Colm dis-
mounted. A small mud-and-timber shack
stood beneath the craggy walls of a cliff. Blue
smoke spit glowing sparks from the chimney
top. Somewhere beyond the small building,
hidden in the trees, horses whinnied.

Thankful he had left his paint at a distance,
Colm crept closer and peered around the
surroundings. No one was in sight. But muffled voices rose from inside the small block-
house. Years as an agent for Wells Fargo had
taught him to be observant and calculating.
How many men did Jordan have riding with
him? He had to know before he could make a
move.

Colm skirted the trees toward the horses. There would be at least one for every rider. He found the tether line and the animals, three in all. Maginn's and two others. He shook his head. No, that can't be it. Jordan wouldn't be out here with only one other man—a snake like that needs lots of varmints t' brace his backbone. They must be standin' watch somewhere.

The hairs on the back of his neck jumped to attention. So how had *he* got through to their camp? Intuition gut-kicked him into action. He reached down and gripped the butt of his Colt. Too late, he heard the sound behind him. Pain splintered his skull, then . . . all went black.

❧ 11 ❧

Sprawled across the dirt floor, her hair fanning over her face, Maginn stared at the flames heating the secluded shack where Drew had brought her. She touched the corner of her mouth and winced. Her cheek stung, and her jaw throbbed from the second blow she had received from the man she had once thought to call friend. In shock, she looked down at the blood staining the back of her hand.

"Get up," Drew commanded, his harsh voice bringing her to her senses. "You're not hurt—not yet."

Slowly, Maginn lifted her gaze. Like the devil himself, Drew's face glowed red in the firelight, his eyes gleaming with an unholy delight. Where was the handsome cavalier who had championed her cause against the monitors so gallantly? The man before her was not he. This was a brutal, unfeeling fiend.

"I said *get up!*"

Pushing herself up from the dirt floor, Maginn felt her head spin. She swayed as she rose, but caught her balance. Tears tormented her composure. "Why did you do it, Drew? Lance was one of us."

"Us? There is no us."

"But the resistance—"

Drew snickered. "Oh, my poor, poor Maginn. You haven't figured it out yet, have you? There is no resistance!"

"What?"

"Are you deaf, you stupid little Mick? I said, *there is no resistance.*"

Maginn could only gape at him. Never had he spoken to her so cruelly and with such hatred. "But I thought—"

Drew shrugged. "You thought what you wanted to think."

She could not believe what she was hearing. He had to be lying, but why? She had to get away. She shot a glance toward the door, but one of Drew's cohorts barred her escape.

Grabbing her arm, Drew leaned into her face. "Don't even think about it. I don't need you anymore, so I'm not opposed to dropping you right where you stand."

"Need me? You mean all this time you were

just using me?" Tears of humiliation flooded her eyes. Unable to bear his nearness any longer, she turned away.

Drew grabbed her face, pinching her jaws in a painful grip. He snorted. "Yeah, and you liked it."

Maginn's eyes widened.

"You look surprised." His hold eased. "Don't tell me you didn't like playing the avenging angel?" He released her, but remained dangerously close. "You told me everything I needed to know. When and where to strike, and oh, yes, who—we can't forget the *who* can we?"

"I did it for my family," she whispered hesitantly.

"Bullshit. Your family's dead. You did it for *you*."

Maginn blanched. His words cut deep.

"Don't give yourself airs, Maginn. You're no better than I am. You loved every bit of destruction we caused the Thimblerigger."

Maginn edged away. "I never wanted anyone hurt."

"Didn't you? Hell, *you* made it easy for me. And I certainly couldn't let all that good hate you had built up inside you go to waste, now could I?"

Anger defied common sense, causing her to momentarily forget the danger she was in.

"You were only supposed to be layin' the equipment to waste, not hurtin' anyone."

"Come on, Jameson," his gangly buddy bellowed. "Can't we just kill her and get the hell outa here?"

"Shut up, Todd!"

"Jameson?" Maginn asked incredulously.

Eyes as cold and unfeeling as steel held her prisoner. He nodded. "Andrew Jordan Jameson. Roark T. Jameson is my father."

Maginn felt sick. Her stomach rolled. "You almost killed your own father?"

"Too bad I didn't, huh? I could've taken care of him for both of us." His voice hardened. "I guess I bungled that too."

"Why, Drew, why? He's your father."

Like a madman, he flew at her, seizing her by the shoulder. "Because I hate that old bastard."

"I don't understand."

"Of course not," he singsonged. "You've always told me what a loving family you had. Well, I didn't. You had a real mother. Not a ghost—an image in a picture to be seen, but never touched. When you were a child and cried out from a nightmare, I'll bet your mother came rushing in and kissed your—"

Todd laughed cruelly. "Nightmares? Did poor little Drew have nightmares?"

Whipping his gun from his holster, Drew

shoved Maginn away from him. He pointed it toward the man. "Get out!"

"Okay." Todd threw his hands up. "Okay."

Any other time, Maginn might have enjoyed the man's blundering movements as he stumbled out the door, but there was nothing funny about any of this now. Drew was acting crazy. She had to find a way out before he lost complete control.

Replacing his Colt, he turned back to her. "You want to know why I hate my father bad enough to kill him? I'll tell you."

Maginn rubbed her upper arms in silence.

"I was three when Indians killed my mother on our way out to Oregon. My father fell to pieces. Hell, he didn't even know who I was. Another family had to take care of me for the rest of the trip. Then, six months after we reached Eugene my father up and left me with the same family to go down to San Francisco. Said he wanted to start a shipping business. I was four then—*four* years old." He held up as many fingers—as if she needed to see them to understand.

"Once he left, I didn't see him much more than twice a year, Christmas and birthdays. He always brought me some lavish toy that I could've given a good damn about." His voice softened. Tears gathered in the tortured man's eyes, and for a moment his expression appeared every bit that of the little boy he described. "I'd begged him to take me with him, but he never did. Said I needed the nurturing of a family." He glared at Maginn.

For a moment she thought he might attack her again.

"The *Jenkens* weren't my family! *He* was, but he didn't want me. I tried everything to get him to notice me. I tried to be good. I worked hard, got good grades in school. And when I was eighteen I joined the army—used the name Jordan like now." He shook his head, his eyes glimmering with a faraway look.

"That didn't work either. I tried to be a regular soldier. Wanted to make myself into something he could be proud of. And finally, when I had worked my way up to lieutenant, *he* snatched everything away. He had known where I was all along. When the war broke out, he bought me a post at Fort Point. You know, not a single shot was fired there in the North's defense? He didn't care how I felt— how humiliated I was. I was just property— like my mother's picture and all that expensive crap he has tucked away so carefully in his house." He chuckled then stared at the fire for a long time before speaking again.

"I fixed him, though. Me and Todd there ran off from our duties one night and got belly-up drunk. Tore up a good piece of San Francisco in the process too. Naturally, we got caught and thrown in the brig. I thought sure the old bastard'd be madder than hell." He looked at Maginn. "You know what he did?"

She held her breath. She did not trust his mood.

"He bought my way out of that too. Not just out of the brig, but out of the army. He didn't even come himself. He sent some hired lawyer. And instead of punishing me, he set me up in his business. Said he wanted to keep an eye on me. But he didn't. He just wanted to keep me from causing *him* any embarrassment. I figured that out quick enough." He grinned.

Maginn's eyes remained fixed on the man.

"From then on, I did everything I could to make him sit up and take notice. But nothing ever gained me more than a lick of attention—except when I got thrown in jail. So, I figured if causing trouble was what it took to get even, trouble was what I'd give him." He snorted. "He looked the other way when I started juggling the accounts and spending the money. He just put it back, and nobody was the wiser. I hated that old man so damn much for ignoring me. And when I was accused of shanghaiing crews for some of the, shall we say, *shadier* captains, he had officials bought off to keep our good name out of trouble. And he *knew* I was doing it."

Maginn trembled. This was not the man she knew, this man was sick.

Drew started to laugh, low at first then louder, until she thought she would go mad listening to him. Watching him, she felt a swell of pity. Tears burned her eyes. Her heart went out to him. "Oh, Drew. I'm so sorry." She barely realized she had spoken.

His laughter stopped. He lunged at her. Clutching her throat, he slammed her hard against the wall.

She gripped his wrists and pulled, but he was too strong for her.

"Don't you dare feel sorry for me." He squeezed her neck. "Save it for yourself."

The door banged open. Startled, Drew released her.

She slumped down.

"Look what we got here," Todd hollered as he and another man entered the shack carrying someone. They tossed the body onto the floor. "Ain't this that gunman your daddy hired?"

"Colm?" Maginn said in a choked whisper.

Drew scowled. Lightning-quick, he snatched her up to him by the hair. His eyes bored into hers with pure hate and meanness. "You led him here!"

"No!" She tried not to yell, but she could not help it. He shook her head so forcefully, she thought he would surely rip out every strand of her hair.

"Don't lie to me, bitch!" He released her only to hit her again. The back of his hand cracked soundly against her cheek.

Pitched atop the one table in the room, Maginn fought to keep her balance. She cut a fearful glance back at the men. Two more entered behind the first pair.

"Now what?" Todd appeared nervous. "If he's here, this means bad trouble for us. I think we should light outa here quick."

"Stop your whining," Drew shouted. His hands flexed dangerously close to his gun.

Maginn held her breath. She did not dare move.

All five men stood silent, staring at Colm.

"Well?" Todd finally asked. "What're we going to do with him?"

"Nothing."

"Nothing? We can't just let him go—he knows who we are. He'll go for the law and—"

Drew glared at the skinny man, then his posture suddenly relaxed. A hellish smile twisted his mouth. "Who said we were going to let him go?"

"But—"

"I said we were going to do nothing . . . right now." He glanced back at Maginn. "It's getting late. I need some sleep."

"What'll we do with him now?"

"Tie him up—the Mick too. We'll take care of them both in the morning."

Maginn looked back at Colm's crumpled form lying beside her. It had been at least two hours since he had been brought inside and he was still unconscious. She scanned the three sleeping men across the room, studying Drew carefully. Except for the steady rise and fall of his chest, he did not move. She bent down. "Colm?"

He did not stir.

She raised her voice. "Colm. Please." She cut a wary glance toward the men. All remained motionless. With their loud snoring, they had not heard her. She nudged Colm with her head. "You must wake up."

He moaned.

"Shh."

His eyes fluttered open and he squinted at her as if she were a ghost. He peered back at their abductors a moment before looking at her. "What happened?"

Maginn shrugged. "You lost the fight."

Colm glared at her. He started to rise, but

195

when he realized his wrists and feet were tied, he glanced at Maginn.

She leaned forward and wagged her hands behind her. "Me too."

He sat up beside her. Grimacing, he lolled his head against the wall and groaned. "What'd they hit me with?"

"Hurts a bit, hmm?"

"Yeah, a lot." With one half-closed eye, he looked at her sideways. "What kinda plans they got for us?"

"Drew didn't say. But you better believe he'll not be takin' us pub crawlin'."

Colm shook his head and chuckled.

"Seriously, we've got to get loose. You think you can get me hands untied?"

"You goin' t' fight them off all by yourself, are you?"

"That crack on your head leave you daft?" Frustrated, she took a cleansing breath. They had no time for banter. "It would take me too long to free you. They've tied me own hands so tight, they're near useless now. You'll have to undo mine first."

It was almost dawn before Colm managed to free Maginn.

"How are we to get out of here without them hearin' us?" Maginn asked as she tugged and pulled on his bindings.

"How many're on watch?"

"Two."

With the knot loosened around his wrist, Colm pulled at the ropes securing his ankles.

A sharp pang of foreboding pricked Maginn's senses. She looked across the room.

Eyes narrow, lips curled in a sneer, Drew lay silently watching them.

Something flashed, and Maginn saw the gun. A startled breath stole her voice.

Colm turned. His stare locked with Drew's. Then, full-tilt, the men lunged at each other.

Colm came straight up off the ground. Pitching dirt in his opponent's face, he knocked the gun from Drew's grasp.

The blinded man yelled and grabbed at his eyes. He staggered backward.

Startled awake, the other men came to their feet.

Before the first was fully roused, Colm slammed a fist into his nose with such force that he sent the man sprawling to the floor unconscious. He dodged the second with a quick turn, then rammed his knee into the man's stomach. But the one called Todd had more grit than Maginn thought. Recovering, he swung at Colm.

Colm's head snapped. Shaking the blow off, he stepped back then lashed out. He shot an uppercut to the man's jaw, knocking him against the wall.

Watching him slide to the ground, Maginn saw a movement from the corner of her eye.

Drew dove for his Colt.

"Look out!" Maginn cringed.

Colm spun back. He leapt atop Drew, his hand gloving his foe's. Fighting for the weapon, they rolled closer to Maginn. A shot fired, barely missing her.

She screamed.

"Get out!" Colm yelled at her.

Terrified, Maginn took a step. She peered at the other two adversaries. They lay unconscious in a heap. She looked at the door. Her heart lurched. The men on watch, they would have heard the gun. She glanced at Colm and Drew struggling on the floor. What should she do? Did he really expect her to leave him?

In the space of a heartbeat, Colm's gaze found hers. "Go!"

The word jarred Maginn into action. She dashed to the door and threw it open. She hesitated, casting a fleeting glance at Colm, but he did not see her.

Locked in blood-lust, both of equal stature, which man would be the victor?

Wheeling around, Maginn ran as if the hounds of hell were at her heels. She bolted for the horses, but the sound of approaching hoofbeats made her change direction. They would be on her before she could reach the forest. With nowhere else to hide, she scampered behind the shack. Something crashed inside.

She flinched, squeezing her eyes closed for a moment. "Get away, Colm. Get away." She scanned the area. She had to find somewhere to hide. They would discover her whereabouts quick enough if she did not.

She looked up at the heavy brush and boulders of the steep mountainside just above her. "God in heaven help me." She had to try—there was nowhere else to run. Taking a deep breath, she pushed herself away from the building and dashed for safer ground.

❧ 12 ❧

Crouched behind a thick shrub, Maginn decided her best chance for making it back to town would be to climb higher up the mountain then traverse the face toward the cover of a nearby timber line. On the opposite side she would swing back around clear of the shack, and on to Cavenaugh's Dig for help. But she did not manage even ten more steps before a shot split nature's tranquillity, pinging against a boulder next to her. It barely missed her hand. Instantly, her gaze zeroed in on the gunmen below.

''There! See her?'' Drew shouted. He and his men all sported rifles, and all were aimed her way.

Maginn's mouth went dry. Bullets flew around her, some too close, near misses. Keeping low, she darted in and around huge rocks and clumps of sagebrush, her sights set on reaching the trees. She fell, ripping her blouse and scraping her elbow on a sharp edge. Scrambling to her feet, she glanced down in time to see the men scurrying up the grade after her. She choked on a gasp and her feet started moving again.

Her ankles ached as she raced up the incline. Her chest burned. Her lungs felt as if they might explode. She was like a scared animal, eyes constantly moving, looking. She ducked and dodged the whizzing bullets, outstripping the wind as she tried to sprint to safety.

Sudden quiet pitched her to a stop. She squatted down behind a large boulder to catch her breath. All remained silent. No one was firing. Strange. Peering around the rock, she squinted down where she had last seen Drew. Nothing. Where were he and his men? She raised up for a better look, stretching on tiptoe.

Someone grabbed her from behind and yanked her back to the ground. Fear flooded her. They had found her. She tried to scream, but a gloved hand clamped over her mouth.

"Quiet!" An all-too-familiar man's voice silenced her.

She fell limp.

The hand eased away and she saw twinkling eyes like hammered copper.

"Oh, Colm." Without thought, she whirled

around and hugged him fiercely. "They didn't kill you. I thought for certain they had. I thought I'd never see you again." She was almost crying. Gripping his shirtsleeves, she looked him square in the eye. "However did you manage to get away?"

"That doesn't matter right now. We've got t' get out of here."

"But we can. They've given up. See." Pushing past him, she stood and looked out at the mountainside.

Another rifle shot, followed by an immediate splintering of the rock shielding her shoulder.

"Get down!" Colm jerked her to him. "Damn it, woman. You want t' get yourself killed?" Removing his hat, he leaned around the base of the boulder concealing them and surveyed the area. "See there? They haven't gone anywhere."

Hugging the rock, Maginn peeked out. She could barely make out their silhouettes.

Drew and his gang had gained a better vantage point up the hillside but were still below them.

Maginn shook her head. She glanced up at the dawning sky. "I can only just see *them*. How in bloody thunder can they tell where *we* are well enough to hit so close?"

Colm tugged on her collar. "This shirt

doesn't need much light t' stand out like a red flag."

Maginn looked down. Elevating her gaze again, she quirked a brow. "So, what're we to do about it? 'Tis for certain I'm not about to take it off an' run round half-naked."

Colm glanced down at her, his stare piercing her with incredulity before returning to the ridge above. He searched the terrain and something appeared to catch his interest.

"What're we goin' to do?"

He nodded up higher. "If we can get t' that crest, I think we just might be able t' lose them over the hard ground."

Something stirred the brush.

"Come on." Colm grabbed her hand. "They're closing in."

Another barrage of bullets exploded around them. Together, Maginn and Colm clambered up the rest of the steep grade.

The shots came faster, the men's aim closer.

"Damn it!" Colm yanked Maginn beside him, flush against an outcropped wall. "They're too close. We'll never make it."

Chest heaving, Maginn closed her eyes and leaned against the cool stone. "So—" she panted. "What now?" Lifting her eyelids to mere slits, she glanced at him.

His mouth twitched. "You think you can run a little farther?"

"Aye, I think so. Why?"

He nodded to the left of them. "We just might have a way out of here after all."

Maginn followed his gaze. Still higher, abutting the mountainside, an elevated flume started its descent through the Sierras. But she barely had time to recognize the structure for what it was before Colm took her hand and yanked her into motion.

As they closed the distance between them and the channel, Maginn heard the sound of rushing water. When they had come up beside it, her eyes rounded with fear as she gawked down the expanse of the giant sluiceway then peeked over the edge. "Sweet Mary, Joseph, an' Jesus!"

About two foot deep, the flume was nearly filled with the churning spring runoff from the mountains. Surely he was not really planning to do what she was thinking? He did not actually want her to— Maginn shivered just looking at the icy-clear liquid. This was madness. She could not do it. "Oh, no—oh, no," she kept repeating as Colm climbed on top of the wooden framework.

He held his hand down to her. "Come on."

In the predawn light, Maginn glanced over her shoulder and peered back at Drew racing up after them. For one brief moment she considered taking her chances with him. At least it would be quicker.

One more shot, barely out of range, sent dirt flying just short of where Maginn stood.

Balancing on the wooden edges of the flume, astride the rushing current, Colm bent down and grabbed her arm. "Maginn. We've got t' get in. It's our only escape. Come on."

Hesitantly, she lifted her gaze to him as well her hand. Secured within his grasp, she scaled the beams until, with his help, she stood in front of him. Her heart raced as she stared down into the roaring water beneath her. Above the noise, she could hear a drawn-out, throaty groan and knew it was she who made the sound, but she could not stop. She had never been so afraid in her life. She knew how to swim, but this was something different. Her imagination took hold of her. She could almost hear the rush of the water calling, waiting to swallow her up.

Colm slid his arms around her waist. "It's all right, Maginn," he yelled. "I'll take care of you."

Feeling his chest against her back, she leaned into him and clutched his hands. She could not stop shaking.

"When I count three, we'll both jump in together. Okay?"

Maginn shook her head. She was not ready.

She would never be ready for this. From the corner of her eye, she saw Drew and his men rushing toward them. If she was going to do it, it had to be now.

His mouth brushing her ear, his fingers entwined with hers, Colm shifted his stance. "It'll be fun."

She rolled her eyes heavenward then squeezed them closed. Fun? Lightning quick, she withdrew one hand and crossed herself—just in case—then nodded.

"Trust me?"

What choice did she have? She clutched his hand again. "Aye."

"Good. Here goes." Colm swallowed. "One. Two."

Maginn took a great gulp of air.

"Three."

Jumping down together, they plunged into the water just as Drew lifted his rifle, aiming straight at them.

Maginn's bottom slammed hard against the wood surface. She screamed. Water closed over her face. Fear sucked her breath away. Colm lifted her from behind, and she saw the gray-lit sky again.

Colm kept a tight grip around her waist, wedging her firmly between his legs.

Knocked from one side to the other, they slammed against the flume walls. Maginn flailed helplessly. They toppled over. Colm righted them, barely missing the razor edge of a metal clamp.

The channel dropped lower. The water raced faster, hurling the couple downward. Waves slapped Maginn's face, blinding her. She blinked. The open flow disappeared in front of her. A planked wall flew at them.

Whipping to the right, the flume took another direction. Colm and Maginn smashed against the side. Hooking his arm over the edge, he squeezed her tighter but the force broke them apart.

She turned, grabbing at him but missing by inches. The pounding flow lashed at her, rolling her facedown. She opened her mouth to scream, but water strangled her cry. Clawing at the sides, she surfaced, feet bobbing helplessly ahead of her. Over the rim, she saw the ground rushing up to meet the flume. A shadow came into focus. She swiped at her eyes, but before she could see what it was, the current sucked her under again. She pushed herself up, smacking into— She did not know what. A scream ripped from her throat. She fought wildly. Striking out, she caught onto something.

Sunshine crested the peak behind her, bringing everything suddenly into light. A huge hideous face with great horns jounced and twitched in front of her. A dead deer.

"Colm!" she shrieked. The water tugged at her. She did not move. Glancing down at her hand, she saw the animal's foreleg. Horrified, she let go. The flow sucked at her again.

Somewhere behind her, she thought she heard Colm call out, but she could not see him in the churning current. Then, nothing. The bottom fell out from under her. Pitched into the air, she felt her sodden skirt flapping against her skin. A shrill, ear-splitting scream tore from her lungs. Down she plunged within an icy, sun-lit shower.

She slapped hard against a watery surface, then darkness. Cold engulfed her. She kicked and struggled fighting for air. She struggled for a breath, but her mouth only filled with frigid liquid. Surging upward, she broke free. Gasping painfully, she looked around. Where was she? An abandoned mining reservoir? Something caught her eye. A body popped up, floating atop the water. Swiping her face, she squinted. Her heart lodged into her throat. "Colm?" He did not move. "Oh, God—no— please!" Throwing one arm out, she paddled sideways toward him. The cold hampered her movements, but with great effort she swam to him. She lifted his face. Her breath caught. Blood trickled down his forehead.

"Colm—Colm! Oh, you can't be dead—you just can't be." Even before she was able to get him from the water, Maginn had started to cry. Colm showed no signs of life. Clutching him tightly, she slowly swam to shore. Then after dragging him onto land, she laid her head to his chest. But with the fury of her own fright, she could not hear his heartbeat clearly. She rolled him onto his stomach and knelt astride him. "Dear God!" she wailed pitifully. Her eyes examined an open bullet wound on his right shoulder, as it turned the buff coloring of his shirt crimson. A gunshot. Drew's last shot had hit its mark.

She set her hands in motion on his back, pushing, kneading the muscles up his spine, repeating the action over and over, in hopes of expelling the water from his lungs. "Hail Mary, full of grace," she whispered tearfully. "The Lord is with thee. Blessed are thou amongst women, and . . ." She recited her prayer diligently. Colm could not die—not now—she would not let him.

Within the ebb and flow of a black undercurrent swirling in his brain, Colm heard the distinct sobs of a woman.

". . . Holy Mary, Mother of God, pray for us sinners now and at the hour of our death. Amen. Hail Mary, full of grace—"

Water choked him. He opened his eyes.

"Colm. 'Tis alive you are!" Maginn pulled him over and hugged him fiercely, a dazzling smile setting her face aglow. "Praise God. I thought I'd lost you."

Focusing on the shimmering green of her eyes, he stifled another cough and flashed her a lopsided grin. He brushed the tiny scar on her bottom lip with a finger. "We made it."

Teeth chattering, she nodded. "Aye. We did indeed."

"But t' where?" He looked around. Above the pool, a torrent of water cascaded from the broken middle of the flume.

Maginn shrugged. "Long as we're alive, I'm not for givin' a care."

"You all right?"

"Aye." Tearing away a piece of her shredded sleeve, she dabbed it to his forehead. "It's you I'm not so sure about."

Colm glowered at the bloodstained cloth. "No need. I'm—" He flinched. It felt as if someone had severed his arm from his shoulder.

"Be still now," she commanded in a gentle tone. "Take a minute to catch your breath. You've hurt yourself most grievously."

Colm was in no shape to argue. He rested his head in her lap. "I'll bet that flow brought us at least five miles."

"You think so?" Maginn retraced the flume's course with a quick glance then shivered. "Five miles I'll not be likely to travel again too soon."

Lifting his brows in agreement, Colm grinned. "It *was* a helluva ride, wasn't it?"

"Now that's a soft-pedal of words if ever I heard them."

His gaze lowered to a huge pine lying beneath the flume. It had obviously fallen across the channel sometime during one of the winter storms and had split the huge trough in half.

"How are you supposin' that happened?" Maginn asked.

"Probably got too snow-heavy." He tried to sit up again. Pain shot down his right shoulder.

She lifted his shirt away from the wound and grimaced. "We've got to be fixin' this before it becomes infected."

Colm took in her wet condition as well as his own. The morning air sent a chill breeze through his soggy clothes. "First thing we've got t' do is get a fire goin'."

"A fire? Isn't that a bit risky with Drew an' his men only a good holler away?"

Colm studied the rise and fall of the mountain peaks. He nodded. "Maybe, but I don't see where we have a choice. If we don't get dry, we'll catch a chill out here." He tried to rise again, but compassionate hands stilled his movements.

"I know you're quite unused to takin' orders from a woman, but I'm here to tell you, you're about to start."

He cut a glance at her bosom. "Yes, ma'am." God, but she was tempting. Her comforting was both soothing and dangerous. Even in this condition he wanted her. He had to look away. He bit back a groan from the pain that pierced his arm. He knew the wound had to be pretty bad, but he did not want to worry Maginn any more than was necessary.

Shading her eyes, she surveyed the area then pointed to a small horseshoe formation of boulders. "You think you can make it up to those rocks if I help you?"

Colm gripped her forearms and pulled himself upright. "Yeah." The words slid out through clenched teeth. "I can do it."

Together, and with great care, the couple rose. Colm tried desperately not to lean his weight into Maginn, but his head felt woozier than if he had been on a week-long drinking bout.

Maginn clutched him snugly around the waist. "I'm not so frail as you might believe, Colm. I'm quite stout of strength, I assure you." She set his good arm around her neck. "Don't be afraid to give me your burden—"

At that moment, Colm's head began spinning. He barely managed to stay upright. Half staggering, half dragged, he pitched toward the rocks, collapsing just inside their circle. He hit the ground with a heavy groan.

"Oh, my good Lord." Maginn's voice filled with panic. She helped him to a sitting position then checked his injury again. "Just look what I've gone an' done. You're bleedin' worse."

His back resting against a stone, he glanced down at the front of his blood-soaked shirt then smiled weakly. "The bullet still in?"

"No. It went clean through."

"It ain't too bad in the front here." He peeked over his shoulder. "But it looks pretty bad back there. It's goin' t' need cauterizing."

Chewing her bottom lip, Maginn stared at him. He almost laughed. She looked as if he had just suggested they remove each other's clothing.

"Do you know how?"

She shook her head.

With great effort, he reached down and pulled a bullet out of his gunbelt.

"An' just what am I supposed to do with that?"

"Bite it open—" His mind was becoming

foggy. He was losing too much blood. "You're goin' t' have t' get that fire goin'. Pour the powder into—" He shot a helpless gaze down at his shoulder before lifting an imploring stare at her. "Understand?"

Round eyes studied him carefully. She took the bullet and nodded.

"Can you do it?"

"Aye." She wiped the cool perspiration from his face. After a long pause, she spoke again. "Then what?"

He licked his lips. It was becoming difficult to concentrate. "Take my shirt—" He started to tug the material out of his pants, but pain shot through his shoulder again.

Leaping to his aid, Maginn stayed his efforts. Gently, she pulled his shirt out from his pants and unfastened the buttons. Carefully, she eased it off. She rolled the cloth into a ball and gently placed it behind his head. "I'll be makin' the fire now."

Colm nodded, but she did not see. She had already wheeled around and scurried away in search of wood.

A few moments later she came back and set the pile of twigs and brush near him. She faced him, her eyes brimming with tears. "I can't start it to flame—I've no matches," she whispered in an apologetic tone. Shaking, she balled her fists at her sides. Her expression contorted into one of rage. "An' even if I had one, it would be as fully drenched as meself."

Colm closed his eyes. He could not think.

"Here now." Her voice suddenly lightened.

But before he could look up, he felt his belt being tugged. "What the—" Peering down to where her hands worked frantically, he tipped his mouth in a slow, but impudent smirk.

Maginn's face beamed bright, her green eyes glimmered with mischief. "Don't be for flatterin' yourself, Colm McQuaid. It's your buckle I'm after, an' nothin' more." Freeing it from his waist, she ran over to where she had piled the kindling. Then sitting on her knees, she turned it underside up and reflected the sunshine at the twigs. It seemed hours before smoke appeared, but finally, she had a robust flame crackling.

Colm's eyelids drooped heavily. He gestured toward the blaze. "Bring fire."

Doing as he instructed, she rushed back to his side and knelt. She brushed her hair back from her eyes.

"As soon as . . . you pour the powder on . . ." His voice faltered. He was losing consciousness. He swallowed against the dryness in his mouth. "Touch fire to—"

"Aye, Colm. I understand."

"Now." Colm's breathing had become labored. His tongue felt thick, his words slurred. "I need . . . stick. Bite down."

She grabbed a piece of kindling and put it between his teeth then leaned him forward. Separating the bullet from the cartridge, she held the burning wood in one hand, the shell in the other. She looked at him, her gaze uncertain, filled with fear.

At that moment he was not sure who was in more pain. His heart went out to her. God, how he hated to cause her this torment, but he had no choice. He offered her the only reassurance he could, an unfocused, but steady gaze. Then leaning his head back, he bit down on the stick and nodded.

❧ 13 ❧

Maginn looked at Colm. God, how she hated to hurt him, but there was no help for it. The bleeding had to be stopped. Readying herself, she lifted both fire and cartridge. Could she really do this? Her hands shook. She took a determined breath and held it. Then, with one last glance at Colm, she poured a small amount of black powder into the bullet hole and touched it with the flame.

He jerked. A deep guttural sound spilled out from between his clenched teeth. His body tensed, and his eyes closed tight.

A tiny cloud of smoke puffed in Maginn's face, assailing her nostrils with the acrid stench of burnt flesh. She flinched. "Oh, Colm. I'm sorry."

But he did not hear her. He was slumped

over and the piece of wood had slipped from his mouth. He had blacked out.

Always the picture of strength, Colm appeared very different now. The sight of him, so helpless and vulnerable, tugged at Maginn's heart. "Damn you, Drew Jordan—or whatever your bloody name—damn you for causin' all this!"

Batting her eyes to stay the flow of tears blurring her vision, she threw the offensive implements to the ground. She eased Colm back then helped him to lie down. After cleaning the wound on his chest, she tore the hem from her shirt and patched it as best she could. There was nothing else she could do.

Though senseless, he had started to tremble. Warm. She had to get him warm. She grabbed the thicker limbs she had found and tossed them into the fire. A sudden chill reminded her of her own sodden condition. She had to get out of her wet clothes. Colm was right. At this altitude, and at this time of year—early spring—they could likely catch pneumonia. Just like Pater, she thought, but she pushed the memory aside.

Forced to strip down to her chemise and drawers, Maginn draped her riding skirt and blouse atop two boulders ringing the enclosure. Taking Colm's shirt, she rinsed the blood out and placed it with her things. When she removed his boots, a large knife fell out of one.

She glanced at Colm. "An' couldn't I just have used that a minute ago." And, too, why had he not used the weapon on Drew? She shrugged. "'Tis not for matterin' now."

She took off his socks and laid them out to dry then went back for his pants. But when she reached for the first button, she hesitated. She suddenly felt shy—yet daring. Her eyes were drawn to the dark bronze of his chest, and downward, flitting a path over his skin and the taut contours of muscle. She noticed his even breathing and found herself hypnotized by the gentle motion of his stomach.

Wanton thoughts gathered in her mind like a maelstrom in a pond, sucking her deep within its whirling current of desire and intrigue. She suddenly wanted to touch him, to know the feeling of his warmth against hers. She shook her head. Merciful Lord! What in heaven's name are you about, Maginn O'Shaunasey?

Heaven's got very little to do with it, me girl, her inner voice chided. 'Tis shameful an' nothin' less.

Nibbling at her lower lip, Maginn looked at Colm. Her cheeks burned. How could she have allowed such randy thoughts to possess her so? "Stop this, Maginn. You've no time to be frettin' over such twaddle now. If you keep this up, you'll be believin' yourself to be no better than one of those bawdy saloon tarts at the Rowdy Rose. Now," she said determinedly. "Get on with it before the poor man dies of the chills."

Gripping the riveted button at the top of his pants, she pushed it through the hole. "See there. Nothin' to it." But her heart's beating told her otherwise. Never in her wildest imaginings had she given such a thing as this consideration. Even when her father was ill, it was the doctor who had changed his nightshirt, not she.

With quicker movements, she unfastened the next stud then the next. "'Tis just a man, he is—an' a sick one at that," she muttered to herself. But this conviction could only disguise the truth of her emotions for the moment. For even as she spoke, her awareness of his masculinity had begun to grow, until she felt as if bands of steel were clamping around her chest. Eyes not quite focused, chest heaving, she unfastened the last button and swallowed. "Done."

But as she grasped the top edge of the denim, her hands stilled. Her heart jumped to an erratic tempo. She could not do it. As she yanked the fabric closed, a turbulent frown worked across her face. "I'll just be for buildin' the fire a wee bit bigger," she announced with sudden resolve. "An' we'll both be the better for it."

Once she was dry, Maginn's next concern was something to eat. But what? Sunlight glinted off the knife lying nearby. She thought of a rabbit and shuddered. No, she could not bring herself to do that. Still, she had to find something. She looked at the reservoir. Surely there would be fish. But how to catch them? Tickling—that's it!

Rushing to the water's edge she walked around the pool until she found a shallow spot where tall grasses had started to grow. She knelt, cupped her hands limply in the frigid liquid and waited.

With the passing of a few minutes, her gaze lifted to the thick stand of pines surrounding them and her mind wandered to their next dilemma. Would she and Colm be able to walk out of these mountains—and without getting caught by Drew and his men? And how much farther was Cavenaugh's Dig? She looked back at Colm resting peacefully. Would he be all right? What would she do if— A cold shiver snaked up her spine. She dragged in a deep breath. *That* would not happen—she would not let it.

Something brushed against her fingertips. She glanced down. A bright rosy-banded trout wriggled closer. Maginn wiggled her fingers.

She had not attempted this since she was a child out with her grandfather in Ireland. She would have to be patient, wait for just the right moment when the fish was settled comfortably against her movements, then— She held her breath. With one quick jerk, she scooped the trout out of the water and tossed him onto shore.

"I did it! I really did it!" She was like a small child, exhilarated by having accomplished a great feat. Laughing, she ran over and examined the small fish floundering in the dirt. Now, for another. By mid-morning she had managed to catch four more. Cleaned and spitted over the fire, the roasting trout gave off a delicious aroma that made her mouth water and her nose twitch with anticipation. Already, her stomach had begun a ferocious grumbling. She had not eaten since her picnic with Colm the day before.

While waiting for the fish to cook, Maginn checked Colm. He felt warm but he was shivering. A fever. She had to break it. After gathering their clothes, and dressing herself, Maginn blanketed Colm with his shirt. She then tore off a piece of her blouse and dipped it into the pool.

"God in heaven, please don't let him die," she whispered as she cooled his face with the compress.

He moaned, murmuring something in a strange and clipped dialect Maginn had never heard before. He began to shake worse. "Mother, I need you," he whispered.

Startled, Maginn stared at him. "Mother?" Well, of course he's for havin' a mother. What had she expected? Everyone did. But this was something she had not considered when thinking of Colm. Though in truth she had never given any regard to his past or his personal life. She had simply thought of him as the consortium's gunman, nothing more.

He swiped at her hand, knocking the rag out of her grasp.

She soothed his brow. "Shh, Colm. It's Maginn—I'm here." Once she had him settled again, she retrieved the cloth and rinsed it clean then replaced it on his forehead. Somewhere in the back of her mind, she heard the sizzle of the fish. She had to eat so she would have the strength to care for him.

Her stomach quieted almost immediately upon tasting the trout and she gave a contented moan. "Thank you, Lord—an' you, too, Grandpater." Enjoying her meal, she sat on her knees and scanned her surroundings. If it were not for their predicament, this would be a lovely place. She smiled to herself. She felt quite pleased with her accomplishments thus far. Now, if Colm would get better and they could just get back to town, everything would work out almost perfectly.

Her meal finished, Maginn bathed Colm with cool water again. His coloring looked better, but he was still feverish. Well into the afternoon, she sat vigil over her patient, keeping him warm, and battling his fever with compresses.

The sun was growing increasingly warmer as it beat down on the couple. Maginn looked for shade, but the only relief was in the shadows of the trees. She looked at Colm. There was no way she could drag him to the shade beneath their boughs. And even if she could, it would probably do more harm to move him. No, best they stay here. She gathered a couple of sturdy branches and wedged them between the rocks above Colm's head. Then removing her blouse, she draped it across the branches to shade him from the sun. This completed, she decided to scavenge the perimeter of their camp to see what else, if anything, she could find for food.

Circling the reservoir, the sight of a small group of tiny parasols caught her eye. She grinned. "Fairy rings." Dashing to a large pine, she squatted down.

Scattered around the base of the tree, the cream-colored mushrooms presented a pleasant picture. She picked one and brushed it off.

She took a bite. A bit bland, but at least they were food. She picked as many as she could hold in her hands then scurried back to the camp. They would feast tonight.

After washing the mushrooms, she skewered them onto a reedy stick, alternating them with thick chunks of fish, then set them over the fire to cook. She checked Colm again. His coloring was better, but he still remained quite warm to the touch. How long would he remain unconscious? Would he ever recover? There was always the chance he would not.

"You mustn't be for thinkin' that way, Maginn. O'course he'll get better." She tucked his shirt up closer to his neck. "He just has to."

Returning to the fish, she pulled off a piece and tested its readiness, but before she had chewed the first morsel, a low growl sounded from behind her. She froze mid-bite. Her eyes moved toward the direction of the sound, but she could see nothing. Slowly, she lifted her gaze and turned to face the intruding animal.

Another snarl.

Maginn's eyes flew wide, her breath catching. A great hulk of a mountain cat sat perched atop the cliffside just above her.

He lifted his nose to the air then roared again, his ears pinned back against his head.

"Don't move," Colm whispered from behind her.

Maginn fought the urge to turn. She remained stock-still. Her heart beat triple time as she stared at the beast. "What do we do?"

"He wants the fish."

"No!" she shrieked.

The cat lashed a paw through the air.

She swallowed. "No," she said again in a much softer voice. "It took me all mornin' to catch them. *We* need them."

"Maginn. That animal's in no playin' mood. He's hungry, and if you don't give him what he wants, he's liable t' take us instead."

She kept her focus trained upward. She knew Colm was right, but that was not the point. Then again, she did not have the upper hand here.

"Very carefully, take one of the burnin' sticks out of the fire and—"

"Sticks? What in bloody—"

"Just do it!" he blurted out harshly.

With no room to argue, Maginn relented. She followed Colm's command. Gripping the burning limb, she cut a glance at him then back at the cat. "Now what?"

"Toss a fish up to him." He paused. "Do it!"

Without thought, Maginn threw the trout up.

The cougar immediately pounced on the food.

"Now, while he's not lookin', throw the stick at him."

Taking great care, Maginn silently rose. She lifted her arm, took aim, then hurled the burning wood, hitting the animal in the face.

With an alarming roar, the mountain lion wheeled away and dashed out of sight.

Maginn withered to a stoop. She released a relieved rush of air then straightened. Her gaze flew to Colm and she ran to his side.

Beads of sweat glistened on his face and his breathing was labored.

Sitting down, she chuckled. "You were just as afraid as I was, weren't you now?"

Colm smiled. "No." He gestured down to the knife she had left beside him. Firmly planted in his grip, he held it up. "More."

"'Twas in your boot."

"Yeah, I know." He glanced down at his bare feet. "Speakin' of my boots—" He raised his brows questioningly.

"Oh." Maginn pointed them out by the fire. "They were wet. I had to be takin' them off if they were to dry."

Gazing upward, he looked at the small sunshade she had improvised. He did not speak, but when his eyes moved back to her, and her skimpy attire, he appeared perplexed. "You took care of me?" He sounded astonished.

Deborah James

Maginn's face heated. She smiled and nodded. She suddenly felt quite exposed beneath his watchfulness. Bending over, she lifted the garment from the branches. Unable to look at him directly, she turned sideways and buttoned her blouse. She could feel his eyes on her movements and knew that it was he who caused this new bout of trembling within her. "'Twill be dark soon," she said as she tugged the length of her hair from out of her collar. "Best I fetch a wee bit more wood for the fire. No tellin' how cold 'twill get up here out in the open."

"Better get more than a *wee* bit. That cat's sure to be back."

Maginn's heart lurched. She darted a fearful gaze around before meeting his eyes again. "Truly, Colm. You think he'll come back?"

"You can bet on it."

It did not take Maginn very long to gather enough firewood for the passing of the night, but by the time she had returned to the camp, the sun had already slid behind a distant peak, draping them in shades of twilight.

Colm had pulled himself up to a half-sitting position and had helped himself to a portion of the food. He gestured to her with one of the pins of wood. "I couldn't wait for you," he said between chewing and swallowing.

When she had piled the last armload of

228

firewood within their campsite, she took one of the sticks and joined him.

"This is really good." He wiped a dribble of juice from the corner of his mouth. "How'd you catch these?"

Maginn swelled with pride. It felt good to have pleased him. "I tickled them."

"You what?" Colm smiled in that lopsided way he always did when he was thoroughly amused.

Maginn laughed. "It's something me grand-pater taught me when I was just a wee thing still in Ireland."

Chuckling, Colm lifted a handful of mushrooms. "So, how did you find these—by whistlin'?"

It was so wonderful to see him smiling again that Maginn did not feel the least bit aggravated by his teasing.

"Would you be likin' more?"

He shook his head. "Maybe later." He watched her while she ate, but did not speak for the longest time.

Finally, Maginn could not stand the weight of his scrutiny any longer. "What is it?"

"Hmm?"

"You're starin' at me."

"Was I?"

"You know you were." Remembering the last time he had looked at her so, she felt her face heat with color and she glanced down at her blouse. She almost sighed in relief when she saw that it was fastened closed. She looked back at him and paled.

He grinned, but cut his gaze away. "You're quite a woman, Maginn O'Shaunasey."

She was not quite sure how he meant that, but she chose to take it as a compliment. She cleared her throat. "Are you for feelin' better now?"

"Yeah." He touched his shoulder and grimaced. "Still hurts like hell though."

"O'course it does," she said. Setting her meal aside, she moved to his side and checked the wound. "It looks better," she offered reassuringly.

"I been out all day?"

She nodded. "It'll be quite sore, but I think you can travel tomorrow."

"Tomorrow, hell!" He made as if to rise, but slumped back to the ground.

Applying her hands firmly yet gently to his chest, Maginn settled him back to his former position. "Don't you go ruinin' me handiwork, Colm McQuaid. I'm none too ready to sear you closed again." She pulled his shirt up over his shoulders and relaxed against the sheer wall at her back. From beneath lowered lashes, she watched him. She could not guess at the thoughts behind the dark depths of his eyes as his gaze remained fixed on the fire. She should say something, but nothing came to mind.

"Thank you," he said quietly. "If it weren't for you, I'd probably be—"

She held up her hand. "'Twas nothin' you wouldn't have done for me. You saved me life as well." She flinched. She had not meant to sound so flip and uncaring. "What I mean is . . . we both helped each other . . . an', well, we're not safe an' sound in Cavenaugh's Dig yet. There's apt to be a wee bit more that we'll have to do for one another before we're through."

Reaching up, Colm took her hand. He smiled. "Just the same . . . thanks."

She was not sure what she had expected from him when he awoke, but it certainly had not been this. Their eyes met. She suddenly saw him quite differently, his usual hard demeanor gone. Her gaze drifted from his only to return just as easily. His eyes flickered in the firelight and she felt the swift return of her earlier yearnings. He moved, ever so slightly, and a strand of dark hair snagged by his collar fell back just above his shoulder. Her heart did crazy things—caused crazy thoughts. God in heaven. She swallowed. Such a dev'l, he is, to make me want—

Somewhere in the not too far distance, the

yowl of a lone mountain cat pierced the quiet.

"Colm?" Maginn lunged toward him, her gaze darting fitfully around the shadowy fringe of their small enclosure.

Wordlessly, he opened one arm invitingly. Flashing red-gold in the firelight, his warm expression drew her into his embrace.

The strange fluttering quieted in her stomach and she felt oddly at ease.

"Rest easy, Maginn." His voice was softer, more gentle than she had ever remembered.

Snuggling down beside him, she was not so afraid anymore. Her eyelids grew heavy. The soft sound of his breathing comforted her.

The great cat called to the night again. But before fear could spear her once more, Colm pulled her closer.

She thought she felt his lips against her hair, but she was not sure, and she did not care. She was safe—safer than she had ever imagined feeling again, comforted more than she thought possible. Fleetingly, she remembered the bitterness that had always ruled her heart whenever Colm was around. She cuddled nearer and sighed. "Not now." And as the many forest animals set up their evening chorus, Maginn allowed those thoughts to take flight on the hushed whisper of the night breeze, and she slept.

❧ 14 ❧

Something tickled Colm's mouth and he opened his eyes. Raising his head, he gritted his teeth against the searing pain that lanced his upper back. He glanced down to look at the woman nestled so close to him, but all he could see was the top of her head. Golden strands of sun-drenched hair teased his lips. Vaguely, he thought back to all that had happened to him the previous day—the cougar, Maginn, the way she had taken charge and cared for him. He smiled. Any other woman would have buckled under with fear, but not his Maginn.

He rubbed his chin absently against the wayward curl still brushing his skin. *His* Maginn? When had he started thinking of her as his? He recalled their past relationship. With their constant battling, who would have imagined that they would come to this? Certainly not Colm. And these strong emotions—where had they come from? He had no words to express what he felt for her.

He stroked her upper arm through the tear in her blouse. What're you doin' t' me, little "Rowdy Rose"?

As if in answer to his silent question, she lifted her face in her sleep and rubbed her temple against his chin. "Colm," she whispered. One small hand slipped up to rest possessively atop the heavy beating of his chest.

The murmur of his name so sweetly on her lips penetrated his resolve, deeper and quicker than all the practiced words ever spoken to him by any of the experienced women he had known in the past. He looked down at her uptilted face. So innocent and trusting. He lifted a hand to her hair and brought a strand to his nose. She smelled clean and cool, of mountain air, yet warm and damp with sleep. God, but she was tempting.

With great effort, he drew his injured arm across his body and cupped her slender jaw. His gaze devoured her. She had been through so much suffering, dare he cause her more? Lost in the moment, Colm forgot all but the sweet pain her nearness caused him now. Desire strained every muscle in his body until he ached with need and want of her. He moved to kiss her, but hesitated.

Her eyes moved behind her lids. Then, as if to entice him further, her lips parted and she sighed softly.

He could not stand it any longer. Straining, he bent nearer. A breath away, the shrill call of a bluejay intruded on his conquest and, startled, he looked away. His gaze gravitated up through the trees to the streaks of golden-pink crawling across the morning sky. With a heavy groan, he lowered his head back to the ground. Another minute and—

Inhaling deeply, he sought to control his emotions, though his thumb continued to absently brush back and forth across the curve of her shoulder. He could take her, but it would not be right—not just for her, but for him as well. He wanted her, true, he had never denied that to himself. And yes, he had had his fantasies about her, yet somehow they had appeared to him quite differently than this. Even with all her fight and fury, he knew she was an innocent—he was sure of it. That in itself was something quite different for Colm. He blinked. Why this sudden attack of constraint? He glanced down at her and his heart jumped.

Pale green eyes watched him, holding him captive.

For one long awkward moment, they lay staring at one another.

He wondered what to do or say. Suspended in thought, he smiled even before he spoke. "Good morning."

Unexpectedly, she stiffened, and her eyes flitted downward. In the next instant, she all but leapt up to a sitting position before squirming out of Colm's embrace and toward the fire. She stood looking down at the pile of wood for a long moment then grabbed a couple of pine limbs and added them to the still-red embers. "How're you feelin'?" she asked as coolly as if they had just met on a church step after Sunday services. When he did not answer right away, she craned her head around and met his eyes with concern. "Is the pain worse?"

He flexed his jaw. Ooo, if she only knew how much—and why. Barefoot, hair tousled, lips slightly open in a pout, she caused him more torment than the worst discomfort of any bullet wound.

She started toward him, but he lifted a hand and shook his head. "I'm okay." To prove his point, he stretched lazily, though with more than a little discomfort. He sat up. "Just a little stiff."

"Here now. Let me help you with that," she offered when he reached for his shirt. The garment was almost completely dry. She held it up for him to put his good arm through the sleeve then patiently assisted him with the other. "Would you like somethin' to eat this mornin'? I can catch another fish if you've the taste for one."

He chuckled. "No doubt you could, but we can't afford t' let Jordan catch us out in the open like this. We were lucky last night, but you better believe he'll be able t' spot our smoke—if he hasn't already. And he's not likely t' be so agreeable if he catches up t' us again."

"Areeable, you say?" Maginn clucked her tongue. Her eyes pierced Colm as she buttoned his shirt, but he knew by her fixed stare she was not seeing him. "That dev'l. He's only pleasant when it suits his purpose, I'll tell you that for nothin'." She rubbed her jaw as if it brought back a distasteful memory.

With Maginn's help, Colm pulled on his socks and boots then stood. Stomping his feet inside his shoes, he followed her movements as she made ready to travel. Once she had her own stockings and boots on, she fussed with the fire, traveling to and fro from the reservoir with handfuls of water. He found it most enjoyable to watch the curve of her round little bottom every time she bent down to scoop up the liquid then dashed back to the circle of rocks and dumped it on the cinders. "How'd you get mixed up with him anyway?"

"Drew?"

He nodded.

"'Twas right after I came to Cavenaugh's Dig. I had just gotten the job with Lance—" She paused mid-sentence and turned toward him. "Did you see him? Do you know what happened?" Her voice was pitched low.

"Yeah," he answered simply. He could see the pain in her eyes and knew that she was hurting for Taggert. He tried to think of something to say that would ease her torment. He would have liked to take her in his arms and hold her. "Don't worry, Maginn. The bastard'll pay for what he did."

There was that look again. A storm of contempt and all-too-apparent loathing transformed her face. Balling her fists, she lowered her gaze and nodded.

He hated to see her like this. God, but he would like to have had Jordan in his hands right then. He moved a step toward her, but her eyes came up sharply to his, halting his step. In that moment, something passed between them—a kind of silent vow, one that left no doubt to the ultimate end of Drew Jordan. "We'd best get goin'," he said finally. "We'll be all day and int' t'morrow before we can make town."

With a dip of her head, Maginn swung around and kicked at the ashes, spreading them flat. She turned and, not quite meeting his eyes, smiled brightly. "I'm ready."

And though Colm could see she was just putting up a front, he did not remark on it. "Let's go then."

For the better part of the morning, they trudged through the forest in silence. By midday, Colm's shoulder hurt like hell.

"How much farther would you be thinkin' 'tis to town?" Maginn asked when they had settled down beside each other atop a fallen tree trunk.

Colm stretched out his legs and flexed his ankles. Grimacing, he moved his arm in a sawing motion. "It's not so much how far, as how long." He nodded toward a distant ridge just visible to the northwest from where they sat. "We got t' cross that yet. If we had horses, I'd say sometime t'night."

After reaching into her pockets, she extended him a handful of mushrooms she had brought with them. She raised her brows. "But since we don't?"

He shrugged. "T'morrow. Early mornin' maybe." Accepting the food, he popped one of the spongy puffballs into his mouth and chewed.

"How's that shoulder of yours?" she asked

after she had finished her portion. He did not get a chance to answer before she brushed her hands together and scooted nearer. Unbuttoning his shirt, she lifted the fabric carefully away from his back and peeked underneath. As if it caused her more pain than it did him, she scowled, then just as quickly smiled. "Looks to be much better."

He could tell by the gnawing heat flaming his flesh that "better" was stretching the truth a mite. He lowered a slow gaze on her. She was dangerously close to him again. And those eyes—those incredibly beautiful green eyes. He heard the soft catch of her breath as she met his stare. Impulsively he leaned forward, his gaze drifting to the slight pout of her mouth.

Again, they fell silent. It seemed as if he could almost hear the pounding of her heart—or was it his? His palms tingled painfully with the recurring need to touch her. He raised his hand to the back of her head. Good God! He pulled back with a start. They would never get back to town at this rate.

Maginn's face flamed red. She straightened and her head dipped down. Then, oddly, she cut a glance around as if someone might have seen them. And all the while she nibbled on her bottom lip, the way she always did when she was nervous.

A thought suddenly gnashed at him. It had bitten him before, but now it left him sorely in need of finding out the truth. He cleared his throat. "You know," he began, a little unsure of himself, but continued quite matter-of-factly, "I thought you and Jordan were lovers."

Maginn snapped her eyes back to him. Her gaze focused on his eyes, yet Colm had the distinct feeling she was peering much deeper.

He suddenly felt uncertain as to how he should continue—or *if* he should continue. "But I . . . guess that's really none of my business." He waited, hoping she would jump in and assure him that it was not so. But she did not, which left him feeling even more unsettled than if she had told him they had been. Unable to withstand the intensity of her watchful stare, he looked away.

Her eyes bored into him with the potency of a red-hot fire iron.

What the hell was wrong with him? Jumping up, he turned his concentration to their trek back to Cavenaugh's Dig. "We best get goin' again." His voice sounded strangely hoarse. "Only a few hours of daylight left." Never had he been in a position like this before—especially not with a woman. He felt cornered by his own curiosity, as if he were being suddenly trapped into revealing something. But just exactly what that something was, he did not know—or maybe knew all too well. Either way, he was not sure what to do with everything he was experiencing.

Maginn did not utter a sound. And for the next hour or so, if it had not been for the forest noises, birds chirping, varmits scurrying, and the like, Colm might have thought himself deaf. And when she did finally speak, he had to train an ear to hear her voice. "Did you say somethin'?"

"In your sleep," she announced straight-out, as if they had been talking all along.

He cocked a brow and peered at her. "What?"

"Yesterday—when you were unconscious, you called out for your mother."

Colm stopped dead and faced her. He hesitated to answer, but she pressed him on.

"You said you needed her."

Resuming his step, he lifted his hands indifferently. "I was out of my head."

"Aye, but you still called for her."

"Is that so strange?"

"Well no, not for anyone else."

He cut her a sidelong glance. "What's that supposed t' mean?"

"Well, you know." She sounded winded.

"No. I'm afraid I don't." He was starting to get annoyed. The subject bit deep. He was not sure he wanted to tell her anything about Jennifer just yet. He picked up the pace.

Quickening her step to match his, she held her hands away from her body as if she were walking a tightrope in a sideshow. "'Tis just that I've not thought of you as havin' a mother, that's all. It came as a bit of a shock actually."

"You think some shaman tossed a magic potion into a fire and I just appeared or somethin'?"

"What's that you say? I've not heard of that before."

Colm frowned.

"What's a shaman?"

"A holy man."

"A priest?"

"Of sorts, I suppose."

"An' of what faith would that be?"

Colm chuckled and shook his head. "Arapaho."

"Surely you're teasin' me. I've never heard of the like." Her eyes suddenly grew large and she pulled him up short with a stay of her hand to his arm. "Surely you're not of a pagan belief. You know, like the druids?"

"Druids? And just who're they?" Her hand felt warm and comfortable against his skin.

"Strange people," she said, her tone becoming low and guarded. Her gaze darted in and around the trees as if someone were watching them. "They lived a long time ago in Ireland an' Gaul, an' are said to have made human offerin's to the spirits of trees."

Colm hid a smile behind a cough. "And you don't believe in such things yourself?"

"Why, certainly not. I'm a good Catholic girl."

"Unlike the bad Catholics who do, hmm?" Resuming his gait, he grinned.

"You're pokin' fun, I know, but 'tis a very serious thing, these spirits. An' nothin' to be triflin' with, I assure you."

"Really?"

"Oh, aye—indeed. They're not at all like the good fairy folk an' impish sprites of the woods. Why, even the leprechauns with their mischievous pranks are not so—"

The more she spoke of the matter, the more she reminded Colm of a very little girl. He tried to imagine her in her native homeland running through the forest. Hair flowing, giggling, and full of wide-eyed wonder. He glanced back at her. She was glowering at him.

"Are you not listenin' to me?" she asked accusingly.

"Heard every word."

"Well, then?"

Obviously, she had asked him a question

and now expected a reply. "Well, now. I'm not quite sure how t' answer that."

"'Tis so difficult a faith, this Arapaho?"

Colm grinned. He felt an immediate surge of relief although he was not sure why. What had he thought she had asked? "No. It's just that most whites don't like t' hear about anythin' that deals with the Indian."

"You mean to tell me you're an Indian?" Her voice was high-pitched.

Colm nodded. "Half. My mother's white."

"So here 'tis again." She smiled up at him, her face beaming devilishly. "We've come back to your mother."

Colm groaned. "Why're you so interested in my mother?"

Clasping her hands behind her back, she tilted her head to one side and peered up at him, her eyes twinkling flirtatiously. She shrugged. "Curious. I've just never thought of a gunfighter like you as havin' one." She giggled. "It paints quite a different picture than the one I've drawn of you in me thoughts."

"Like in your sketchpad?" He had not meant to sound so cold and unfeeling, but she was pressing him into something he was not sure he wanted to discuss. Then again, what harm could it do to tell her? "She's the reason I became a gunman."

"How's that?"

"Livin' with an Indian and havin' a half-breed son by one didn't gain her much respect when she was brought back into the world of the whites."

"Brought back? You mean someone forced her to go to the fort? She wanted to stay with the Indians?"

"Damn it!" Colm halted abruptly. His eyes bored into hers. "Why the hell is that so hard t' believe? Indians are like anyone else—better in some cases. If they steal, it's only from an enemy. Whites'll steal from their best friend if they're given half a chance. And Indians don't lie—how many white people can you say that about?"

Maginn looked shocked. "I—I'm sorry, Colm, truly. I wasn't for—" She reached toward him, but withdrew her touch. "I mean, I didn't think to—"

Colm could see by her sincere expression that she was trying to apologize, but he did not care. "No one *ever* thinks. No one knows the hell she's been through. They don't care how hard it was for her t' return with the soldiers t' the fort with an Indian son." He knew he had already said too much, but he was past the point of stopping now. He leaned into Maginn's paling face and sneered. "Not that the good white women at Fort Kearny didn't allow her int' their world—so long as

246

she washed their husbands' dirty laundry and kept her mouth shut. And it was even worse after Jameson wouldn't acknowledge her as his lost wife.''

"Jameson?" She clutched her chest. "You mean to stand there an' tell me Jameson's your father?''

Colm could feel his temper mounting. He had to end this now. He stalked away from her, but she ran up behind him.

"Colm, please. I'm sorry. I didn't know—''

Anger marking his stride, Colm became blinded to the terrain. He caught a rock with the toe of his boot and lost his balance. Pitched to the ground, he slammed hard against the leaf-littered incline. His face smashed into the earth and he groaned. He rolled to his side and tried to right himself, but the angle of the slope was too steep. He somersaulted, tumbling over and over. His head spun with the fall. He grabbed at rocks, plants, anything that would hold him, but he could not stop himself from sliding steadily downward.

❧15❧

"Colm!" Maginn shrieked. Neither of them had noticed the gradual ascent their path had taken until it was too late. She trained her eyes on the man tumbling down the steep incline. Taut fists held in front of her, fear binding her motionless, Maginn saw him slam against the ground and flip end over end. She screamed again and started after him. Her heels dug into the soft earth and leaves as she bolted downward. Her heart pounded. She had to help him.

Running as fast as she could, she could not catch up to him before he hit the bottom. "Colm—Colm!" Her voice strangled on his name. Halfway down, she lost her footing, smacking her backside on the ground with a heavy thud. She scrambled to her feet. She looked down and spotted him.

Sprawled faceup, he did not move.

"Dear—Lord—nooo!" Her breath came in heavy pants. She took a great gulp of air and started after him a second time. Almost down, she heard his groan. Falling to her knees, she started to slide, managing to stop herself beside him. She scooped up his head and cradled him in her lap. "Colm?" she whispered frantically. "For the love of God, look at me."

His eyelids fluttered.

Through a flood of tears, she examined his face. The only wound she could determine was a tiny gash trickling blood near his hairline.

He moaned again.

"Talk to me, Colm—say somethin'!" She shook him.

He raised a hand to his head and opened his eyes.

"Are you all right? Is anythin' broken?"

It took a moment, but then he smiled, that same heart-wrenching lopsided smirk that he had taunted her with ceaselessly in the past. "I'm—ah—" Obviously still disoriented, he glanced around then back at her. A bit shaky, he gripped her arm and pulled himself upright. "I'm fine—I think." He wiped his forehead then stared down at the blood staining his fingertips.

"Oh, Colm," she wailed against her hand.

Spilling in great scalding streams, the tears came faster. "You scared the pure life from me body. I thought I'd lost you. I thought I'd never get to you—an' when I finally did, I thought you were dead for certain." She swallowed hard against the terror still lodged in her throat. Her lungs heaved painfully against her chest.

His expression sobered. "It's okay, Maginn."

"Oh, Colm," she repeated in a sobbing whisper, her body sinking limply. She traced his features with an imploring gaze. She had lost so much. She could not stand the thought of losing him too.

"Shh, everything's all right, Maginn. I'm fine." He brushed at her tears, but it only made her sob all the harder.

How much more pain could she take? What would she have done without him?

"I'm okay," he said reassuringly. He pulled her into his arms and hugged her close. He held her there like that for a long time.

Clutching her shirt, she cried against his chest, feeling more comforted than she thought ever possible again. Months of pent-up anguish spilled out, soaking into the torn and dirty fabric where her cheek rested against him. Her mother had died so tragically, and there had not been time on the trail for Maginn to mourn the loss. She had never wept for her father, and had only spent angry tears for Tommy. But now, after so long and after so much, she finally gave in to her grief.

Colm rocked her within his embrace like a small child. Head resting atop her hair, he stroked her back, soothing her sorrow with a tenderness Maginn had never imagined he possessed. He felt hard and strong. The firm and steady beat of his heart against her ear soothed her, encouraged her, allowed release for her suppressed agony.

Acutely aware of the wonderful, but strange, security she felt, Maginn snuggled closer. Exhausted, she remained within the strength of his warmth even after she had stopped crying. She clutched a handful of shirt and rubbed her nose against its softness. Then sniffling, she took a deep cleansing breath and lifted swollen eyes up to him.

He smiled, his regard glimmering dark and secret.

Why had she never taken the time before to notice how truly handsome he was? She studied the play of his blackish-brown hair as the breeze stirred it against his collar. And his eyes. The color of buttered toffee, they melted her insides like honey-sweet candy.

Their gazes locked. She felt a sudden rush of heat flood her body. Her hands grew moist where they touched his shirt. She was drawn to him like a bee to its hive. Forget their circumstances—forget he was her enemy—God help her, she wanted him.

Without a movement, the silence that passed between them warned them both, yet promised each much more. But before either had time to gather reason and step back from their emotions, the signal passed between them.

They met in a heated rush.

Maginn leapt to her knees. Colm sat up straight. She almost toppled them over as she threw her arms around his neck, but he held them steady. Her lips burned to be touched by his. Her heart set up a fierce flutter of wing-beats within her breast.

The instant their lips met, his tongue pushed inside her mouth. His hands pressed against her back, drawing her even closer to him.

She met his kiss with equal fervor. Following his lead, she pressed her tongue boldly against his, tempting, tasting, seeking the core of the fire lapping greedily at her insides, flaming, melting her body until she felt liquid-hot.

As he entwined his hands in her hair, a low-pitted growl sounded in his throat, vibrating against her mouth.

She wriggled against him. So quick did the

charge of need and desire bolt through her that it left her dizzy, breathless. Shuddering, she pulled him closer still. Her hands slipped to his back and she suddenly remembered his wound. "Your . . . shoulder," she murmured apologetically.

"Doesn't hurt," he breathed into her mouth. His lips slid to her cheek and down to nuzzle her ear. "You always smell so damn good."

She closed her eyes and leaned back, letting his mouth roam where it would.

His lips were everywhere, searing her skin. He nibbled her chin, kissed her throat, tasted the vee of her collarbone as if he were parched and she were a cup of warm sweet wine. His hand moved to a breast straining against the inside of her blouse.

His palm, so hot she thought it would surely burn through the fabric, forced a gasp from her. She trembled against the unfamiliar male touch, silently begging for more. Her hands gripped his hair. Her stomach tightened. Her nipples hardened. Without thought, she arched back.

His mouth found a breast. He licked the thin material covering it, sucking it until he had saturated the tip through the cloth.

Her body went crazy inside. Blood pounded in her temples. She could not think—only react. Knees digging into the ground, she thrust her head back and moaned. Then she smothered her face in the damp strands of his hair and gritted her teeth. Moisture, like hot, sweet honey, poured out from every pore of her body, and somewhere down below in the depths of her being she felt another drizzle of heat.

His head suddenly lifted. His hand moved to the buttons on her blouse.

Her eyes slitted languidly. Both fascinated and frightened, she watched him unfasten her shirt and yank it aside.

One hand slipped underneath her chemise. He circled her body with the other strong arm, pulling her up tightly against him.

Her breath caught.

"Don't be afraid. Not of me—not ever again."

She swallowed against the dryness in her mouth and shook her head. "I'm not."

Leaning forward, he kissed her once more. His hand never stopped kneading, teasing, driving her body out of control. She found herself thrusting toward him in joyous welcome. "You're so beautiful, Maginn."

Drawn to the thickness in his voice, she peered down at him.

He had lifted her chemise.

Naked to his gaze, trembling with pure

sweet desire, she was not sure how to react. She turned her eyes away.

He bent nearer, making her forget her shyness as he tasted her mouth, the hollow of her neck, and returned to her breast again. He bit the tip lightly, causing her to moan deep in her throat.

Blindly, she twined her fingers tighter in his hair and pressed him to her bosom. Never had she felt so alive. Her body ached for more. She arched against him and squeezed her eyes closed.

Sucking her into his mouth, he found her other breast and thumbed its tip. He pinched it lightly, and she groaned again. Trailing a path of fevered kisses over her skin, his mouth abandoned the first to tease the other. He brushed the light stubble of beard on his chin against her softness before sucking her wholly into his mouth.

"Colm," she gasped, dying of need.

Unfastening her skirt, he inched his hand down her belly.

Too late she realized his direction. She tensed, digging her nails into his skin. "No," she whimpered fitfully. But even as she said it, she knew she did not want him to stop.

His fingers trailed a fiery path to the downy mat shielding her womanhood. He pushed his knee between her thighs, forcing them apart.

Her heart leaping, lunging within her, she could not resist his commands. Awash in the splendor of his touch, she moved, allowing him entrance. Delicious agony seized her emotions and she lost all sense of caution then. She was his to tutor, command at will. With the heat of his first touch against her softness, his name escaped her throat in a rasping cry.

While he suckled each nipple in turn, he slipped a finger inside her womanly flesh. In and out, he drove her on, never allowing her an ebbing moment.

Warm and wet, she was ready for him. Her mind reeled. Her mouth flew open in the throes of passion and she cried his name again. Her hips thrust against his hand.

With agonizing swiftness, he worked her body until she was a quivering mass of dewy, impatient flesh. His head came up and he flicked his tongue across her burning mouth. Sweat broke over his face in a fine mist, bathing hers wherever their skin touched.

With a low, savage growl, he jerked his hand away and pushed her to the ground. Tugging and pulling, he could not get her skirt off fast enough. He lunged up onto his knees. Gripping the coarse fabric, he tore it down over her hips and the length of her legs. "Woman's frills!" he railed in a frustrated whisper.

She flinched and opened her eyes. What had she done to anger him? She followed the path of his tortured stare. She had forgotten about her pantaloons.

He nearly ripped them from her body as he pulled them to her ankles and off her feet. His eyes were focused on hers as he pulled his shirt over his head without unfastening it. Then, snatching at the buttons on his britches, he peeled them down.

At the sight of him, Maginn heard her own pleasure rumble in her throat. She noticed a queer thrill charge through her body; it felt wickedly delicious. So this was what a naked man looked like. He was a glorious sight. Dark eyes shimmering, mouth tempting, he tossed his hair back from his face and kicked his pants aside. Hard muscles rippling across his chest, he seemed to be moving in slow motion.

She was burning up. Gazing heatedly at him, she lifted her arms and encircled his neck as he covered her nakedness with his. The smooth skin of his chest teased her breasts, making them tighten even more. As she writhed against him, the moisture sheening his body felt hot and slick and good.

His engorged flesh made itself known, pressing hard against her, probing, slipping, prying her open.

When he entered her, she stiffened. Her eyes

widened. He was hurting her. The pain growing, she raked her nails across his lower back and squeezed her eyelids shut. She thrashed her head from side to side. And all the while she whimpered, "No—no."

He stopped moving.

The pain died and she looked at him.

"Maginn, please," he commanded in a tormented whisper. His glittering eyes were filled with desperation. "Don't fight me."

"No—oh, no," she begged into his soft hair. But he was so tender, so gentle, the intermingling of pain and pleasure so sweet, she stopped thrashing and listened to him.

"I want t' make it good for you—ah—for both of us." One hand shifted to her bottom, holding her softly. He moved, eased into her again.

She opened her mouth to scream, but he smothered it with a loving kiss. She struggled uselessly, praying for the torment to end. And then, it did. Maginn's mind cast aside all thought of pain. Now, she only thought of Colm, of the swift pleasure he created inside her. There was suddenly no wrong or right of things, only wonder and need, and sweet desire until she thought she would explode . . . and suddenly she did.

In the next moment, Colm rose up and lifted her buttocks to meet his rhythmic lunge again and again until, with one last powerful thrust, his seed spilled into her, liquid-hot.

She basked in the excitement, cried out with joy and release in the sensation, and reveled in the power of this new experience. Where pain and sorrow and fury once dwelled, now there was only peace and pleasure. Instinctively, she wrapped her legs around him and held him there until their strength gave out.

Falling down beside her, Colm slipped his good arm under her head and encircled her shoulders, gathering her to him. They lay wrapped together for a long time, neither moving. When finally his heartbeat slowed beneath her hand, he moaned against her ear. "That was so good, Maginn—so *damn* good." He nuzzled her hair then kissed her temple.

One hand resting atop his chest, she smiled. She traced the subtle arc of his muscles with her fingertips, and nodded. "'Twas the first time, you know?"

"I know."

Maginn's head snapped up and she bit her lower lip. "You could tell?"

Through half-slitted eyes, he looked at her. His mouth pulled to one side in a crooked smile. "Don't do that."

"What?"

"That." He plucked her mouth with his

finger. "You always bite your lip when you're upset."

Maginn's brows shot up. "I do?"

"Mmm-hmm." He closed his eyes then squeezed her reassuringly. He pressed her head back to his shoulder. "But there's no need for it now, sweetheart. You were wonderful."

Maginn grinned. "You really think—" But before she could get the last word out, his steady breathing halted the question.

Beneath the whispering canopy of pine boughs, Colm fell asleep holding her.

Something bright jabbed Colm in the eyes and he was roused from his sleep, flinching against a shard of sunlight cutting through the trees. His head bolted up and pain sliced through his right shoulder. Grimacing, he rose up to rest on his good elbow. He flexed his arm. It still hurt like hell.

He peered around. Everywhere, streams of sunshine poured down from the sky, piercing the shadowy Sierra forest surrounding him. Where was Maginn? A soft chuckle drew his attention and he looked behind him.

Fully dressed, she sat on a tree stump watching him. Her beautiful face beamed, outshining nature's own radiance. "'Twas wonderin', I was, just now, how long I should let you sleep."

Standing, he found his pants and pulled them on. He looked up at the sky. The sun had already dropped low, signaling the lateness of the day. "You should've woken me up," he said a bit too sharply.

Maginn flinched. Her posture went rigid.

He should not have said that—at least not so harshly. She was too fragile yet. He had awakened her emotions, and now they were too new, too vulnerable. Making love for the first time was always disarming, especially for a woman like Maginn. Releasing a breath, he bent down and picked up his shirt then flung it over his shoulder. He lifted his hands and motioned for her to come to him.

Head lowered, mouth turned down at the corners, she did not move.

He smiled apologetically. "Come here, lady. I didn't mean t' snap at you."

She met his gaze with a defiant, hurtful stare but remained seated. After only a minute or two of silence, she finally relented and approached him, halting an arms' length away.

Reaching out, he pulled her to him. Her body tensed, but he did not let that weaken his intentions. She needed reassuring and by damn he would give it to her—even if he had to make her take it. He kissed the top of her head. "How do you feel?" he asked, hoping the tender tone of his voice would soothe her fears. When she still did not relax, he hugged her tighter, gently rocking her back and forth. The tension in her body eased almost immediately.

She lifted a timid smile and shrugged. "I'm not sure. Different. Good." She shrugged again. "I'm not sure."

Looking down at her, he saw the glimmer of a woman newly born peeking out from her eyes. He leaned down and kissed her nose. "It's okay. It'll be better next time, and then you'll know—"

"Next time?" Her voice was filled with a kind of childlike hope.

Yes, damn it. What kind of man did she think he was? Surely she could see how much he cared for her. She could not still believe him to be the heartless gunman she had always claimed he was? Colm chuckled and touched his forehead to hers. "Aye, Maginn, me sweet . . . next time."

Her lips spread into a smile and her eyes sparkled bright green. Rising on tiptoe, she surprised him with a peck on his mouth. "Well, then," she said, spinning away from him. "We best try an' get as close to town as we can before dark." That said, she flitted off through the stand of pines like the fairy plume of a dandelion seed blowing in the wind.

Pulling his shirt from his shoulder, Colm shook his head. The woman amazed him. She did not fully realize what had passed between them. But Colm knew—much more than he wanted to acknowledge. His chest tightened as tautly as did his shirt across his back when he put it on. Watching her, an odd feeling, one he had never felt before, stirred deep in his stomach. He was confounded by the change in his own emotions. He wanted this woman for himself and him alone. He glared at her retreating back, but he was not angry—more stunned by his own thoughts. How had this woman managed to wield her way into his heart so quickly? Absorbing his own thought, his mouth pulled to one side with a smirk. "I'll be damned."

By early evening, they had made it to the foot of the last ridge before Cavenaugh's Dig. They had to stop and make camp before the sun completely slid behind the mountain so they could make a fire.

Using his buckle as Maginn had done, it did not take Colm long to coax a flame into a small but comforting blaze. "Too bad there's no pond or stream close by," he said when they had settled down in front of the fire.

"An' why's that?"

"I'm hungry." He grinned. "I'd have you *tickle* us up a string of trout again."

Maginn's back stiffened and she arched a brow, a knowing smile pulling her mouth up. "Oh, you would, would you?"

"Mmm-hmm."

"You're the man. *You're* supposed to be the provider." She flipped her hand haughtily. "So provide."

He gestured to his wounded shoulder help-lessly. "Yeah, but I'm hurt—remember?"

"Saint Jude, be merciful! I forgot all about you bein' hurt." She bolted to his side and raised his shirt. Immediately upon checking his wound, she fell limp and sighed. "'Tis not broke open, but I'm not for knowin' how you pulled that one off without causin' yourself more damage."

"Pulled what off?" he asked with a faint smile.

"Why, takin' the fall of course," she answered matter-of-factly. "What'd you think I meant—" Her gaze shot to his and her mouth fell open. Her cheeks colored a bright pink.

As they exchanged glances, Colm knew she understood. *Damn, but she was a tempting vision—embarrassed and all.*

She pulled her lower lip between her teeth, then peering up, just as quickly released it.

Tugging his shirt down, she moved just as hastily back to her place.

Colm watched her turn her gaze away, looking everywhere but at him, her hands clasped tightly in her lap.

Crickets had set to chirping and the moon had captured its full glow, winking through the wagging pine boughs, before either spoke again.

"Colm?"

"Hmm?" His gaze lifted across the flames to where she sat.

"I—"

"What?"

She shook her head. "Nothin'."

He could see something was troubling her—but what? "Sounds like somethin' t' me."

"I . . . just want you to know how sorry I am for makin' you angry back there." She gestured behind her with a nod. "'Bout your mother, I mean."

Colm tensed then relaxed. He shrugged. "It's okay. I guess I just get more than a bit riled when somebody says somethin' about Jennifer."

"Your mother?"

"Mmm-hmm."

Maginn smiled. "Pretty name, Jennifer."

"Yeah. She's prettier still." He envisioned

his mother's face. Auburn hair and large blue eyes, she always had a smile for him.

"Is she still alive?" Maginn asked, caution marking her tone.

He nodded. "If you call washin' grungy underwear livin'."

Maginn pulled a frown. "Whatever are you talkin' 'bout? I'm not for understandin'."

"She's the soldiers' washerwoman back at Fort Kearny."

"But I thought you said she was Jameson's wife."

"That don't mean nothin'. She's still an army washerwoman."

"But didn't he send for her? Didn't she— didn't someone write him an' tell him about her?"

"Yeah, they wrote him, but he just sent a wire sayin' his wife was dead. That's it, just dead. He didn't even try t' find out if it was true."

Maginn rolled her eyes and clucked her tongue sarcastically. "Why in heaven's name not?"

"He thought she was a four-flusher."

"A what?"

Colm glared at her. He did not want to talk about all of this, but he knew she would not be satisfied until she heard everything. He would have to tell her sooner or later. So it might as well be now.

"I'm sorry, Colm. You don't have to tell me any more."

But he did. He suddenly wanted her to know and be done with it. Taking a deep breath, he began. "About thirty years ago, she was captured on her way t' Oregon, by Windchaser, my father, a warrior of the Arapaho. He had seen her traveling with one of the wagon trains from the east and thought her beautiful. After watching the train for several days, he stole her from her husband and son, and brought her back t' his village t' make her his woman."

Maginn gasped. Her hand flew to her throat. "Son? You mean—"

Colm chuckled, though not with amusement—disgust. Knowing what she had been about to say, he nodded. "Andrew Jameson, 'Drew Jordan,' is my half-brother."

Maginn's eyes widened to their fullest. "Does *he* know?"

Colm shrugged. "Prob'ly not. I doubt Jameson did himself before—" He caught himself, not finishing his thought. "Anyway, you can just about figure the rest out for yourself. Jameson was too busy makin' money t' check out the colonel's story about Jennifer, and nobody else would take in a white Indian slave and her half-breed son. So she was left t' take care of the two of us as best she could."

"Washin' laundry?"

"Yeah, washin' laundry."

Maginn's brows pulled together. "But I'm still not for understandin'. Why would you go to work for that man, Colm? Surely you knew who he was?"

"Not till I came t' Cavenaugh's Dig."

"Who hired you then? That Mr. Willard?"

Leaning back a space, Colm stared hard at her. He was not sure what to say. Should he tell her? He expelled a heavy breath. "Maginn, I'm not a gunman—at least not anymore."

A puzzled frown creased her forehead. She tilted her head to one side and peered at him questioningly.

"I'm half owner of the Thimblerigger Mining Consortium."

With a disbelieving grin, she laughed. "Oh, now. Don't be foolin' with me, Colm. 'Tis a poor joke you're playin' here."

"I'm not foolin', Maginn. It's true. I won it."

"Won it! What a lot of potty-twaddle! How could you win it? The company's owned by Mr. Jameson, Mr. Willard, and the man that you—" Her gaze locked with his, fear marking her stare.

"I *didn't* do it! Cross shot himself. I guess he

couldn't handle losin' everythin' t' me like he did."

"How?"

"I told you. He shot himself."

"How'd you win?" she said between gritted teeth.

"Poker."

Maginn cocked a brow. Her expression soured. "I see."

Colm watched her small hands tighten into fists atop her knees.

"So that's why you're protectin' the monitors. You own them! You're as bad as Jameson!" Her face contorted with rage. She pinned him with a glare then gasped. Her expression fell and shame filled her eyes as she clutched the top of her blouse together. "God in heaven. I let you—"

"What?" He was starting to get mad. "Make love to you?"

She sneered. "Love?"

"Yes, love, damn it!" he yelled. He wanted to jerk her to him, shake her, make her see what he was telling her was true, but she was across from him and the fire was between them.

Her eyes filled with tears and, covering her mouth with one hand, she shook her head. She leaned her head back and batted tear-filled eyes. "How easy a conquest I musta been for you after all the worldly ladies you've been with." She laughed bitterly. "You must be quite pleased with yourself, I'm sure."

"Damn it, Maginn. You've got it all wrong."

"Wrong?" Her chin trembled. "No, Mr. McQuaid. I'm only too right. You're no different than Drew. You used me to get to him."

"Cut the Mr. McQuaid crap!" He jumped to his feet.

She flinched.

He took a step toward her, but she stiffened before he made another move closer. He had to do something—say something to make her understand.

Her chest rose and fell with her hurt and angered breathing.

"Look," he said, sitting beside her. He tried to touch her but she leaned away.

"Don't!"

He grabbed her face, forcing her to meet his gaze. "Damn it, woman! Look at me!" Seeing true terror in her eyes, he softened his tone and loosened his hold. He lowered his hand to her waist. "I didn't use you. And even if I had, why would I make love t' you if I didn't really want you?"

She stared at him for a long minute.

"And as for the consortium. I only wanted it t' get my mother out of that hellhole of a fort. I wanted her to have some comforts. But after seein' all the destruction caused by the monitors, and what they did t' you and your family—" He hesitated. He caressed her side with his fingers, hoping his touch would say more than he could speak. "I'm real slow at comin' t' terms with my own feelin's, Maginn, but—"

She swallowed, tears spilling down her face.

This was not working. He could not find the right words. How could he make her understand? Just tell her, Colm, tell her, his inner voice whispered. I love you. But he could not. She would not believe him.

She shuddered against his hand.

God, she was so fragile, so susceptible to pain. He could not cause her more. He wanted to protect her, stop anything—anyone—from ever hurting her again. The way her eyes pleaded with him raised the hair on his arms, and he was suddenly seized with the ache and want of her all over again.

He would make her understand the only way he knew how. His blood surged, stirring his groin. He touched her cheek, caressing the curve with his thumb. "Trust me," he said simply, then leaned forward and kissed her. He slid his arm fully around her waist and pulled her to him.

She shivered, but did not resist.

Cupping her chin, he moved a space nearer.

Her eyelids fluttered. "Kiss me," he whispered against her mouth.

"No." But she did not move.

Closing his eyes, he touched her lips. "Kiss me." He grazed her mouth with his tongue and he heard her breath catch in her throat.

Her gaze drifted downward, watching his advance.

The rapid rise and fall of her chest ignited his passion. A breath away, he hesitated, hoping she would respond willingly. When she did, it surprised him.

She moved toward him, but just enough to touch.

He could not wait any longer. His body sprang to life. Penetrating her mouth with his tongue, he cupped her breast in his palm, felt her quiver, and knew she had given in to him.

Falling back, he pulled her on top of him, leaving his hands free to roam down the length of a slender back and to knead a small firm bottom. He groaned against her lips.

She answered him with a like moan. And, slipping one arm around his neck, the other atop his chest, she braced herself up and tipped her head back in complete surrender.

He remembered his earlier promise. "It'll be better this time," he murmured in a voice husky with hunger. He nibbled down along her jaw then farther to her throat and to where her blouse exposed the swell of her breast. "And *this time* you'll know what you're feelin'."

❧16❧

Half a mile outside of Cavenaugh's Dig, Maginn smiled up at Colm. Thumb hooked through his belt loop, she hugged his side. Though she was dirty, hungry, and tired she almost wished her adventure in the woods with Colm was not over. Almost, but not quite. They had endured so much these last two days, but what had passed between the couple would last them a lifetime.

Maginn withdrew her arm from around his waist and combed her fingers through her hair, reweaving her braid. Without losing her step, she brushed at her ripped and grimy clothes, but it was no use. "I must look a sight with meself all tattered an' torn."

"You *sure* do."

Looking up, she saw that the space where he had been was now empty. Colm had stopped

273

and now lingered behind her. Bent over, she halted and glanced back.

Standing feet apart, elbow resting atop one hand, Colm rubbed his chin, that ever-present devilish grin marking his amorous mood.

Straightening, she smiled, genuinely pleased that he approved of the view. "Come on, now. We've got business to attend to."

"That we do," he said, strolling up and patting her bottom.

"Here now—not *that* kind of business," she said, laughing. It felt so good to laugh again. She had not been this happy in a long time. "Remember Jameson? Drew?"

Colm's jaw tightened at the mention of the two names. "Only too well."

"Well then, let's get goin'."

"Yeah, well, when we're through with them, we've got another bit of business with the parson, right, lady?" Clutching her upper arms, he kissed the tip of her nose.

She smiled demurely. She still could not believe he had actually asked her to marry him last night—or that she had agreed. It had all happened so quickly between them, she was almost afraid to answer—afraid it might break the bond between them and they would be as they were before. Two desperately lonely people. Taking the chance, she relented shyly. "Aye, love, we do indeed." Her voice was but a whisper, yet very clear. She turned from his grasp and took a step.

"Wait a minute," he said, taking her hand and pulling her up against his chest. He folded his fingers behind her back and smiled down into her face. "One more kiss before we go into town?"

She squirmed against him, though she was not trying to get away. "We're too close to town, Colm. Someone might see us."

He shrugged. "So what? They'll be seein' a lot before too long."

She pushed against his chest playfully. "Please, Colm."

"Kiss me," he said in that rich, sultry voice that turned her insides all warm and honeyed. The heat of his palms seeping through her clothes to her skin was almost unbearable.

This was what she had been made for—to be loved by Colm McQuaid. Slowly, seductively, his hands waltzed up and down her spine, while his lush dark eyes lured her to him. He leaned nearer, his mouth moving dangerously close, dispelling all thoughts. She groaned inwardly. In another minute she would not be able to stop him. In another minute, she would not want to.

Sanity broke his spell. They had to get to town, see the sheriff, and Jameson. Blinking, she bounced up on tiptoe and pecked him lightly on his lips. "There now. Satisfied?" She grinned and twirled out of his grasp.

"Not by a long shot." He reached for her, but she sprinted ahead of him.

With easy strides, he caught up to her again.

"*Colm*," she said with a warning, her finger poised in his face. "One kiss, you said. *One*."

"Some kiss."

Maginn had to giggle. He sounded like a rejected little boy. She tucked her arm in the crook of his elbow, and together they finished the short distance into Cavenaugh's Dig.

Entering the edge of town, Colm steered Maginn around to the back of the boarding house. "No sense gettin' everybody all riled up—the way we look and all. No tellin' what the good townsfolk would think I've done t' you. Me bein' such a notorious gunman."

"An' just wouldn't they be thinkin' the pure truth of things too." She flashed him a saucy grin.

"Knock the stuff off, woman, or I'll throw you down right here and now and give this town somethin' t' really think about."

After sneaking across the yard of Penhaligon's Boarding House, they came to stand beneath the veranda outside of Maginn's room.

"An' just what're you thinkin' to do with

me?'' Maginn asked when Colm had climbed over the rail and onto the sun porch.

He reached down. "Give me your hand. I'll pull you up." Taking hold of her, he hoisted her up, though she took note that lifting her weight caused him more than a little strain.

"Are you all right, Colm?"

He nodded, but she did not believe him.

"I'll just be a minute. Then we'll be goin' to see the doctor about that bullet wound," she stated as he helped her through the window.

"Yeah, okay. Anythin' you say." Colm rubbed his shoulder, a frown creasing his features.

Quietly, Maginn walked over to her bureau. She gasped at the sight of herself in the mirror's reflection. Disheveled hair, dirt smudging her forehead and cheeks, and her clothes— She shuddered. Lord in heaven. She was a mess. Grabbing the pitcher from the toilet set she had left sitting on the bureau top, she poured some water into the bowl and splashed it in her face. She sighed. What she really wanted was a bath—a long, hot soak. But that would have to wait until later. First she had to see that Colm's wound was all right, then they had to go to Jameson's and warn him about Drew.

Toweling her face dry, she looked into the mirror. That was one thing she was not looking forward to doing. Jameson was not going to be easily convinced, especially about his own son. Humming from across the hall drew her attention. Mrs. Penhaligon. She would have to be quiet so as not to cause the woman undo alarm. Yet she had to change. Disgusted with the condition of her clothing, she stripped off her shredded blouse. Then moving to her wardrobe closet, she searched through her four other shirtwaists for the simplest style. She glanced down at her chemise. It, too, looked a sight, but there was no time to change. And her skirt—it would have to do for now as well. Colm was waiting.

Quickly she buttoned her blouse and tucked it into her waistband. Then unbraiding her hair, she ran a fast brush through its tangled mass before hurrying back to the window. "Colm?" she whispered as she climbed over the sill. Once she stepped outside, she saw him standing at the opposite end of the veranda, peeking around the corner. "What're you 'bout down there?"

He gestured her to silence then motioned for her to join him. "Look." He pointed toward Jameson's house.

Following Colm's direction, Maginn felt her throat close over a gasp. Barely visible behind the plants hanging in and around Jameson's portico, the tall, lanky man Drew had called

Todd leaned against one corner of the house next door. Maginn covered her mouth. Her gaze flew to Colm's. "Whatever's he doin' here?"

"I don't know, but there's another one over there." He directed her to one of the other cronies who had been with Drew at the line shack. "Somethin's up. Come on." Colm swung himself over the railing and down to the ground. Then after helping Maginn, he took her hand and led the way out of Penhaligon's yard and into Jameson's.

"What're we up to?"

"Not us—them." Colm moved to the back of the house, and around to the opposite side from Todd. "I've got t' find out what's goin' on inside. It's too quiet. Those men ain't waitin' out there 'cause they're bored." Finding a window ajar, Colm pushed it open then signaled Maginn for silence as he crouched beneath it.

"Shut up, ol' man. I've heard all I want to hear from you."

At the sound of the familiar voice, Maginn's eyes flew wide. Drew Jordan was inside the house, and by the dangerous tone in his voice, not the least bit agreeable.

"You go get the sheriff," Colm whispered, his fingers gripping the windowsill. He started to pull himself up, but Maginn grabbed his arm and yanked him back. He grimaced, glaring first at her, his hurt shoulder, and back at her.

Maginn flashed him a look of apology. "Whatever do you think you're 'bout, Colm McQuaid? You're not really goin' in there?"

He nodded. "Jameson might be in trouble." He started to rise.

"No!" she rasped. "You can't. Drew'll kill you."

"He'll try." Colm grinned and winked. "You just get t' the sheriff and bring him back. I'll be okay."

"But your arm."

"Forget my shoulder!" He lashed the words at her.

She flinched, staring at him as if he were mad.

"Look," he relented. "One of us needs t' stay here in case somethin' happens. And one of us needs t' go for the law. It's that simple." He paused. "You want t' stay?"

Biting down on her bottom lip, Maginn glanced nervously at the window. She had no desire to see Drew Jordan again—ever! She shook her head.

"Good." Giving her a quick kiss, he motioned her back the way they had come. "Keep t' the alley as long as you can."

Taking only a few steps, Maginn glanced

back over her shoulder just in time to see Colm pull himself in through the window.

This is crazy! Did he really expect her to just run off and leave him? He did not even have a gun. How would he protect himself? He only had a knife and what good was that against Drew's Colt?

Something crashed, like glass shattering against the floor in the house.

Maginn jumped. Colm. Something was wrong. She had to help him. Racing back to the window, she peeked inside but she could not see him. She leaped up, scraping her feet against the wood siding, and hoisted herself up to her stomach. She lost her footing and started to slip back. This was harder than it looked. Groaning, she wriggled in a little farther. Draped across the sill, she let go of the wood frame and reached for the floor.

Someone grabbed her.

She tried to yell, but was yanked back so hard against the base of the window that all she could manage was a pain-filled yelp. She struggled, grasping for a chair, anything to hold on to, but found only air. Jerked outside, she hit the boardwalk with a thud. Her head slammed against the house. Terror and rage bolted through her body. Readying herself for an attack, she fixed her eyes on her assailant.

"Well, would you look at this?"

Chest heaving, Maginn swallowed.

Leering down at her wickedly were the man called Todd and two of Drew's other cohorts.

Colm hesitated at the foot of the stairs. He had to find a gun. He glanced around the parlor. There, in the entry behind the door, a pistol hung in a holster from a hall rack. Careful not to arouse attention, he crossed the carpeted floor and pulled the weapon from its leather case. An older gun, the Navy Colt .36 was a smaller caliber than Colm was used to. He clutched the unfamilar grip. A little unbalanced, but it would see his purpose done. He checked to see if it was loaded. Three shots. They would have to do.

"Listen to me, son."

Colm heard Jameson's muffled voice echo from the study behind the staircase. Moving to the door standing ajar, he strained to hear the conversation.

"I told you we've got nothing to talk about. You had your chance while I was growing up, but all you wanted to do was wallow in your own self-pity." Drew Jordan sneered bitterly. "Momma wasn't the only one that died out there on the trail."

"But that's what I'm trying to tell you, boy. She's not dead—your mother's alive."

Jordan snorted. "You been drinking, ol' man?"

Colm eased the door wider. Standing on the opposite side of the room, Jameson was partially hidden behind the blond man. He could only see the older man's face and his crutches.

Drew took a step toward the table nearest Jameson. He picked up the decanter of liquor and pulled the stopper. Straight from the bottle, he took a swig and coughed. "Well, now that's good. But it ain't good enough to make me believe fairy stories. Hell, I didn't even believe them when I was a kid. But then, you wouldn't know anything about when I was a kid, would you?"

"It's no story, Andrew. She's really alive."

Colm could see a glimmer of tears in Jameson's eyes.

"Look." Jameson picked up a piece of paper from the chair behind him. "I got this late last night. It's from the commanding officer at Fort Kearny. I was awake all night reading it over and over." Hand shaking, he held out the telegram to his son.

Jordan took the paper and read it aloud. "MAY 27, 1875. TO ROARK T. JAMESON. CAVENAUGH'S DIG, CALIFORNIA. HAPPY TO CONFIRM. JENNIFER JAMESON ALIVE AND WELL. AWAIT YOUR REPLY. MAJOR WINTHROP HARRINGTON. POST COMMANDER, FORT KEARNY, NEBRASKA."

Colm cut a glance to Jameson. So the man

had believed Colm after all. Colm was not sure how to feel. The old man looked like a cow-eyed schoolboy. He could see Jameson was truly excited at the prospect of finding his wife again. He wondered at his mother's reaction to Jameson's query.

Jordan wadded up the telegram and tossed it onto the floor. "You believe that crap?" Shaking his head, he laughed. He lifted the lid of a carved wooden box on the table where the decanter sat and retrieved a slender cigar. Then taking a match from the tray beside it, he struck it to flame and lit the stogie. "Some money-grubbing bitch says she's Jennifer Jameson and you believe it?"

The single word used against his mother sent Colm's blood to boiling. His jaw tightened as did his hand around the butt of the gun. He started to enter but Jordan chose that moment to turn. Colm stepped back from sight.

"It's not just her. You read the telegram. Major Harrington of the U.S. Army answered in her behalf."

"What in hell does that prove?" Jordan sneered. "He's probably in on it with the little tramp."

"That's enough, Andrew! I'll not have you speak about your mother—"

Colm heard a thud, a groan, wood clattering, and a body fall to the floor. He leaned around the door and peeked inside.

Sprawled in front of a bookcase, Roark Jameson lay unconscious. A small gash oozing with blood creased the left side of his temple.

"I'll say, or *do*, anything I damn well want, ol' man." Standing with his side to Colm, Jordan hovered over his father. Replacing his pistol in his holster, he picked up the lamp on the table. He took off the chimney then, grinning, he doused the senseless man with kerosene. "Once you're gone, *I'll* have everything—everything, that is, but *you*."

Silently, Colm stepped inside, his gun aimed at Jordan.

"Damn you, ol' man." Drew's voice faltered, as if he were about to cry. "All I ever wanted was for you to notice me. But you never did— Never had the time—" The word caught in his throat as he saw Colm.

Colm lifted his gun higher, aiming at Jordan's chest. "Step back," he commanded.

Jordan's lips slowly spread into a deadly smile. He made a smacking sound with his mouth. "I didn't expect you'd make it here this fast." Rolling the cigar between his fingers, he raised his brows. "Where's me darlin' Maginn?"

Colm's eyes flicked to the lamp, the smoldering tobacco, Jameson, and back to Jordan. "Put the lamp down. Now put the stogie out in the tray," he added when Jordan had complied with the first.

"I never really wanted to hurt him." Drew's expression changed almost immediately. His body began to shake and he squeezed his eyes closed. He suddenly dropped to his knees and covered his face. "I never wanted any of this to happen. But he just kept pushing me, ignoring me like—like I was nothing." Drew's voice trembled.

Standing there watching the man rock himself back and forth like a small child, Colm's resolve wavered. He had never seen a man dissolve into tears before. The truth was almost too painful. How tragic this circle of events they had all been victims to. A lost wife, a pathetic husband, a wayward son, and Colm all trapped in the same vicious wheel of pain and suffering waiting to run headlong into one another.

Pity for the men warred with the vengeance he had set out to obtain. He felt sorry for them all. He moved within a foot of the whimpering man. "Get up, Jordan. I'll see you get a fair—"

Colm's legs flew out from beneath him and he slammed to the floor on his back. The gun soared from his hand. Pain tore through his shoulder and he groaned. When he looked up, he saw Jordan scramble to his feet, grab the cigar and toss it into the puddle of kerosene next to Jameson.

Burning oil assailed Colm's nostrils. He heard the sound of flames igniting, and some-one running. He saw a boot, grabbed it, pitched its owner onto the floor in front of him. He focused on Jordan's twisted smile, but only for a second. In the next instant, Drew rammed his heel into Colm's face.

White stars burst in his head. Liquid warmth gushed from his nose. He had to fight the blackness threatening his consciousness.

Heavy footsteps echoed through the house, and somewhere in the distance he thought he heard Maginn's voice.

"No, Drew. Let me go! Colm—"

Grabbing onto the small table, he tried to pull himself up but fell back down, spilling the lamp and bottle of whiskey to the floor. He made another attempt and stood. Squinting, he looked around. Blue fire lapped greedily at the oil spreading to Jameson. His shirt sleeve was already engulfed.

The flames were out of control, snapping and gnashing, gulping up everything in the room. With Maginn's cry ringing in his ears, Colm grabbed a rug and threw it over Jame-son. Smoke so thick he could hardly see burned his eyes and lungs. He could not breathe. He could not see Jameson anymore. Falling to the floor, he groped around next to him. He felt a hand, wrapped his fingers around a thick wrist, and pulled. The man was heavy. Heaving and yanking, fighting the black cloud stealing his breath, Colm reached the door leading out of the study.

Once in the parlor the smoke was not so thick. He sucked in air then dragged Jameson across the room and out into the front yard. By the time he made it outside, a bell had started to clang. He took a final step and fell beside the older man. His lungs felt as hot as the roaring flames within the house.

"Fire! Fire!" voices railed above the roar of the flames.

Someone grabbed him under his arms, another took his feet. He was being carried out to the street.

"It's McQuaid. And Jameson. McQuaid musta pulled him out."

Colm opened his eyes to a blurry face and a scrambling of bodies scurrying around him, forming a line up to the house. "Mag—inn." He coughed, trying to clear his lungs. "Maginn. Where— Where is she?"

A crowd of puzzled faces looked down at him, but no one answered.

❧17❧

"Can you hurry it up, Doc?" Colm glowered back at the white-haired doctor.

"You want this shoulder infected? Pure wonder it isn't already."

The old man's gruff voice did nothing for Colm's growing agitation. He felt restless. He did not have time to be dallying around. He glared over at the man. "Just bandage me up and let me get outa here."

"And just where do ya think yer off to so quick, Mr. McQuaid?" A small rail-thin man with the fullest crop of gray chin hairs Colm had ever seen squinted out of one large brown eye. "I got some questions to ask ya about that fire yonder." He pointed at the wall of Penhaligon's Boarding House as if he could see the still-smoldering house next door.

"You can find out anythin' you want t'

know from Jameson." He looked back at the doctor. "You said he's all right, didn't you?"

"Yep. His lungs might be a little smoked out, but other than that, he's doing pretty good, I suppose."

"I already got Jameson's side of the story. Now I want yers."

The sheriff looked determined, but Colm was even more. He had to catch up to Drew and the other men before they hurt Maginn. He looked down at the lawman's gun. "You plan on shootin' me, do you?"

"What the hell ya talking about, boy? You gone loco or something?" The man's face pulled into a frown, causing his skin to stretch into a skeletal mask.

"Okay. You're done," the doctor interrupted. "Just slip this on and take it easy with that arm."

Colm looked at the black sling the man was holding up. He shook his head. "Sorry, Doc. I got plans for usin' this arm, and I can't manage it with that thing on." Standing, he directed himself to the lawman. "Look. I'm goin' after Jordan—Jameson—whatever the hell his name is. So unless you plan on usin' that thing on me here and now, I'm leavin'."

"Now hold on, McQuaid. My deputy is getting a posse together right now. I understand yer worried about that li'l O'Shaunasey gal, but I can't just let you waltz outa here alone and—"

"You ain't *lettin'* me do anythin', Sheriff." Colm stretched his arm. "I'm goin', and right now. I don't have time t' wait for you t' round up a posse."

Pulling on a clean shirt Mrs. Penhaligon had given him, he glanced up at the stocky woman. "'Preciate the shirt, ma'am."

She smiled from across the room and nodded.

"You got a gun 'round here that I can borrow?"

"I'm sorry. I don't keep weapons in my home, Mr. McQuaid," she answered softly.

"Damn. Jordan took mine up at the shack. And that Navy Colt I found at Jameson's is a piece of crap. I need a good one." Colm looked at the doctor, but he just lifted his hands helplessly and shook his head.

"What about it, Sheriff? You goin' to' help me out here?"

Rubbing his beard, the lawman stared at him for a long minute. "Can't do it, boy. I won't take the responsibility." He wagged a finger at Colm. "Now if ya wanna ride with me and my men, I might be able to acommodate ya."

"Never mind." Disgusted, Colm tucked the

shirt into his pants. "I'll find one somewhere else."

"Here." A familiar man's voice called from the landing at the top of the stairs.

Colm's head snapped up toward a very shaky Lance Taggert leaning on the wood railing.

Mrs. Penhaligon gasped. The sheriff snorted and the doctor, on in years though he was, hurried up the stairs to his other patient.

Supporting his weight with one hand, holding out a holster and ivory-handled Peacemaker .45 with the other, Taggert looked as if he might collapse at any moment.

Colm dashed up behind the physician. He took one glimpse of the agent and grimaced.

Head still bandaged, Lance's coloring was bleak. A sheen of sweat beaded over the uncovered portion of his face and his one visible eye registered terrible pain.

"What the hell're you tryin' t' do t' yourself, Taggert?" Colm took the holster and slipped his hand through the cinched belt. Taking one of Taggert's arms, the doctor grasping the other, they helped the injured man back to his room.

"That bastard's got Maginn?" Lance asked when he finally lay back in his bed.

"Mmm-hmm."

"You going after him by yourself?"

Strapping on the gun, Colm flashed his friend an unflinching look. "You know I am."

Taggert nodded. "Good." He sounded winded. "I guess I don't need to warn you what he'll do to her if he gets too far ahead and he doesn't need her—"

"I ain't goin' t' let him get that far." Colm waited for the doctor to finish fussing with the agent and leave the room before he continued. He moved up to stand beside Taggert. "I'm goin' t' get him, Lance. For you—for Maginn. The bastard's sick with his own self-pity. No tellin' what he'll do if he's left t' roam free."

"You aren't feeling sorry for him, are you?"

Colm chuckled sarcastically. He remembered the scene in Jameson's study. "Maybe once, but not again."

"You got a rifle?"

"Nope." Colm shifted the weight of the Colt on his hip. "This'll have t' do."

"In the wardrobe." Taggert nodded toward the oak cabinet standing against the far wall of the room.

Crossing over to the closet, Colm opened the two doors.

"In the back on the right."

Retrieving a rifle from the corner indicated by Lance, Colm stared awestruck at the gun. "Winchester forty-four-forty, walnut stock, nickle-plated butt, and rear sight." He whistled.

"Damn, Taggert. This is some kinda weapon you got here."

"Just bought it before I came up here." His voice was strained with the effort of talking. "Only sighted it a month ago."

Colm flipped up the sight and looked down the barrel. "You got cartridges?"

"Top shelf."

Colm found the box. Opening it, he picked up one of the long bullets.

"Only holds half of what the Forty-four does and one up the barrel. But with the right man squeezing the trigger it can take the wings off a fly two hundred yards away."

Arching a brow, Colm glanced at his friend in amazement. "That far, hmm."

Lance wet his lips and nodded. "Don't let him get the upper hand, Colm. Kill him if you have to. I don't care whose son he is, don't take any chances with that bastard."

Surprised, Colm arched a brow. "You know who Jordan really is then?"

Lance dipped his head and swallowed. "Been after him for a long time. He was into shanghaiing in San Francisco for a while. Never did catch the son of a bitch. Couldn't get any evidence. Jameson must of had it buried." He took a long breath before continuing. "Sure was surprised to see him involved in this, though—his own father!" He cut Colm a confused glance. "Can't figure that one."

"It's a long story." Colm set the box of ammunition down on the foot of the bed, shifted the rifle into his right hand and loaded it. "I'll tell you about it when I get back." Taking up the rest of the bullets, he turned to leave.

"Colm?"

"Yeah?" He spun back to his friend.

Holding up his hand, Taggert smiled uneasily. "Get her back, Colm."

Colm swallowed against the lump in his throat. He had not known the agent long, but what he knew of him, he liked. God, how he hated to see him cut down to such a disabled state. He took his friend's hand in a heartfelt grip and squeezed gently.

"She's in love with you, you know," Taggert said in a throaty whisper.

"I know."

"You love her too."

Colm took a struggling breath, though there was no hesitation in his mind. "More than I can tell you."

His gaze glinting with moisture, Taggert returned the pressure to Colm's hand with equal fervor. He smiled weakly. "I hope I find someone like that someday."

Colm's eyes stung. He had to get out before

he gave in to tears himself. "You will, partner. You will."

They stared at each other for a long, indulgent moment. Each knowing, feeling the deep abiding friendship that had grown seemingly overnight and flourished into something more powerful than either could describe.

"Get out of here," Lance finally said, his voice breaking up on a cough. "Go get that woman of yours. And don't you dare let anything happen to her, or you'll answer to me personally, Colm McQuaid."

Leaving Penhaligon's, Colm headed for the livery. "You got an animal that's sturdy and fast, Mason?" Colm asked.

The sandy-haired stable boy turned a quizzical look on Colm. "Wouldn't you rather have your own horse, Mr. McQuaid?"

"Scaramouch?"

"Ain't he that black-and-white paint I always seen you ridin'?"

"Yeah."

The boy pointed to the corral behind the barn. "He's back there. Came in by hisself late yesterday. Your saddle and gear's hangin' on the rail in the tack room."

Colm had never been so happy to see an animal in his life. "Hey, boy," he called to the horse.

With a shrill whinny Scaramouch trotted up to the corral gate and nuzzled Colm.

Within only a few minutes, he had saddled the paint and set out after Drew and Maginn. A short while later, he picked up their trail heading north toward Reno. Every hour or so, he would stop, check for fresh signs, and search the distance with his binoculars.

His first break did not come until a little after noon. Looking through his field glasses, he spotted movement in the trees. He waited, studying it from a ridge about a quarter of a mile away. He had to be sure it was not an animal. But it was—the two-legged kind. He focused the lenses for a better look.

Jordan rode in front of the pack with Maginn sitting behind him. The other four fell in behind him.

Lifting his sights, he studied the terrain. They were heading back to the line shack.

"Now that ain't too bright," Colm said under his breath. He lowered the glasses. "Unless they got supplies stored there. Or maybe want t' set a trap." He quirked a brow then took another look. He would have to catch up to them before they could make it to the shack. Pick them off one at a time. He glared at Drew's receding head, and his blood turned blue-cold. His fingers tightened on the binoculars. "But not you, Jordan. When we meet, it'll be face t' face."

Even through the trees, the afternoon sun shone hot, heating Colm's head. He wiped his brow and raked his fingers through his damp hair. He wished he had picked up a hat from somewhere before he came out.

He pushed Scaramouch on, forcing the animal to a fast pace, until finally about a mile away from the gang's shack, he got close enough to use the rifle. Circling around in front of the men, he tied Scaramouch up to a tree as he had done before. Then picking a spot on the rise, he took up the Winchester and raised the sight. He aimed at one of the men off to the side. Not being familiar with the gun, he did not want to risk a shot too close to Maginn. Sucking in a breath, he squeezed the trigger. The rifle cracked, kicked into his left shoulder.

The rider's hands whipped into the air from the impact and he dropped to the ground. Startled, the others wheeled their animals toward some nearby boulders. Drew jumped down from his horse and yanked Maginn along behind him. A round of gunfire pinged in Colm's vicinity, but none came close enough for him to worry. They obviously could not pinpoint his location.

Colm heard the men call out to each other.

"Can you see him?"

"No. You?"

"Drew? You see him?"

"Who got hit?" Jordan yelled.

"Rydell." A long pause. "He ain't movin',
Drew."

Colm peered down his sight to the downed
man. Sure enough, he had not stirred. He
pointed the barrel at another of the gang
members.

"There he is. See that flash. Up there in them
rocks."

Gunfire split the silence in a barrage of
whirring explosions.

Colm emptied the Winchester's magazine.
He wounded one and killed another. When
the round of gunplay stopped, Colm's cheek
burned from the heat of firing the repeated
shots. He reloaded the rifle then pointed it
back down at the shelter of brush and boulders hiding the men and Maginn.

"McQuaid?" one of the men called out to
him.

Colm did not answer. He tried to get a fix on
the voice, but could see no one.

"You want the woman?"

Colm moved the barrel from side to side. He
still could not see anyone, just rock and scrub
brush. There were up to something. He looked

around. One of them would probably try to get around behind him.

"Hey, McQuaid? I said, do you want the woman . . . *alive*?" A wicked laugh followed the question. "She sure is purty."

They had not harmed Maginn—not yet. He was pretty certain of that. They had not had time. But he would have to do something and damn quick. Maginn's life depended on it. He had to have time to think. With no more bullets than were in their belts, they were pinned in tighter than a drum. But if he was not careful, while the other two kept him busy, one of the men might be able to slip out from the rocks, grab a horse, and get to the cabin for more ammunition. He had to force them into his line of shot. "Jordan. I only want Maginn," he called out, training his sight down to where the voice hollered up. "Let her go and I'll let you go."

"Can't do that. Why don't you come down here and we'll figure somethin' else out . . . friendly like." A moment passed.

A plan formed in Colm's mind.

"What do you say, McQuaid? You comin' down, or do we take turns havin' some fun with the woman? We'll make her sing real loud and purty so's you can hear."

"Okay," he shouted. Taking off his gun belt, he removed the Colt and tucked it into the waistband in the back of his pants. Then lifting the rifle above his head, he stood and raised his hands out to his sides. "Don't shoot. I'm comin' down."

"Get to comin' then. But watch yourself. Remember the woman."

They had to know he would not give up so easily as this. But hopefully they would let him get close. And when they did, he would make a play for his Colt. And hopefully, they would not use Maginn for a shield. Hopefully, Lady Luck still clung tight and this would work. There was a lot riding on hope, but it was all he had at the moment. That, and a damn fast gun hand.

"That's far enough, McQuaid. Throw down that rifle," a man called out when Colm stood at the bottom of the rise.

He tossed the Winchester off to the side. A movement caught his eye and he squinted past one of the boulders. "Where's the woman?"

One of the men, the tall, skinny one with the nasty laugh, stepped out from behind the rocks, his gun drawn down on Colm. "Oh, she's okay. Just a little scared."

"Bring her out." Colm glanced around. He could not see anyone else. "You said you wanted t' figure somethin' else out—now let me see that she's okay and we can get down t' business."

The skinny one snickered. "Now you didn't really believe we was stupid enough to go through with that crap, did you?"

Colm felt the hairs on the back of his neck stand on end. They were not coming out. His plan was not working. "Where's Jordan—I want t' talk t' him."

"But he don't wanna talk to you, gun-slinger." He laughed wholeheartedly. "You know, you don't look so fast and tough without your gun."

Colm gritted his teeth. This did not feel right. Something was wrong. He could not wait any longer. He would have to move now.

The man's expression grew serious. He lifted his pistol and aimed at Colm's chest. "I ain't never killed a gunfighter be—"

But Colm did not let him finish. He yanked his Colt from his pants, lunged for the ground, and shot.

The man groaned, jerked to the side, and fell to his knees before sprawling belly down in the dirt.

When the dust cleared, Colm saw pale blue eyes gaping at him, fixed in a death stare. He did not move for a minute. He had to locate Drew and the other man. Nothing stirred. Slowly, he got up. Kicking the pistol away from the dead man's hand, he moved to the boulders.

Carefully, he wove in and out of the rocks. He heard a noise. There, behind that clump of bushes and pile of rock. His heart jolted. What if it was Jordan? He would have to be quick. He took a deep breath. Leaping out from behind his cover, he dashed for the mound. He dove over the rocks with a flip and landed on the ground—gun up.

"Don't shoot, McQuaid." One of the men, no more than a boy really, whimpered next to a split boulder. "I ain't got a gun." Chest heaving, he held his belly, blood gushing from a bullet Colm had obviously plugged in him.

Keeping his Colt trained on the boy, Colm rose then moved to check on him. "Where's your pistol?"

"Drew took it." He was panting. "Said I was as good as dead and didn't need it." He looked up, true fear glazing his eyes. "I ain't gonna die, am I?"

Colm looked around the surrounding rocks. "Where's Jordan?"

"Tell me, McQuaid. I ain't really gonna die?"

Colm did not have to check the wound to know that the boy did not have long to live. He was bleeding too badly. "Where's Jordan?"

Closing his eyes, the boy began to cry in earnest. "I don't know. He lit out a few minutes after I got shot."

"Which way?" Colm gripped the kid's shirt.

"I don't know."

"Come on. You must've seen which way they went. Is he on foot?"

"Yeah, but I don't know where they went."

"And he took the woman?"

The kid swallowed noisily then nodded.

The meanness of Colm's temper surged through his body. Jordan had Maginn. But where? They could have gone in any direction. He started to rise, but the boy grabbed his sleeve.

"Please, McQuaid. You gotta help me. Don't let me die."

Colm looked down. There was nothing he could do for him. He could see the kid was scared, but he would not let his anger soften. He could not afford to. Maginn was in danger. She needed him. And he needed to hold on to every ounce of hate he could muster.

"You ain't gonna let me die, are you?"

Colm turned his mind away from the compassion that usually rode hard on his heart. "Everybody's got t' die, boy." Gripping his Colt tighter, he lifted a scowl and glared into the surrounding tree line. "Everybody."

❧18❧

The sky grew dark. And somewhere off in the distance, the low rumble of thunder echoed the hammering of Maginn's fearful heart. Where was Drew taking her? Forced at a hectic pace, she stumbled and fell, scraping her knee. She slid a couple of feet down the gravelly hillside, but Drew was quick to grab her wrist.

"Get up, damn you!" he snapped, wrenching her to her feet. "Quit trying to hold me up."

"You're not for wantin' me, Drew. Let me go now."

Breathing heavily, he glanced up at the top of the slope then blotted the sweat from his face with the crook of his arm. With a grin he nodded toward the crest. "Up there."

Leaning forward, Maginn dug her fingers into the sandy earth. She grabbed and pulled at shrubs, protruding rocks, anything that would aid her in her ascent. "Please—Drew," she panted. "Let me go."

"Shut up!" Hand on her bottom, he shoved her ahead of him.

When they had climbed to the top, he pushed her down behind a wall of stone. "I don't like being followed, so we'll wait right here for our gunslinger-hero."

"Colm?"

"Colm, is it?" He pinned her with a glare that left her feeling even more uneasy. "You don't seem quite as scared of him as you were a few weeks ago, Maginn me sweet. What happened out there in the woods with him?"

Maginn's face flamed hot with embarrassment. She did not like the implication of his tone.

"I see. Something *has* happened . . . or has it been going on all along?" He shot a glance downward and grinned lecherously. "You couldn't get enough information from bedding down with Taggert, you had to—"

"I've done no such thing!" she shouted, forgetting herself. Her temper soared. "I've not slept with Lance—ever!"

"Yeah, well I don't hear you boasting the same about our gunman there. Oh, yeah, he's fast all right, but it isn't with a Colt." He winked. "Is it, me darlin' Maginn?"

"'Twasn't like that atall—" Eyes wide, she covered her mouth. She had not meant to blurt out like that. Damn her temper.

"Ooo. Wonder what mommy and daddy Mick are thinking up there in heaven about their girl right now? Vengeance never tasted so sweet, hmm?" He raised his brows up and down suggestively. "You know, you really had me fooled for a while there. Every time I touched you, you turned to ice. You had me believing that you were serious about all that revenge crap. Guess I didn't have a fast enough gun, eh?" He grabbed his crotch.

Maginn winced, but for once, held her tongue silent. She seemed to be making matters worse for herself.

"Then again, we've never tested it, have we?" He leaned forward, his gaze traveling hungrily over her body.

Aghast, Maginn clutched her throat and pulled back. Her heart lurched, beating triple time. Her gaze darted from side to side, searching for an escape. The grade was too steep. She could not get away fast enough. There was no way out. He was too close. His gun too near. Think, Maginn. Save yourself. She gulped for air.

Suddenly, he laughed. "Don't get all lathered up. I don't want you—not yet." Returning his gaze to the ground below, he narrowed his eyes. "First I want McQuaid. Don't worry, though. I just want to hurt him bad enough so's he can't do anything." He smiled wickedly and rubbed the length of the gun's barrel down his cheek. "Then I'll let him watch me take you."

Lord in heaven. He was mad. "Drew, there's things 'bout him you're needin' to know."

"Like what? I know all I want to know about that bastard." He looked at her quizzically. "What's got you so all-fired high-and-mighty about him anyway? He's nothing but a hired gun. Hell, he's no better than me, really. 'Cept that somebody else pays him to do their killing." He chuckled. "I do it for myself—because I want to."

Maginn shivered. She had to think—do something before Colm found them. Drew would not give him a chance. He would kill him—she had no doubt. "I'm not for understandin' you, Drew. I know why you hate your father, but why him—why me? I thought we were friends."

"Friends?" He sneered. "I don't need friends. I thought I made that clear at the shack the other day. You were just a way of getting to my father. And McQuaid? I don't know why—it's just . . . I don't know . . ." His gaze slid back down the incline. "Something."

Noting the uncertainty in his voice, Maginn

decided to take advantage of the situation. "He's your brother, you know," she said, her voice all but smothered in the breeze that had picked up.

A low, deep-throated laugh rumbled against the backdrop of a growling thunderhead above. He looked at her curiously. "What? He's my what?"

"Your brother."

He shook his head. "You know, for two people who're such embittered enemies, you and that ol' man of mine sure have a lot in common."

"Your father?"

"Yeah. He tried to give me some bullshit story about my mother." He wiped his upper lip with the back of his hand and chuckled. "Tried to tell me she was alive. After her being dead for almost thirty years he tried to convince me—"

"Oh, but she is, Drew. She really is." Hopeful, she raised up onto her knees and clutched the craggy edge of the boulder she was sitting behind.

He quirked a brow. "How the hell would you know?"

"Colm told me."

Frowning, he darted a gaze between the foot of the hill and Maginn. "How would *he* know anything about my mother?"

"I told you." Maginn hesitated. She could not read his emotions. Could he accept what she was about to tell him? And if so, would it make a difference? She swallowed. She had come too far—said too much to turn back now. Colm would be here soon. She had to try. "He's your brother—half-brother, really."

Disbelieving, he met her stare. He shook his head, his expression turning black and foreboding like the scudding clouds overhead. Lightning flashed, revealing a hate-filled glint in his eyes.

Maginn had to bite down on her lip to keep from shuddering. She could not let him see how frightened he made her. She had to go on. "Your mother, Jennifer, wasn't killed at all. She was captured . . . by Colm's father, an Indian called Wind—"

Like a rattlesnake, Drew struck her. The back of his hand met her jaw with a resounding crack.

Pitched to the ground, her cheek stung, her head reeled. Sucking in a breath, she stared at him.

Drew trembled from head to foot, pure hatred gleaming in his pale eyes. Shoving his gun in his holster, he grabbed her by the hair and hauled her up to face him. He closed his hands around her throat and squeezed.

Her eyes flew wide and she gasped for air.

She grabbed his wrists and pulled, but he was too strong. She tried to scream, but only managed a strangled groan. She could not breathe. Her vision blurred in an explosion of stars fusing to white. She twisted and kicked, clawed at his grip.

Suddenly, Drew flinched. His attention was diverted to something else and his hold relaxed, releasing her.

Falling limp, Maginn gasped for air. Slowly, she became aware of gunfire. Someone was shooting. Colm! It had to be. Careful not to gain Drew's notice, she peeked over the boulders.

At the foot of the hill, behind a fallen tree, a thin wisp of smoke flew up, followed by a resounding ping splintering a rock near Drew's face.

Drew returned fire, shot for shot.

The sky was charged with lightning. Thunder split the sound of exploding guns. Something crackled. The smell of burning grass surrounded them.

Startled, Maginn turned and looked behind them. Panic filled her being. Lightning had struck the ground and fire lapped greedily at the brush. The breeze shifted, blowing a thick gray-white cloud of smoke directly toward them.

At once, Maginn's eyes burned. Her lungs

clogged. She had to get away. Jumping up, she dashed for lower ground and Colm. But strong hands jerked her back.

"Where are *you* going?"

Terror shaking her body, she pointed to the fire. "We've got to get out of here," she shouted above the growing roar of flames.

Drew held her tight. He glanced back at the orange-yellow blaze burning toward them. He grinned. "*You're* not going anywhere." He swung his gun.

Maginn screamed. The pistol crashed against her forehead and she fell to the ground. She fought the blackness, but she was sinking, drowning in an ebony current. She felt hot, as if she were in an oven. Something stole her breath. She heard someone scream her name, but it echoed from so far away. Squinting, she saw Drew turn and run.

"Maginn!" The voice sounded familiar.

"She's dead, McQuaid. I killed her," Drew yelled from somewhere off in the distance. His wicked laughter rose above a dull roaring sound.

Gunshots splintered above her in deafening explosions. She glanced up. Someone stood above her. Drew? She was not sure. She tried to break through the darkness, but the tide carried her off. Farther and farther away . . .

"Maginn! No!"

She coughed, choking on the thickness of the air. She opened her eyes. Smoke blurred her vision. She blinked, squinted, peered deeper, and a man's fear-stricken face moved into focus. She touched his cheek. "Colm?"

"Yes, Maginn." He hugged her to him then pulled away, his gaze darting all around them. "We've got t' get out of here—fast."

Smoke and flames, heat and wind whipped at them and she suddenly remembered the grass fire. Her eyes grew round with fear. She tried to jump up, but her head spun, forcing her back down with a groan.

"Can you walk?" Colm asked.

The tension in his voice ignited her panic to the point of terror. She shook her head. Everything was fuzzy.

"Come on. Hold ont' me."

Maginn turned tearing eyes up to him. Her throat burned. Her limbs did not seem to work.

Colm bent low and lifted her into his arms. He dashed away from the smoke and toward their only hope, a tree line as yet untouched by flames. He charged forward. But the wind changed and the fire jumped. Flames leapt into the pines, forcing Colm and Maginn back the way they had come. All around them the blaze raged, turning them again and again. There was no escape.

"Son of a bitch!" Colm shouted. He plunged them to the ground, falling atop Maginn. His face next to hers, he hugged her to him. "Hold your breath!"

Maginn stared at him. Why? What's wrong? She tried to stand but he held on tight.

"Hold your breath, damn it!" Shielding her body with his, he ducked his face down, clutching her beneath him. Then a strange noise like a thousand growling, snapping dogs gnashed all around them.

She panicked. She had to get away, but Colm held her fast. He was scaring her.

"Do it, damn it. Do it now!" he commanded again.

With his weight and the smoke, she could barely breathe. Straining, she looked up just in time to see a dark shadow thick with smoke rolling toward them. She sucked in breath as hard and fast as she could, gulping for air. Burning heat flamed her face, stung her eyes. Her head felt as if it might explode. Her body tensed.

Colm flinched, pressing them hard against the ground.

A moment later, she opened her eyes. The cloud of gray passed over them. "Blessed Virgin."

"It's clear. Let's go," Colm rasped.

But as Maginn moved to stand, something

stirred nearby. She wiped her eyes and looked again. Lord in heaven! Only a few yards away, Drew stared back at her. With all her power and strength she screamed. "Colm!" She pointed in Drew's direction.

Rolling, pulling her with him, Colm tumbled them away. He released Maginn and whipped out his gun. He fired, an ear-shattering shot. A blast, up high, answered. A groan. A thud. Then nothing but the roaring flames.

"Get up! Come on!" Colm jerked her to her feet. The blaze was getting closer. Gripping her arm, he pulled her to him.

"McQuaid!" Drew's strangled voice rose above the deafening snarl of the wildfire.

Maginn halted.

Colm yanked her a step forward.

"I've been hit. McQuaid! Help me!"

Through the rolling smoke, Maginn looked at Colm.

"Come on!" he yelled. He would not meet her gaze. "We've got t' get out of this."

"McQuaid?" Drew's voice faded. "Don't leave me— I'm hurt—" The words were swallowed.

The fire grew hotter, the smoke thicker.

A hand clasped in Colm's, Maginn covered her face with her other arm and ran as fast as she could. Everywhere animals scampered, screeching as they ran past them. Something shrieked above them in the trees. Looking up, she saw a terror-stricken porcupine in a high bough of a pine. A terrible scream—a squeal, and the animal exploded.

Still they ran, ducking and dodging falling timber, so fast, Maginn thought her lungs would burst from the strain. On they ran, cutting a zigzag pattern through the forest, searching out a clear path of escape.

Suddenly the smoke fell away and she felt something wet. Coming to a clearing, she glanced up as a sprinkling of raindrops splattered her face. Her gaze darted to Colm's and she grinned. "Rain!" She looked back at the red-orange flames licking the forest. "Oh, Lord, Colm . . . it's rainin'." They had made it out of the fire.

Out of breath and tired, they fell to their knees in a heap. Amid a mixture of tears and happiness, Maginn hugged Colm. "Oh, Colm—we've made it out!"

He did not speak, but she could feel the rush of happiness and relief flow from his body as he clutched her to him.

Their eyes met.

Maginn batted her eyelids against the warm droplets. Her heart swelled. "I thought we were dead for sure, I did," she said in a soft rush.

"No, Maginn. No more death—no more pain," he murmured. "That's over. Now there's only us . . . and happiness." He kissed her then, sweet and warm.

And though she had not felt such joy in a long time, tears seeped beneath her lashes to mingle with the rain. "I love you, Colm McQuaid." Hugging him, she sighed. But a sudden thought pricked her mind and she pulled away. Her eyes grew large. "Drew." Turning to stare at the burning trees, she covered her mouth. "My God, Colm. Drew's still in there."

Colm's body tensed. Following her line of vision, he shook his head. "He's dead, Maginn. We can't help him."

Shivering, huddled together, they sat for a long while watching the misting drizzle beat out the fire.

When finally the mountainside only smoldered and hissed, Maginn's gaze shifted toward the west and the distant mines. "I never wanted all of this, you know?"

"What?" Colm turned to face her.

"Those fiendish monitors," she heard herself repeating as she had done so many times before. "They're responsible for all this. If Jameson hadn't been so involved with them, he wouldn't have ignored his son. He would've been more open to your mother." She shuddered. "An' Pater an' Tommy an' Lance— Oh,

Colm. An' just look what they've made of me-self."

Colm hugged her to him. "It's all right, Maginn, it's all right."

She allowed him to console her for only a moment before pulling back and looking into his eyes. "No, Colm. 'Tis not. I never knew before what a terrible fury I've in me. An' I'm not for likin' it, I'll tell you that."

Meeting her gaze, Colm stared at her long and hard. He brushed a sodden tendril from her brow. "I guess we've both been goin' after things the wrong way. I never realized how much I had till I nearly lost you." He took a breath, a long silence stretching between them. "I'm selling my half of the consortium, Maginn. It's not worth it t' me anymore. If Jameson wants it, he can have it. We'll start over somewhere else—maybe your farm down in the valley. Would you like that?"

"Really, Colm?"

He nodded. "It'll be rough; we won't have quite as much money as I'd planned t' have when I settled down."

Maginn shrugged. "'Tis of no consequence to me. We have each other."

Standing, he pulled her up beside him.

"Funny," she said after a few minutes.

"Hmm?"

"'Twas the damn monitors that brought us together."

Nodding, Colm chuckled. He squeezed her shoulders tenderly. "You know . . . we'll still have t' fight those damn water cannons." He took her hands in his and grinned tenderly, his smudged and dirt-grimed face more handsome than Maginn had thought possible. "But at least we'll be fightin' them t'gether."

She smiled, and as they turned away from the smoke and ash, she leaned her head against his shoulder. And in that same brief moment, she thanked the golden fury that had raged so strongly in her until now—thanked it because it had brought her to Colm. "Aye, me love, together."

Epilogue

California, November 1875

Inside the stage depot in Cavenaugh's Dig, Maginn studied her reflection on the window glass. Turning sideways, she pressed her gloved hands flat against her stomach to check her shape. No change yet.

"You look beautiful." Colm stepped up behind her and clasped his hands atop hers.

"You're for sayin' that now," Maginn said playfully. "But when I'm as big as a melon full-grown—"

"You'll still be beautiful." Nuzzling her ear, Colm pulled her back against him.

"Here now. None of that, Colm McQuaid." Her gaze darted frantically around the empty room. "Whatever will the good townsfolk be for thinkin' of us?" she scolded in a whisper, though the chastising tone in her voice was barely noticeable.

"We're supposed t' act like this. We're still newlyweds."

She reached back and caressed his head then moved out of his grasp to peer through the window. "Look there. Poor Roark's pacin' up and down the walk like a nervous schoolboy." She laughed softly and shook her head. "If his constituents could just see him now. They'd likely as not find another to back as their congressman. Right now, he doesn't look like he could fight Mrs. Beeton, much less battle the monitors in Washington."

Colm chuckled. "I know. But he wants t' be the first one t' see Mother's stage when it comes int' town." He stepped up beside Maginn and looked out the frosted pane. "I don't know how he's standin' that cold out there, though."

"I know what you mean. It's colder than Jack Frost's nose even in here." Pulling off her gloves, Maginn took a couple of steps toward the black potbellied stove in the corner near the window. She rubbed her hands together for warmth. Feeling the ring on her finger, she glanced down at the gold band, then traced one of the two rubies. "Colm?"

"Hmm?"

"You think she'll mind me havin' this for

my weddin' ring? An' what 'bout me? You think she'll like me?"

Colm turned away from the glass and took her hand. "I think she'll be very pleased with both—you and this." He kissed the spot where the gold touched her skin. His eyes met hers with tenderness. "Don't worry so much, Maginn. She's goin' t' love you."

Pulling her lower lip between her teeth, Maginn frowned. She was not so sure. Pretending to be colder than she was, she slipped her hand from his grasp to hold it near the heart of the stove. "Maybe not."

Colm cocked his head to one side and scowled. "What's this?" He grazed her mouth with a finger. "Why're you so nervous all of a sudden?"

"'Tis just—oh—I don't know. I'm just for wonderin' what she'll think once she actually hears everythin' that happened—with Drew, I mean." She sighed heavily. "He was her son, too, you know. An', well, I guess now that I'm goin' to have a child meself, I quite understand how she might hate me for gettin' him involved with all that monitor mess and the resistance."

"I told you before." Colm's expression was stern, though his voice was gentle. "You didn't get Drew involved. He got himself int' everythin' that happened t' him. He was a sick man. And besides . . ." He lifted his brows.

"Roark and I both explained everythin' t' Mother in our letters."

"Everythin'?"

Colm nodded but he averted his gaze back out the window. "Everythin' but what he did t' Lance. I didn't want t' upset her any more than I had t'. I'm just glad he was able to go back East for that eye operation before Mother could get here. I think seein' him and knowin' Drew had done that t' him would've been too much for her t' bear."

"Aye, you're probably right 'bout that." She slid her hand back into his, and followed his gaze down the road where the stage would be coming in. Her heart felt suddenly weighted down. She missed her friend terribly. "You think he'll be okay?"

"Sure."

"You think we'll ever see him again?"

Colm shrugged. "Maybe." He sounded sad, yet hopeful.

At that moment, a tiny flutter of life tickled her insides and Maginn smiled despite her concerns about Lance. How differently things had turned out from the way she had imagined that they would. Though indeed ten months ago standing over Tommy's grave she had not given her future any consideration at all, now the fury that had incited her need for vengeance had been replaced with love, a husband, and a new family.

She thought of Tommy's death and the child within her. This was what it was all truly about—life replacing life. Her gaze lifted to Colm and her heart swelled with happiness. She suddenly felt very lucky to have found such joy, and very complete.

"Colm! Maginn!" Roark Jameson leapt in front of the pane of glass, jerking her from her reveries with an excited wave of his arms. "It's coming in. She's here—my Jennifer's here!" His round face glowed with anticipation.

Just as Maginn caught sight of the team of huge horses kicking up snow as they trotted into town, Colm turned to face her. He pulled her hand up to his chest and squeezed her fingers, an endearing smile lifting one corner of his mouth. "You ready?"

She swallowed. Another step to take toward her future. The monitors had cost her much, but what they had given in return was immeasurable . . . and now, here was Jennifer. Yes. She was ready. She took a deep breath and nodded.

"Good." As light as the down of a feather, he kissed her. Then tucking her hand into the crook of his arm, he led her to the door. "Now. Let's go introduce my mother to her new daughter and grandchild."

Lifting her head high, Maginn beamed up at Colm. "Aye, love. Let's."

Afterword

Not until January 7, 1884, did the Caminetti Act legally put the matter of the monitors to an end. Now the once great mining pits lie silent, the connecting dirt roads go little traveled, and within its steep banks the Yuba River flows serenely by Marysville. There are still vast heaps of silt in the upland creeks and the beds of the four Sacramento Valley rivers where they cross the flatlands. But they only remind residents of a fight that even after some one hundred years has left no heart untouched.

Dear Reader,

I hope that you enjoyed reading Maginn and Colm's story as much as I enjoyed writing it. Since *Golden Fury* is my first published novel, I would be delighted to hear any opinions that you have.

You can write to me at:

P.O. Box 60631
Bakersfield, CA 93386-0631

—*Deborah James*

411